RESURRECTED

KATTY'S STORY

BONNIE LACY

FROSTING ON THE CAKE PRODUCTIONS

To Our Lord and Savior, Jesus Christ

"What About the Moms?"

"Now, if anyone is enfolded into Christ, he has become an entirely new person. All that is related to the the old order has vanished. Behold, everything is fresh and new."
2 Corinthians 5:17 Passion Translation

"The cross is the center and mother lode of all joy and satisfaction, because it is there that your old self has *already died with Christ*." ~ Mystical Union by John Crowder

ONE

Katty Randolph picked up the cup and breathed the aroma in.

Coffee.

Never been a fan before. She had always preferred booze … and lots of it. But since Katty and her daughter Bea had been living with Noell Carpenter, they visited Mrs. Gelda's thrift store. The woman carried a full-range of everybody's household cast-offs, from old leather pouches for pencils, to vintage blank notebooks that no one could ever bring themselves to mess up by writing in, to everyday dishes, clothes and old bedspreads. Plus, a complete coffee bar. In Katty's opinion, it was the best coffee ever. Even the hot chocolate that Mrs. Gelda served was the best.

Bea begged for it when they drove by the hot chocolate packets in the grocery store. "Can we go to Mrs. Gelda's store today?" She'd rub her tummy. "I'm hungry for her hot chocolate."

Katty smiled even now, as she sipped the coffee. She loved the fact that they could buy Mrs. Gelda's coffee beans, grind them, and drink the coffee at home, too. Er, at Noell's. Adding cream from the store cooled it down to where Katty could sip and enjoy it. Even if she let it cool more, it was still delicious.

She blew out a breath and glanced at the creek a little ways down the hill from her. Bubbling and tumbling over rocks that they all three had dropped into the stream last summer. Playing in a little creek. Never before. Not even when she was a kid and allowed to play here—what? Once? Twice? Next to Noell's kitchen, this was her favorite place on the property, so far. A place to ponder, to breathe, and … to figure out how to pray.

Well, as she thought again, Gamma's closet was her favorite place. They continued to leave the door open and read from as many journals as they could—learning more about Gamma, her life, her thoughts, her gifts.

Amazing woman.

Tears threatened as Katty tapped on the journal she now hugged on her lap. Not letting it get wet. Not getting it dirty. Her heart burst in just holding it.

Noell had said it the other night. "This journal is your journal. Katty's journal. We should tape a piece of paper on the front with your name on it, because it's all about you."

For sure. Gamma seemed to have written it to Katty, alright. Like she knew, even back then, that Katty would live at Noell's. And that Katty would need words of wisdom to find out who she was after all the evil and crazy. After all the abortions and booze and drugs. The abuse.

The air smelled so sweet, so clean down here. Dark clouds hovered behind the trees in the west, but that didn't dampen Katty's mood. Beautiful rays of sunshine peeked through from behind her, sparkling off the leaves and warming her back. So sweet. She glanced behind her at Grampa's old shop. He'd been a skilled craftsman with a full woodworking shop. Other than some rooms inside the house, that was the only place left that she and Noell hadn't explored. Well, Noell had, but she wanted to do it again with Katty and Bea.

There was the camper, too, but they just hadn't had time to

go in there either. All the journals still to be read in Gamma's closet drew her, lured her so that nothing else really mattered.

Katty shook her head. If someone had told her she wouldn't even think about booze and the next fix because of some old lady's journals, she'd have told them they were crazy. But now, she treasured those journals. Even the ones not about her. All from Gamma's heart for her, Noell, and Bea.

Noell. Katty was just learning what Noell had been through from very young to now. She blinked. She had always been so overwhelmed with her own life, her own troubles, that she hardly even thought about what Bea might be going through. And now Noell.

Noell was so generous with her property—her house, this garden, her food, all her stuff. It was all hers, but yet she shared it. She shared Gamma's room, the bed. She said all this was Katty's, too.

She set her cup down beside her on the old slate bench and picked up a pen. Noell had uncovered a whole box of blank journals, just like the ones in Gamma's closet, waiting to be written in. She had counted them out, "One for you Katty, one for me, and one for Bea." All through the box, until it was empty. She'd emptied it and shaken it upside down. Fifty for each of them. That might be enough. Had Gamma planned that? Had she known that she was finally done writing in her own journals and saved the rest for … Noell, Katty, even Bea? She must have paid a fortune.

Katty opened the first journal. It even creaked. No one had opened it before. Old, but still new.

Blank.

She smoothed her hand over the page. The lines waited for the words.

How does a person even write in a journal? She shook her head. What does one say? She had barely started to open up to Noell about her life, much less writing in Gamma's journals. She normally kept her thoughts so locked up, chained inside her for all her life.

Don't tell them at school how you got that bruise. Don't uncover that burn on your leg. The burns from hot macaroni take a long time to disappear and heal. Don't tell them at the Sunday School what happened. No, you can't stay overnight. They'll see. They'll see the wound from being stabbed with your colored pencil. At least it's your favorite color.

How could she find a key to unlock her heart, her pain? To free even those awful thoughts and memories and write them down? Katty hugged both journals close to her chest. Gamma's journal felt … holy. Somehow a warmth, a delicious hug back.

Open up to Noell? Well. Katty guessed she didn't need to. Every time Noell picked up one of Katty's forks after dinner, or a glass, Noell would be overcome by what she saw of Katty's life.

How? How had Noell gotten that gift? Noell herself confessed that she had mostly called it a curse. When she forgot to cover her hands and opened a door, the what? The molecules left by another human touched her own skin and visions exploded in her head, revealing all about that person. Bad and good. When Noell had picked up Katty's suitcase that first day they'd moved in, Noell dropped it or at least set it down quickly. Katty thought it had been too heavy, but later found out that Noell had seen the babies, the blood.

Blowing a breath out, she opened Gamma's journal and skimmed along a few lines. "Katty, seek out who you are. Let God take you there. Find YOU." Gamma had drawn a big beautiful pink heart around the word you, all decorated with various hues of reds and pinks, with little circles colored in with yellows and greens. Beautiful.

She read more: "Learn to listen. Learn to hear. Learn to see what is truly around you."

What did that mean? Learn to see or to hear?

She blew out a breath and stopped. Listened. Birds twittered.

A distant airplane zoomed. Even though Noell's house was blocks or more from the highway, a semi truck roared along the highway.

Was that what she had meant?

"Breathe. Quiet your heart, your thoughts." Impossible. Katty's thoughts constantly poured through her mind, a thousand thoughts per minute.

More.

Deep sigh. Gamma had drawn that heart when she had been thinking about … Katty. Katty only. "Find you. Then God can lead you to the man He has for you."

She swallowed and wiped her face. Her hands trembled. Something was going on today. Something was up.

Gamma's powerful, intuitive, prophetic words reminded Katty of the little blind lady at the convenience store a couple weeks ago. Nelly? "Find yourself a faithful man. You'll know, dear—you'll know when you've found him. He sees you like a queen when you know you're still a scullery maid." Or something like that.

What was a scullery maid?

And how had Nelly known Katty was a female? The lady was … blind!

Where was that little couple now? Katty shook her head. "Please God, keep them safe and make them well." Memories of that day—the accident—tried to distract her from Gamma's beautiful heart and words.

"No." She said it out loud. Surprised herself. "No. Not today." She opened her own journal and picked up the pen. Lots of white page there. What to write? What to draw, if anything? How did Gamma do it? How had she filled maybe a hundred journals? Maybe more?

Had Gamma balked at the blank page just like Katty did now?

Maybe Gamma had paused for a few minutes just letting the

page speak. Or had she gathered her thoughts? Drawn a tree first to find what was on her heart? Or maybe, just like Katty was now, Gamma feared messing up the purity of the blank page. If she knew anything about Gamma, Gamma prayed. Was that how she'd written all those journals?

Katty had been stumble-down drunk when she first opened a can of paint back at the trailer house and slapped it on the wall. Not to cover up or paint over the crappy paneling—although that needed to be done—but to reveal. To reveal the pain of the past. To face the pain of *her* past. She had slapped it on at first in a drunken rage, but soon began to let the paint speak from her wounded heart inside.

And now, today, she did the same thing. Or tried. Tears threatened. Fear lurked. Lies tried to stop her from seeing. From seeing and remembering the truth and writing it down on this pure white page in a journal provided by Gamma herself.

Thunder rumbled deep. Almost like it echoed from heaven into Noell's yard.

Into Katty's heart.

Katty shook her head.

Something was going on today.

TWO

Jasper unsheathed his sword and held it high as he guarded his charge, Katty. She had walked down to the little stream behind Gamma's old garden and sat on the bench there. She carried with her journals from that multi-dimensional closet. As she walked into the garden, she also—unbeknownst to her—entered another realm.

Jasper, as her personal angel, operated in every dimension: the human physical world among the planets and all creation, and also in every other realm, every heaven. When Katty had entered the garden, she also stepped into the angelic realm through a golden portal or ring. The Shining One. The visual of the golden portal layered over the colorful beauty of the garden —all surrounding his beautiful human. Her brown eyes glowed, dark hair knotted on the top of her head, and with curling strands framing her shining face.

He'd never seen her appear like that before. She had opened her heart to the Father, through Jasper's Master, Jesus Christ, and left behind her old world of darkness. She just needed to see herself as Jasper could see her—as the Righteousness of God, in Christ Jesus! That she would rise and shine in His Glory!

Jasper couldn't help it. A shout of victory burst from his throat that startled and stirred the other angels around him until they were all shouting and singing and praising the Living One.

"To the King! To the Ever-Living One!"

Each angel, and there were many as the host gathered in Noell's yard. Each angel raised a sword and a shout broke out across myriads of angels. A shout of victory embedded itself in the lives of the humans that they served with, no matter if they could feel it or know it was there. Victory was in their hearts.

Every angel knew that a battle happened before that victory, but they had served for a millennium and knew that the God of the Ages always won. He won in the beginning. He won in the end.

As Jasper walked and inspected the ranks, the loyalty and grit of these beings overwhelmed him. Very different from the humans, but every bit as persevering.

As he passed a certain one, the angel would nod. "Hail to the King!"

Jasper nodded back. "All Glory to Him, King Jesus."

Some angels readied their steeds. The horses stomped and pounded their hooves as the angels tightened the cinch on the saddles and adjusted bridles and reins. Heavenly horses stirred up golden dust as they stomped. The sounds broke through to open the hearts of the prayer warriors on the earth. The horses sputtered and blew, eager to get into battle. Eager to stretch out their powerful legs. Almost in a stampede—free to pound and fly. The angels mounted them and the two beings—horse and angel—became one powerful force.

Each angel wore different garb: from deeply embroidered flowing, belted robes to leather vests over fabrics not made of this earth. Huge in their own being, according to even angelic standards, the swords they carried and the metal that linked weapons and bags were heavenly.

Angels of every kind were present to protect and guard the

property and the humans who lived there. Many had that heavenly metal hanging from their ears, their necks, every possible place on their bodies. Piercings. Every color of skin etched with beautiful patterns and the most exquisite inking that spoke of the Glory of the Lord, of many prior battles and victories they had won. Weapons of every color, every design, spoke of the Living Power within. Some stringed, some portals, all materials and essence unknown to humanity. All to the Glory of their King.

The clamor might have been deafening to someone or something else, other than the angelic realm or the Kingdom of God, but with each minute that they prepared, the roar grew louder and more anticipatory of battle—exactly part of all they were created for.

It was a sweet picture. Jasper glanced from the angelic realm to the natural realm, and back to the angelic, wishing Katty could see it. Maybe someday. All the angels, thousands of them, surrounded a beautiful, strong woman sitting outside beside the small stream, sipping her coffee and holding some books. If she could have seen the fire lining the pages of some of those books, she would have screamed, dropped them, and ran. The breezes that ruffled her own hair stirred every angel around her. The angels turned their faces into the wind, breathing in the fragrance.

The fragrance of the One, from one realm to the other.

Thunder erupted, along with shouts of the angels. The noise was deafening, but it empowered and strengthened. Always the voice of the Lord stirred up a heart to worship in these angelic beings as they prepared for battle.

Along with the thunder came an exhilarating fragrance of peace and freshness that cleansed the atmosphere. The smell of freshening. It was what humans might call fresh air, but in reality, it was the fragrance of the One Himself.

It drew each heart of the angels to Him in service, in loyalty, and in truth.

Jasper passed another as he walked among the troops. "Holy, holy, holy!"

He could feel the prayers of the humans, both living on the earth, and humans in heaven. Humans on earth, like Mrs. T. She might be frail-looking to other humans, but if they could see her in the invisible world like Jasper could, they would back away from her. She'd become even more powerful since marrying Clarence Timmelsen.

Humans seemed to find it funny that Clarence and Mrs. T had married in the nursing home. Both in their eighties. She had prayed for him ever since he'd been kicked out of prison into that nursing home where she lived. When Katty and Bea had become a part of Clarence's life, Mrs. T—then Mrs. Hatly—had taken on praying for them, too.

And today, as per Mrs. T's prayers, the angels lined up along the border of Noell's property, side by side, creating a fence or hedge so solid that no evil could penetrate. She knew, better than most, how important and imperative it was to protect the borders.

It was a beautiful sight to see, with each angel dressed in different garb and supernatural colors. The colors represented every color of the earth and of heaven. Flags trailed many yards, flew from staffs, catching the wind of the Spirit. Even the long hair of each angel, in every color possible, flowed in that Wind.

A certain band of angels played instruments from King David's time and of his design in worship to the King and God of all Time.

Gabriel nodded as Jasper passed him. "Greetings, Brother." He was extraordinary in his stature and heart. Every one who encountered him bowed low as he brought messages and plans from the Father's heart.

Jasper bowed now. Gabriel lifted him back up. "We worship the King."

"Greetings, my Brother Gabriel." Jasper grinned. They

embraced and pounded each other's backs, bumped fists. "What message do you bring from the Father, our Jehovah? Our King?"

Gabriel seemed to grow even taller. As his eyes glittered and sparked, his chest expanded with the Breath of the Lamb. "He is always with us. He is!"

The host gathered around them to hear the words. At the same time, the enemy gathered outside of the ranks, outside of the border, ready for any opening, any moment that the prayer stream might let up and a portal might open.

Michael landed in the middle of the yard and raised the battle cry. "To Him!" Each angel lifted their weapons and added to the cry until it matched the thunder and beyond.

Jasper marveled at the sound. The battle was over from the beginning.

A demon dropped inside the border. Gutsy fellow.

Another one.

And more.

There was no fear amongst the angelic host, just loyalty to their King of Glory.

As the sound of the battle cry ramped up, the demons began to morph. First one and then another melted, dissipated into tiny flecks that blew away with the wind of the Spirit.

Even though the humans, too, carried on the battle in their realm, people like Mrs. T knew that when they prayed, it was a unique collaboration between realms—the human, physical realm, and the invisible world of the Spirit. Each prayer that layered over another and another won more hearts to the Kingdom of God. They protected more people and aligned with Father's plan. Even though the humans couldn't see that, it was true. They only needed to never give up—never give in.

Each prayer, each word, was precious and gathered into golden bowls in heaven. Perseverance in prayer in the battle was enough to shatter the enemy's plans and advances.

Take on the offense. Step out in faith, dear humans. Jasper

wanted to speak it and he did many times to Katty. Sometimes she even heard him.

Even though the angels knew the battle was won, sometimes the human will changed the direction. Sometimes an individual choice for good or for evil, changed the course of the battle, changed the outcome of the situation or relationship.

Changed the course of history.

Jasper knew his charge and her young daughter, Bea, both had that ability.

They both had the ability to make moral decisions, the strength to follow the Lord in all things.

They also had the freedom to follow their past choices and paths of abuse and pain.

THREE

Sigh. *Breathe.*

Pen up. Katty shook her head. She had raised her sword—kind of. Her pen was a weapon. Where had she heard that? Couldn't have been from high school days. Sounded like Mrs. T. Or Clarence.

She swallowed.

Her paintbrush was a weapon.

Well, if lies tried to stop her, then she would meet them head-on by writing truth.

So, truth or lies? Had her mom ever told the truth? "You are a slut." Something must have changed in Katty, because there had been a time when Mom said that to her and Katty laughed in her face. Hearing that in her memory just now made her cringe. When Mom started telling Katty she was a slut, it was probably before she really was one. When she was too young ... to be ... a slut. Realization hit home. Mom had programed Katty into believing that about herself until she became a slut for real.

Katty wrote at the top of the first page, the day and her name. Formatted it kind of like Gamma had in her own journals. Gamma had dated each entry. She had almost written a history book from the very minute her pen touched the page. A memoir of her life.

Okay. Cast aside what Mom used to say.

Katty tapped the pen against the paper. Who was she *really*? What was truth? She gazed toward the creek and a spark of lightning crackled from behind the trees, making her jump. Thunder rumbled in the distance. Was God telling her something?

Back to the journal. She wrote, "I am a mom."

She wrote slowly and carefully—best penmanship ever—thinking of who might read her own journals someday. Maybe she should address them with "Dear Reader." Or, "Dear Bea."

The flowers, or what Noell called weeds, waved in the early morning breeze. The air smelled so sweet this time of day, but it smelled like rain. Almost as good as the coffee. She scribbled a flower in one corner, then sipped from the cup. That flower was not as pretty as Gamma's. No eraser on her pen. The flower looked really stupid. Katty sighed. It was a start.

"I am a woman."

She spoke the words out loud as she wrote them.

Deeper.

"I am an addict. Addicted to all kinds of things." She glanced over at the cup of coffee beside her and wrote, "Now I'm addicted to coffee." It had to be better than whiskey or drugs.

What else?

Deeper still.

Recent memories opened up. She'd hit Bea many times in the past, although that was getting better. She shuddered. She never wanted to end up like her mom. She didn't want Bea's childhood to end up like her own. Awful, awful memories. Beatings. Nightmares.

She swallowed. "I am an abusive mom."

She spoke it out loud again, as she wrote it. After she added the period, she stared at what she had written for a long time. A tear dropped onto the letters and ran down the page. Another one fell, almost in slow motion. She blinked as it fell from her own eyes onto the page. And another, until a tiny pool of ink-tinged water blurred the words, drawing black ink to the edge of the paper.

Quickly, she wrote, "I … " But she couldn't finish that sentence. Babies. Awful. How could she write that? No. How could she have *done* that? How could Phil have done what he had? He was one evil man.

Tears slipped down her cheeks, and she didn't wipe them away. The sound of water flowing through the creek was comforting to a point—even more so after it rained. Tears. Water. Same stuff except one with salt and one without. One from pain. The other from … the rain?

Something so real was happening.

"Oh Gamma." She whispered it, even though she was alone. Why disturb this beauty, this peace, this presence? "Gamma, I wish I had known you. Maybe I wouldn't be those things." She glanced down at the first pages of her journal. "The 'I am a woman' one is okay. The mom sentence is good. But the rest is awful. If I had known you, would I have turned out better? What if I could have run away from Mom to live with Gamma? Mom was bad. Gamma was good."

She wrote that down. Why not? Get it out. She'd done enough puking booze up. Why couldn't she puke out her feelings, her thoughts? Those words.

Thunder growled again. A drop landed on her journal. Should she go inside? They'd had what Noell called a teaser, but she said they needed lots more. Katty used to hate rainy days.

She suddenly realized she was nodding. She also realized that she might be listening—listening in a deeper way, a more thoughtful way.

"Who am I? Really."

She was so alone.

"Abuser, druggie, addicted, murderer."

There. Katty shook her head as she wrote those words. She choked a sob down and sighed.

Gamma had loved her. She had even written that in the journal on her lap. "I love my little Katty." Or something like that. Gamma loved her. Gamma hardly knew her. But right now, Katty could almost feel someone, someone near her. Someone? Who? Here. The magic. Just like in Gamma's closet? What Gamma had written about her. What if her art was really a gift, something she was meant to do? What if none of that had been the booze, but a true gift?

The trees seemed to rustle in response to that thought. The water in the stream below gurgled with joy.

Katty wasn't even drunk.

But if Gamma had loved Katty, nobody else did.

Well, there was Bea.

And she guessed Noell loved her, too. Yeah, Clarence and Mrs. T.

But.

Who would ever love her—like a guy? If she told some guy what she had done—how she'd lived—they'd never stick around. Some guy like Mark.

Phil had said he loved her, but she knew guys like him. They only stuck around for the sex. When that was all used up … poof! They were gone.

"Katty?" Noell called her. Bea must have broken something or was driving Noell crazy. Katty didn't expect Noell to babysit. They were only cousins, for Pete's sake.

Katty wiped her face and turned to see Noell rushing down the slope, her beautiful blond hair floating behind her. She rarely wore it loose, so it was a treat to watch it flow behind her, in the breeze. Noell was one beautiful female. Blond hair. Blue eyes. How on earth could they be related?

"Katty." Noell glanced behind her. "I tried to beat her down here. I wasn't sure if she'd get upset."

"Upset. Over what?" Katty glared at Bea. "What'd she do?"

"She didn't do anything." Noell whispered. "It's the trailer."

"The trailer."

"Yes. They just called."

"They."

Little Bea followed, her brown eyes wide. She was so mesmerized in something that she tripped and tumbled down the hill. She pushed herself to sit upright and stared. Pointed. "The angels are here." Her eyes darted all around the yard. "Mommy. Noell. Look. There are even horses." She stood up, trembling, "Angels riding horses." She spun in a circle, almost tripping again. "Lots and lots of … angels."

Silence.

Katty glanced at Noell.

Noell seemed to search the yard, then back to Katty. Her eyebrows arched up, her eyes wide. She rubbed her arms.

Both back to Bea.

Bea must have realized where she was, blinked, and swallowed. She faced Katty, but glanced away several times. Back to Katty. "Mommy, they're tearing the trailer down. What about my bedroom? My stuff?" She started to cry. "My books. My rocking chair."

Katty shook her head. She didn't care about her own stuff at all. Was there anything in that old crappy trailer that she wanted? Maybe the old rocker? She moved the journals, held out her hands to Bea, and pulled her onto her lap. "Bea. We have most of our stuff with us here. We brought your books here when we moved in with Noell. You counted them, remember?" She glanced up at Noell and spoke. "Them destroying the trailer makes it kinda hard to get rid of us for a while longer."

Noell shook her head. "You never have to move out." She sat on the bench beside them. "This is your home, too. For as long as you want. Until you don't need it anymore." She gave Katty a look that she couldn't interpret.

"What? Until you kick us out?" Katty moved her coffee cup closer.

"You're gonna kick us out?" Bea's last word ended in a wail.

"No!" Noell grabbed Bea and hugged her onto her own lap. "No. No. No." She turned Bea's head, one hand on each side of her face, to look into her beautiful brown eyes. "Never. Ever. You can live here until Daryl and Dumpty—

"Uh, Katty?"

Katty jumped. Was that Mark?

All three turned to follow the voice speaking from behind, but the sunlight was blinding. When the figure moved, blocking the rays, there he was. Mark walked toward them in full police uniform, a paper in his hand.

Noell nudged her. There was that look again.

"Hi."

He looked so handsome, all dressed up. Well. In his uniform. His hair—

"This looks like a party." He smiled.

Bea popped off Noell's lap and jumped for him.

He almost tripped, took a step back, but held onto her, the paper wrinkling. "Bea. Good morning." He laughed. "You are so fast. I'm going to have to work on my reflexes."

"Your re-flexes?" She frowned. "Is that like a gun? Or 'quipment?"

He laughed.

Katty could watch him all day. Listen to him laugh all day long. Watch him with Bea, every day.

"C-could I talk to you for a minute?" He raised his eyebrows, one side of his mouth in a smile, and tilted his head toward Bea, still in his arms. "Alone?"

What was this? Was he asking her for a date? He was still in uniform, but maybe. "Uh, sure." She stepped to him and picked up Bea. Those eyelashes. Those green eyes. "Um."

"Just for a minute." He looked behind him. "Maybe in the front? Alone?"

Breathe. "Sure. Noell, can you—"

Noell hopped up and took Bea from her. "We'll go inside. You need a snack, Bea? You didn't eat all of your cereal, did you?"

Bea nodded, a very serious expression on her face. " This is 'dult talk, right?" She was so intent. "That's why they don't want me to hear." She whispered in Noell's ear, loud enough for all to hear. "It's about my Christmas present, probly."

Noell chuckled and nodded as she carried Bea to the house. "Probably." She arched one eyebrow as she looked back at Katty.

There was that expression again. What was Noell thinking? Katty needed her own gift—the gift of … mind reading.

"Well, with them in the house, we can just sit on the bench here. Is that okay?"

Mark nodded and followed her. He perched on the very end.

"Is this about the trailer? Because we can go over today to make sure—"

"The trailer?" Mark blinked. "Um. What's happening with the trailer?"

"I thought deputies knew everything that might be going on in town." She sighed. "They're tearing it down. We've been kicked out." Almost to herself. "What about Mrs. Nosy?"

Mark smiled. "You mean Agatha?"

"What? Who's Agatha?"

He chuckled and nodded. "Mrs. Nosy. She demands that I call her Agatha."

"Huh. I never knew her name. I guess I just called her that because she was so …."

"Nosy?" Mark finished her sentence. He chuckled.

"Yeah, well, I deserved some of it." Katty shook her head. "All of it."

Awkward silence.

"So, they're tearing down the trailer?" He shook his head. "I did not know that." He flipped the paper over and back again, smoothing the wrinkles out. "Do you need any help? We could use my pickup."

We? Katty raised her eyebrows and almost smiled. "That would be great." She hesitated. "Uh, if you have time." She shook her head. "We won't keep much from there, if anything. It's all junk. It's—"

His head jerked up. "What about the art wall? You can't junk that." He looked directly at Katty. "It's beautiful."

She knew her face must be red, because it felt like a dragon had just breathed fire onto her skin. "Thank you." She swallowed. "But … what would I do with it? Where would I put it?" As soon as she asked the question, she thought of Grampa's shop. She looked that direction the same time Mark did. "But how do I get it down?"

"I can help." He rustled the paper. "Uncle Ted left me his tools. We can figure it out." He leaned toward her and spoke softer, but firmly. "You have to keep that, Katty."

She blinked. "O-Okay. Yeah."

He blew a breath out and turned over the paper in his hand. "I hate to do this."

Katty cringed. She'd heard those words before, spoken from any number of legal, law enforcement personnel.

Even her mom had used it on her. *Sit up straight. Be strong.*

Mark still hesitated. "We had word from Phil Daynton."

"Phil?" She shook her head. The last word she'd expected him to say. "I thought he was in prison—or at least on his way there. I thought we didn't ever have to see him again." She pushed her hands out as if Phil had been standing in front of her. "Ever!"

Mark nodded. "I know. I can't imagine." He showed her the

paper and right at the top it said, "Acknowledgement of Paternity and Rights."

Katty blew out a long breath. "No." Another breath as tears welled up. "He can't do that." A thought entered her head, and she perked up. "He has no rights. There's no birth certificate." Not one that she could find or remember. She had been in a drunken stupor when she birthed Bea by herself. Drunk even after that. She had nothing. Phil had nothing. She folded her arms across her chest. "He can't prove it." She straightened. "I bet Clarence would agree with me."

Mark tapped the paper. "Maybe. But Phil is asking for a DNA test."

FOUR

Jasper blew out a breath. He could feel Katty's pain, even though as an angel, he didn't have authority to change things for the humans.

The confusion on her face, and then anger mixed with pain, was enough to make him cringe. He had been through it all with her—every wound, every slap, each and every attack. More than anything, he wanted freedom for her—from fear, from pain.

But at this moment, on this day, even with the host of angels still surrounding her, there was no freedom. She seemed doomed to always live under Phil Daynton's evil intentions. Under lies from the enemy.

Jasper knew Father God had plans for her and little Bea. He glanced toward the house. Bea peeked out the window, but Noell grabbed her away, and then peeked herself.

Jasper saw nothing particularly interesting. Well, there were thousands of angels in their yard, but only Bea might be able to see some. Yes, she had seen them all … here … today. Jasper knew she had seen her own angel before and sometimes, maybe even him. Little Boy especially.

Jasper knew these humans. They always wanted to make

everything work out pretty or happy. No matter what every difficult opportunity might bring with it, they had to learn, to grow, to create. But all they ever wanted was a happy ending.

He shook his head. His heart broke for Katty and Bea sometimes. He loved them. He wanted the best for them. He wanted to protect them from … from themselves and their own poor decisions. Plus, from other people who might harm them. Especially from the demonic beings.

The night when Katty had run away to the convenience store, maybe five or more years ago? Jasper had done his best to distract her from even seeing Phil, much less bumping into him like she had. She was starving that night. Hadn't eaten all day.

But more than that, she had been starving for love her whole life.

And then Phil showed up, flashed his charm and a candy bar.

Jasper wasn't sure which had attracted Katty more: Phil's magical seduction or food. She got both. After all she had endured with her mom, he seemed to offer yes, immediate safety and gratification, but also a way out. He offered Katty an escape into something she had always dreamt of—someone who would truly love her and treat her as a princess.

That's what Phil had called her that night.

Princess.

He had been her savior, her rescuer.

In the end, she had been duped. Phil's rough, rugged good looks lured her. In his younger days, he might have been model-worthy.

Hard to think, as an angel, about a human that God loved, but Phil was a user. Truth. He came from a long line of users. Well, his dad was a master user. Fact.

Phil had opened the door to the house with flair, like it was grand—a palace for his princess. In real life, it had been kind of grungy, but her eyes had been blinded. Katty must not have seen that part. Or since she was away from Mom, maybe she didn't care. It didn't matter. She was free and with a good-looking guy. He would take care of her.

And take care of her, he did.

Jasper shook his head at the scenes stored in his memories. It had been subtle, but he remembered the moment the scene had turned brutal. Katty was already smitten with the fact that she was now free from Mom, but even more so, she was smitten with Phil's charm and his lovemaking, his good looks. She didn't know any other way. She'd never had a lover before.

But when his hand cupped her throat, her eyes popped wide —terrified. And even though she was drunk, all it took was a bop to her temple, and she was out. He'd already poured enough booze down her to get her drunk, but when she came to, Phil made sure to warm her up with pizza and more booze, laced with something else that Jasper had no name for.

By then, she was his.

FIVE

Phil Daynton paced the floor of the jail cell. Eight steps one way. Ten the other way. Same painted concrete block walls. Next time around, he could count the blocks. There was a crack in the mortar, from the floor to the ceiling. Without thinking, he stopped and pushed against the blocks. Nothing budged. Stupid. Stupid. He had to do that. Almost involuntary movement. Another lap around the cell. Same gray paint. Same transom windows. Same toilet and sink. Pine Sol smell piped into the cell somehow. Instead of the air he breathed, it was a cell full of Pine Sol air. Going to prison might be a welcome change.

Stupid.

Going to prison wasn't just for a week here or a week there. A weekend vacation.

It was for a lifetime. Or at least, he guessed, for the rest of his remaining years. *That* lifetime. His past deeds with Bea and Katty, but before them, had caught up with him and his record was overloaded with escapades from his past. Some of what he'd done at the demand of his dad was piled in there, too.

It all came back to box him in. His turn to go. How Dad had forever beaten the rap and never gone to prison was not fair. He had started it all. He had been the founder of the cult. He'd been the one who pretended to accidentally kill a neighbor's cat in the backwoods. Soon he had progressed to sacrificing larger animals in an abandoned grain elevator in the country. People showed up. Seemed either they had nothing else to do, or the evil lured them in.

Dad should have to serve his own time. Somehow, he knew the right people to escape the punishment he deserved. He knew who to kiss up to and knew when to call in favors. Where was Dad now? Not that Phil wanted to see him. Just curious about how his dad had dropped off the face of the earth. Curious how Phil now would serve time for the crimes Dad had committed.

Phil tapped on the sink as he looked in the mirror.

He didn't know anyone that he could call in favors from. He didn't have friends in high places or know any corrupt judges or lawyers. The only one he knew that had any credibility had been caught and imprisoned himself. Or so Phil had heard through the druggie nation. The warden was serving time for his own escapades as the evil warden of the prison back then.

Deep sigh. At prison, they had windows low enough to see out of. Not here. If the windows were lower, that would help with the boredom. He could at least watch the coming and going of people getting mail or coffee. Would pass the time a little.

Knock, knock.

"Yeah?" Like he could say, "No entrance. Not today. I don't need any. Come back when I'm good and ready."

"Not home." That was stupid. Actually, it was stupid for the deputy to knock.

The door pushed open, and the big, black deputy stood waving a paper. "Looks like you're on your way. All that has to happen are the paternity tests and then we'll bus you to prison."

"Yippee. Wait. I need to pack or something." He held his hands out. "Oh, what shall I pack my toothbrush in?"

The deputy smirked and shook his head. "Ya wanna sign this

or not?" He held the paper out and clicked a pen open. "Sign here, Daynton, and then we're done."

Phil took the paper and held it against the wall and signed. "Guess I should read this, but. They talk about signing your life away and I guess this is it. At least I'll have proof she's my daughter."

The deputy took the paper and pen. No comment. Just a pause. "You have no idea how much you don't deserve that kid."

Phil jerked his head back. "What?"

The man turned around and glared at Phil. "She's a sweet kid and you have already abused her in so many ways. How on earth did you get away with this?" He shook the paper in the air. "How did you get paternity test rights?"

Phil squinted and emphasized each word as he spoke. "Because I'm her fa-ther."

"Just because you had your way with her mom—probably drugged her and abused her—and she got pregnant, does not make you any kind of a father." He started to shut the door. "You are such a loser. Stuff is coming to the light—stuff you used to do with your dad. Is that where you got your parenting skills, your standards? From him?" The deputy was building steam. He blew out a couple of breaths, but came back at Phil again. "And those losers you turned loose on Katty and Bea that time. Those guys broke in and Katty had to lock her and Bea in the bathroom till we got there."

"I could sue you, ya know."

"Right. With what? Your good looks? Your lily-white past? Your record?"

"Bastard!" Phil rushed the man, but the door slammed in his face. He pounded his fist onto the door hard. "Ow! Damn." He hit the door over and over and yelled, "Watch your back! I still have friends in … somewhere."

He leaned against the closed door and slid down, clutching his throbbing fist against his stomach. As he landed on the floor, something fluttered. First in one corner, something dark, some dark mist or shadow? Was there a gas pipe that burst? Some sort of leak? Smoke?

He pounded on the door. "Hey! We've got a fire in here. Or a leak!" He pounded again.

The dark smoke grew and floated upward and onto the ceiling. More appeared in another corner.

He sniffed the air. Didn't smell like smoke. Pounding the door, he yelled. "Help! There's smoke in here. Bring in a fire extinguisher. Bring a gas mask. Help!"

They shoulda heard him by now.

He watched as the black mist on the ceiling crept toward him, like dirty black fingers clawing their way toward him. From the ceiling, the darkness slithered down the block walls.

It wasn't smoke, he realized, with a jolt. He sucked in a breath, only to have his throat constrict. He couldn't breathe. He remembered. This wasn't the first time that the darkness came for him.

Arms reached out for him, fingers ending in talons.

"No. No!" His last word ended in a squeak.

Just before it reached him, the darkness parted to reveal a face. Wicked yellow eyes. A wide grin taunted him.

"No!"

SIX

Jerum, Phil's angel, stood guard next to the cell door.

Phil screamed and screamed. The sound shattered one of the ceiling lightbulbs. There'd be no explanation for that when the deputies discovered the light out. It always interested Jerum how a sound from within the invisible realm could damage something inside the physical realm.

Powerful lungs on that guy.

Amusing how Phil always touted himself as manly, strong in body, full of courage. But he screamed so loud and high-pitched that he broke glass. To Phil's defense, the glass in a lightbulb was very thin and fragile.

Part of what the demons were doing was visual, but most of it must have been inside Phil's mind. Those demons. Planting thoughts of terror. Planting seeds of what they would do to him.

Boy appeared next to Jerum. "He screams like a girl." Boy's arms crossed on his chest as he leaned against the wall. "Those demons aren't so big. They aren't so strong."

Jerum smiled down at Boy, then glanced back at the scene before them. It looked ridiculous to him too, but he'd learned from experience in all the realms of heaven, on the earth, and under the earth, both past and future, that things oddly weren't as they appeared to be.

"I know, Young One. But you've never seen the Realm of Darkness from the human point of view, as I—"

Boy sputtered. "You haven't!"

"I was just saying, as I haven't either. There is an abundance of learning in every realm. Every heaven."

Just as the black mist fully covered Phil's body, it began to glisten and bubble as if Phil's body was in a cauldron, simmering and smoldering. Steam rose from his body, bringing with it the odor of burning flesh.

Jerum winced. That couldn't feel good.

Boy wiped his nose. "Phew! That stinks." He reached for Jerum's hand. "But he's my dad. And he's naughty. He is evil." Boy blinked and wiped his face. "He's Bea's dad, too. A bunch of us are his kids. Makes me sad." Boy gripped Jerum's hand tightly. "Makes me sad that he didn't want us."

Jerum lifted Boy to his chest.

Phil's body shuddered and shook until the demon got the fit right. Several layers were visible to them. The human, physical body, but also the demons within as they writhed and twisted.

Boy leaned his face into Jerum's's shoulder, as Jerum patted his back. "Let's go. Let's go talk to Jesus." He peeked down at his dad and shivered. "I don't want to watch."

Jerum hugged Boy. "I have to stay, Buddy. He is my responsibility until Father says leave him, or until he leaves this earth. Only then will I leave him." Jerum breathed deeply as he listened. "When your dad was little, a baby, he was like Bea is. Happy." Jerum breathed a breath from heaven. "He was sweet from the minute he was born. God's spark was within him … as it is now."

"Wait." Boy checked his dad's body. "God's spark?" He pointed. "In him? No way."

Jerum smiled. "Yes, it's there."

Boy shook his head. "No way. I can't see it. There's not any God in him."

"Yes, there is. There is a God spark planted in each and every human at the exact moment they enter earth." Jerum nodded. "Pretty amazing."

Boy stared at the blackened, gruesome sight before him, gave Jerum a questioning look, then squirmed to get down. He walked up to where Phil lay on the floor, unconscious, and leaned over to inspect the body. He pinched his nose and whispered, "Jesus, help me see."

Something glimmered. A tiny light twinkled through the muck.

Boy jumped and backed away. "I see it, Jerum. It's true!"

Just as Boy stepped closer again to see, Phil groaned. Then he growled, pushing himself up on one elbow. His eyes flashed open and for a split second he stared at Boy. He pushed himself up to his hands and knees and barked and growled again.

Boy jumped away and ran to hide behind Jerum's robes.

Phil roared and growled, like he was figuring out who he was —who the demons had changed him to be.

Jerum shook his head, patting Boy's head to comfort him. Phil had been evil before, but now …

SEVEN

Today, with Mark and Katty together within his view, Jasper couldn't see the future, but something was already set up in the Kingdom. Something that would change the world. Something that would change Mark, Katty, and Bea's world, but also many other humans on the earth. He knew how Father worked in the Kingdom on this earth and sometimes He had to let the situation get down right dirty and evil, before the humans woke up.

Jasper hated that part.

Mark straightened his slumped shoulders, gave a sigh, and stood. "I'm sorry to have to serve you that."

Katty glanced up at him, then at the paper in her hands. Then back at Noell's house.

Jasper knew she was seeing every one of the problems in front of her. Each one had to seem as huge as a house to her. Impossible. Crushing. Each one could change her and Bea's life forever. Her life was an entire street of houses to deal with.

She sighed and stood.

Mark started to step away, but then turned. "Katty." He hesitated. "I'm here for you." He tapped his hand against his pant leg.

At the same time, and in the same cadence, a rod appeared beside Jasper, pounding the ground. Each time Mark tapped his side, the rod pounded the ground in unison. Another rod appeared. And another. All pounded the ground. All lined up, circling Mark and Katty. All moved on their own. All part of the creation of heaven.

Jasper backed away in order to view the full scene. To experience the full effect of the powerful cadence of battle. Somewhere, someone was preparing for war and these rods of authority, of power, made it clear: they would not back down, they would not give up.

Several angels landed next to Jasper. They glanced first at Jasper, then at the rods. Then back at Jasper, some with a questioning expression on their faces.

Each time the rods landed, the ground shook. The sound echoed, vibrated through the humans standing there, reverberated all across time from the past and into the future, affecting not just the two humans standing there, but others who had been involved from the past and more humans into the future. The ground. The towns. The businesses. The families. The marriages. The schools.

Something was changing—beginning now—with these rods of authority.

One angel leaned close to Jasper. "What set them off?" He shook his head. "I've never seen this many in one moment of time, in one season even."

Jasper shook his head. "Not what."

The angel appeared perplexed. "Not what?"

"Who." Jasper folded his arms across his massive chest. "*Who* set them off is the question." He smiled slightly and stepped into the midst of the rods, lifted his own sword, and turned to face the angel. "Someone is learning who they are in Him and taking back the ground the enemy took from them.

Someone is becoming more like Him!" He lifted his sword and pounded it down hard in time with the rods.

The sound exploded, shaking, vibrating with the frequencies of heaven onto the earth.

Shaking the very foundations.

EIGHT

Mark stood beside Katty for another minute.

Breathe.

She wiped another tear away.

What could he say? He had just read the document to her that basically locked her and Bea in with Phil. They both knew Bea was Phil's child. They didn't need a DNA test to clarify that. Bea was Phil's and nothing could change that. Katty had birthed Bea months after escaping from Phil with baby Bea intact—safe within Katty's own womb. The only reason Mark knew was because he had taken liberty with the department archives to read Katty's history. They both knew.

He should get back to work. But … he guessed he was at work right now. With Katty. He delivered the document. She'd signed it. He had done his job. And he could buy more time here just by trying to help her deal with the news. That was part of his job, too. Helping people adjust and maybe accept what life had dealt them.

"Mark. You there?"

Mark flinched and pushed the button to respond. "Yes, Chantelle. What's up?"

"Well, we are just finishing up the paperwork for Daynton to go to prison." She stopped.

He knew. They needed the copy of the paperwork that Katty held in her hand. He could tell by Chantelle's voice that she realized that he was still with Katty and she'd said too much. "Sure. Thanks and I'll be right there."

Katty held up the paper. "Oh. You need this back?"

She wouldn't tear it up, would she? Mark shook his head and reached for it. "I just need the department's copy. The other one's for you." He pulled the copies apart and handed Katty hers.

"He's in prison." She visibly swallowed. "Isn't he?"

Mark hesitated. She had a right to know. The man had terrorized her and Bea. They had a right to feel safe. He nodded. "Almost."

"Almost?" She fully faced him and the paper floated to the ground. "He's not *in* prison?"

Mark sighed. He didn't want to tell her. "The judge won't push him through until this paperwork is done. And the DNA tests are done."

She sat back down on the bench—hard. "I thought … I thought he was gone. I thought he was out of our lives —forever."

Mark eased down beside her and retrieved the paper. "When the DNA tests come back—"

"Wait." She grabbed his arm. "How do we do that?" She glanced toward the house. "Is there a blood test?"

Mark couldn't stop himself from looking in that direction himself. Back to Katty. "Possibly. They do it through saliva or … blood. Both can be very conclusive. So you'll know for sure."

Katty shook her head slowly, again and again. "I already know." Her voice cracked. She looked directly into Mark's eyes. Tears filled those beautiful brown eyes and flowed down her cheeks.

Mark, without thinking, lifted his hand to wipe them away. He almost caught himself to stop, but he did it anyway. "I—"

She pressed his hand against her cheek with her own and kissed his, before she realized what she had done. She released his hand and stuttered. "I-I'm sorry. I shouldn't have done that."

He quickly grasped hers and kissed it. "Not sorry. No. I'm … I'm … " But he couldn't go on. It wasn't right. What if it didn't work out? What if when they did the test and Bea proved to be Daynton's daughter, Katty decided it was best to be with Phil? He quickly kissed her hand again and released it.

"What do we do? How can we get out of it?" Katty held up the paper. "Does this say we have to?" She glanced up. "We need to show this to Clarence. Is there a law or something that says we have to?" She swallowed visibly. "Why can't we ever be free of that man and his evil?"

She started to pat her pocket, but Mark caught her hand. "I know. This has to be unbelievably hard." He didn't let go. "Katty." He swallowed and plunged in. "I will do whatever you need me to do. I'll be there when they do the DNA test, and I'll be there when they give you the results … even … though we know." She was so beautiful.

Katty blew out a breath. She blinked a couple of times, wiped her eyes, then looked directly into his.

"I'll help you take the art wall down and bring it here. Or we can store it at my house." He tried to laugh, but her expression made him stop. "You need to keep that."

She bowed her head, tears flowed and dripped onto her jeans.

He lifted her head again. "I'll go with you to prison--"

She gasped. "To prison?"

Dang. He should have stopped at the art wall. "If Daynton gets rights, you might have to take Bea to visit him in prison."

She shivered.

"I'll go. I'll take you and stand beside you with Bea." He tried to get her attention again. "Look at me." He lifted her chin again. "I already talked to Sheriff Dennison. I will be the one to take him to prison and I will be the one to drive you and Bea there, too. Anytime. You will not go alone." He blinked. "You will not be alone."

Oh, Lord, how far should he go? He knew beyond any doubt what he wanted. How much should he say?

"No matter how this turns out." He swallowed and began again. "No matter what the tests show or don't show, I'll be there for you—with you." He blinked. "Beside you."

NINE

Bea peeked out the window again before Noell came back downstairs from her bathroom. Mommy stood now, talking to Depdy Mark. She wiped her eyes. "Mommy's crying." Bea whispered. Louder. "She's crying."

She immediately knelt beside the window and folded her tiny hands. "God?" Bea wiped a tear away with the back of her hands, never unfolding them. She bowed her head and started again. "Dear God in heaven. Uh … please help Mommy. She's crying." Bea stretched to see out the window. Mommy wiped her cheeks. Bea wiped her own. Mommy looked scared.

"God, please help Mommy feel better. Please help Depdy Mark be nice to her. God … please make Phil go away. I don't want him for a daddy. Ever. Please make Phil be nice to everybody. Make him be like … Clarence. Make him be like … You, Jesus. But please move him away." She paused. "Please help me be a good girl, so Mommy never hits me again. Please … please … uh, help me be more like Mrs. T. Please God." Another thought. "Thanks for getting Mrs. T married to Clarence."

She stood to peek out the window, standing just behind the curtain. Mommy followed Depdy Mark to the front of the house.

"Amen!"

Bea started to rush out of the bedroom and ran smack into Noell. "Oof!" Bea stumbled back and landed on her bum. From where Bea sat on the floor, Noell's face was far above, almost at the ceiling. "Noell. You're as tall as the angels."

"As the angels—"

Boy, his tiny wings outspread, suddenly appeared from behind Noell's legs. He was laughing hysterically. Bent over, he pounded his chest. He snorted and pointed at Bea. "Ha, ha, ha. You encountered Noell in a harsh way." He disappeared, his laughter still echoed in the room, even though he was no longer visible.

Bea jumped. "Boy, where'd you go?" He wasn't under Noell's legs. He wasn't behind her. "Boy?"

"What?" Noell reached down to pick her up, but Bea moved away. "Who's Boy?"

Boy popped right back in front of Bea, still laughing, wiping his eyes.

Startled, Bea bounced away, clapping her hands. "Boy. You're back. How'd you do that? You disappeared." She scooted closer to him and stood, tapped his chest with her finger. "I could still hear you laugh, but you were gone. How'd you do that?"

"Bea." Noell acted almost angry. "What is going on? Who are you talking to?" She held her hands out and scanned the room. "Who is laughing?" She paused and shook her head. "Never mind. Where were you going in such a hurry, little one?" Noell leaned over to look right into Bea's eyes. "You wouldn't be spying on Mommy and Mr. Mark, would you?"

"Bet she *was* spying on them." Boy shook his finger at Bea. "No, no, Bea."

Bea tucked her chin in, head down, and hands behind her back. "Well." She popped her head up, glanced at Boy, then at Noell. "Mommy was crying. Mr. Depdy Mark wiped her cheek, like this." She imitated his movement on Boy's face. "And Mommy kissed his hand."

Boy backed away. "I'm not gonna kiss your hand."

Bea halfway giggled and halfway cried. She didn't know what that meant—to do both together—but she did it, anyway.

Boy didn't make it any easier. He put his hands on his hips and stuck out his tongue, then hid behind Noell.

"And then … and then something happened." Bea tried to remember. "There were two mommies. One like my mommy. Like what she has on. Jeans and T-shirt." She pointed outside. "But the other one was my mommy all dressed up." She jumped up and down, clapping her hands. "In a white dress. All pretty! And Depdy Mark was there like he is now, in his depdy clothes." She pointed again. "But then there was an-another one—all dressed up in a white shirt."

She pulled on Noell's T-shirt. "What does that mean? Does that mean they're in love, Noell?" She swallowed. "What does that mean? White dress? They kissed. They touched. Are they in love, Noell?"

Before Noell could respond, Boy skipped around them both, clapping his hands and laughing, singing, "Mommy's getting married! Mommy's getting married."

Noell blew out a breath and twisted her head to see behind her, tried to see what Bea seemed to be looking at. She reached to pick Bea up. "Anyway. Slow down." She looked toward the front door. Bea could tell that she wanted to run and see Mommy for herself. But she stood up and hugged Bea tight. Tighter.

The best ever. To be held in Noell's arms. To be hugged there with both arms around her. She waved at Boy and stuck her tongue out at him. Noell's hug was almost as good as Mommy or Depdy Mark. Or Clarence. Noell breathed in her ear and her chest moved up and down with each breath. And Bea breathed up and down with her. Together.

Bea tried to match each breath with her own and almost had by the time they reached the kitchen.

Noell sat slowly, cuddling Bea onto her lap. She kissed Bea's forehead, still holding her tight.

Something Bea didn't understand, but never wanted to stop, was happening between her and Noell. She closed her eyes. She'd live forever on Noell's lap with her hugs. They continued to breathe together, as one person. Two people. Breathing together. Two girls breathing as one. One lady.

Deeper breath. From both of them.

"Aww. I want a hug." Boy pouted, his chin tucked to his chest.

Bea's eyes leaked tears, but she didn't move to wipe them away. She almost said something to Boy, but didn't want to stop what was happening. Through the tears, a pretty picture opened of a white cloud, twisting and swirling up from between them. Pretty colors swirled, winding like ribbons, up and around. With each breath they took together, the cloud circled up, seeming to go through the ceiling and up into the sky. Bea blinked. Where'd the ceiling go? She could see the sky!

Noell didn't want to stop it either, because her eyes were leaking too and she didn't move to wipe them. Did she see the swirls and colors? The cloud?

They raised their heads, and the Cloud turned into a huge bubble that flowed over them both, covered them like a blanket.

The front door squeaked open and quietly closed.

Bea's head popped up, and she looked at Noell. "Mommy."

Noell smiled and wiped Bea's face. Then her own. "Mommy. Maybe."

"Aww. Maybe Mommy will hug *me*." Boy disappeared.

They waited, Bea still on Noell's lap. She searched the room. "Where did the cloud go?"

"Cloud? What cloud?" Noell combed Bea's hair behind her ears.

Soft footsteps tapped from the front porch through the living room.

"Mommy's coming."

When they both heard the door to Gamma's room close, Bea said, "She didn't come in here."

"Probably had to go potty. She's been outside a long time, drinking—"

"Coffee!" Bea giggled. She had heard both Mommy and Noell comment that drinking so much coffee made them have to potty. She started to jump down, but Noell pulled her back onto her lap.

"Let's let her have some time." Noell hugged Bea. "Okay?" She squeezed Bea. "Besides, I'm not done hugging you."

Bea settled back onto Noell's lap, her head against Noell's shoulder. Her eyes stayed wide open, searching the room. Without lifting her head, "Didn't you see the cloud?" Boy hadn't come back either. She listened for Noell's breathing and breathed in when Noell did. And again. But a deep breath pushed out of Bea, breaking the pattern, the timing.

This time, Noell breathed with Bea. "What cloud, Bea?"

"The cloud that fell down over us." She raised one arm, but then closed her eyes and listened to Noell breathe, matching her own with Noell's again. Until Bea's tummy growled and they both giggled.

"Is it time for a snack, Bea?"

They both opened their eyes. Mommy stood in the kitchen doorway, a paper in her hand.

Boy peeked from behind her.

Noell caught Bea again, before she could jump down.

"Hi Mommy." Bea said it at the same time that Boy did.

Mommy smiled, but she had a funny look on her face. Not happy, but not sad. Not mad. Bea knew mad. "Hi Bea." She walked into the room and sat across from them at the kitchen table. Just sat. Didn't say anything. But she breathed.

Boy sat on a chair next to her.

Bea watched her and matched her own breathing to Mommy's.

Mommy watched Bea and then Noell. Back to Bea. "You've never been so quiet, Bea."

"We're breathing, Mommy." Bea put her head back onto Noell's shoulder. "Like this."

Mommy's mouth opened. "Breathing."

"Yes. Together." But when Bea tried it again, Noell started to giggle. "I know together. That means both of us. We breathed at the same time."

Boy watched closely and breathed with them.

Noell giggled again.

Mommy smiled.

Bea remembered. "Did you see the cloud, Noell? All pretty and swirling? Did you see it? Is that why you are laughing?"

"Cloud? Um … " Noell combed through Bea's hair and looked out the window, squinting. "What cloud? Those clouds?" She pointed.

"I saw it." Boy nodded.

"No, silly." She sat straight up on Noell's lap. "The cloud that swirled up from between us. I know between." She waved her hand between her body and Noell's. "It swirled and twirled up from between us, up to the sky." Oh, if she could wave her hand that high. She checked Mommy's and Noell's faces. "To the sky outside." She leaned against Noell. "So pretty. Lots of colors. Pretty." She used her arms again. "And it fell down around us like a bubble to the ground."

Their eyes were wide open, and their mouths were open, too. They looked at each other. They didn't believe her.

They didn't believe.

"It's true."

Neither said anything.

"An-and I saw something else, too." Bea jumped off Noell's

lap and stood facing them, like she was in charge or in a play and she had to speak her lines out loud. She cleared her throat. "I saw—"

A sudden, loud clap of thunder made Bea jump. She screamed and ran for Mommy. "Mommy! That scared me."

Mommy pulled her close. "Me too. I jumped!"

Another loud boom made them all jump. Rain pelted the windows. The wind blew the back door open.

Noell jumped up to shut it. "I need to check my windows upstairs."

Bea could hear her clomping up the stairs.

"I'll check ours … Gamma's bedroom. Oh, the front door might be open." Mommy rushed out.

A flash of light and another boom of thunder.

"Mommy!" Bea stood alone in the kitchen and began to cry. "Noell?"

TEN

The next day at the sheriff's department, Katty jumped up from her chair and yelled. "You've got to be kidding!" She grabbed at Bea's arm and stomped away, dragging Bea with her. The air sucked out of her. Couldn't breathe. Gut punched. She blinked. Might either scream or cry.

"Katty, please come back and sit down." Sheriff Dennison motioned to the chair she had vacated. "This is what the paper was about."

She stared at him. "I didn't think you'd actually make us do that."

The sheriff pointed at the chair again. "Please sit down. It only takes a little bit of time and you'll be out of here."

"Not on your life!" Katty choked. "I thought you wanted me to come here to check on the adoption or something. They're tearing down my trailer. Not this." She belched. Not now stomach. What the hell? Screw these guys who were supposed to protect the innocent. "Screw you!"

"Mommy?" Bea clung to Katty's leg.

Sheriff beat them to the exit and stood between them and the door, blocking them from leaving.

Something burst from within her. "What are you doing? You can't keep us here." Katty wiped her mouth and tried to step around him. "Can you?"

Memories of being trapped in her closet when she was growing up flooded her vision. Her mom's voice was still loud—after all those years. "I'll teach you to sneak out at night."

The very reason she always tried to escape—because her mom locked her in the closet.

"Mommy."

That wasn't Bea.

Katty blinked. Only kid in the room was Bea.

But that voice was not Bea.

Bea started to cry. "Mommy. Let's go." Her chin quivered as she pulled on Katty's purse strap.

"Katty." Sheriff held up the paperwork. "I'm so sorry to put you … to put Bea through this." His chin dropped to his chest—his eyes closed. "This is a court order." Head back up. His brimming eyes locked on Katty's own. "And it needs to be done before Daynton goes to prison."

"Prison." She faced him. Her face wet. Snot running. Stomach doing flip-flops. "You don't know that man." She wiped her nose with her sleeve. Yuck.

A door pushed open into the room from the cell block and Guy and Mark escorted Phil in, hands cuffed behind his back, ankles shackled.

Katty pointed at Phil. "He deserves prison. Yeah." She choked. "But Bea deserves a dad so much more than he'll ever be."

Chantelle hung up the phone. "Clarence will be here in a minute."

"Good. Clarence can get us out of this." Katty picked up Bea and positioned beside the exit.

"Please come and sit down." Sheriff Dennison waved her to the chair again. "At least until Clarence gets here."

"No. Staying right here." She buried her face in Bea's hair. Poor kid needed a bath. Or maybe that was her own body odor. She should have let Noell come with them. She'd offered, but what was the big deal?

This was a big deal.

"Mommy?"

"Bea. I'm right here." Katty lifted her head and realized too late that she was the only one who had heard that.

Those voices were back.

Chantelle smiled and ducked her head as she worked on the computer. Obviously, *she* thought Katty was crazy.

Katty had always thought Mom was crazy, so Katty was probably inside that same nightmare. But how could she explain hearing those voices now that she was sober? She'd heard them drunk and now sober.

Katty set Bea down.

"I know he is her father. I don't need some kind of test to tell me that. I've never had sex with anyone else!" She landed hard on the wooden chair, crumbling. Wiping her face, she looked directly at Mark. "Ever." She realized what she'd just said, but couldn't stop herself. She pointed at Phil. "He is evil, and I don't want her to live knowing that he's her father." She slapped at the paperwork on the table. "That's it. That's all." She pointed at Phil. "You are evil. You aborted every baby—either by taking me to a clinic or … doing it … yourself."

She collapsed in sobs.

Phil snickered.

No one moved.

No one said a word.

Chantelle pulled a chair up close.

Katty turned away from her. Away from Bea.

Bea was left standing by herself and began to whimper. "Mommy. Up me." She turned to Chantelle but must have realized she didn't know her and turned away.

She turned to Mark.

He released his hold on Phil and gently lifted Bea into his arms.

She wrapped her arms around his neck and hid her face.

The door opened, and Clarence just stood there and stared at the people in the room.

No one spoke.

Finally, Sheriff Dennison stepped forward, holding out his hand. "Clarence. Thank you for coming."

At that name, Bea lifted her head, scrambled down Mark's legs, and ran to Clarence.

"Clarence. Up me." Her voice cracked as she held out her arms, bouncing up and down. "Up me."

He reached down and hugged her. "What is this baby talk, little one?" He slowly lifted her and scanned the room. "I take it things are going well?"

Katty's head popped up at his voice. "Clarence. Please say we don't have to do this." She threw the papers on the floor. "Please tell them Bea doesn't have to get tested."

Clarence sat in a chair across from her, still holding Bea.

Sheriff picked up the papers.

"Clarence please."

Clarence's stomach tightened as he sat at the table holding Bea.

How could he say no to his girls?

How could he push them to do something so painful as legally letting that murderer know he was Bea's father?

He pushed Bea's head against his chest. His head covered hers.

She was trembling, and he knew if he could get his arms around Katty, that she was too.

God Almighty! Help!

"Clarence." Katty shoved the tissues away that Chantelle offered her. She wiped her face with her sleeve again and leaned forward. "Please. You're a lawyer. You're our family. You adopted us." Katty sniffed. "Please. Just let us go home."

Twist the knife.

Clarence slowly shook his head. Judge ordered the test. He'd experienced life at the hand of court orders himself.

Trapped, but senseless.

Sheriff nodded at Chantelle.

"No! No!" Katty jumped up.

Sheriff restrained her.

Bea wailed in Clarence's arms. Little Bea had no idea what was happening. She couldn't have any idea. But she knew it was going to be bad, and it had to do with her.

Terrified.

God, Clarence loved his girls.

He would do anything on the face of this Earth to protect them.

But he couldn't protect them now.

***

Phil was almost sorry for all the commotion. He knew he was the cause of it all. And he almost regretted it.

Almost.

Something in him twisted.

Katty was screaming, and that didn't help the kid.

The kid. He knew Bea was his. She looked like him. She acted like him. Hell, she screamed like him.

Could things have been different for all of them? Could he still be her dad? In spite of his own childhood? In spite of it all?

Phil jumped.

The boy appeared. Right behind the Sheriff. That kid. Again. "Damn that kid." Phil stretched forward—like he could reach him—with handcuffs and shackles on his ankles. "How did he get in here?" Phil jerked his head up. "Even better. How did he get inside that nursing home? He was there, too."

"There's no kid in here except for little Bea, sitting on Mr. Timmelsen's lap." The black deputy almost yelled it, pointing at Bea.

"Get outta here, kid!"

The boy hunched behind the sheriff.

"Enough." Sheriff Dennison stepped toward him. "You've been tested for drugs and you're clean. You will have a full psych test when you get to prison. And if your little boy follows you there, it will not go well for you."

The boy shook his head.

Hands in his pockets.

Head down.

Huh. Just like …

Mark turned away and wiped his eyes.

Holy God. Help. Mom, pray.

He cleared his throat.

Turning back into the room, he stood beside Daynton and grabbed the handcuffs behind the man's back, a little rougher than he should have. As if to cancel the first time he jerked the handcuffs, he yanked them again. Guy must have felt it from where he stood on the other side of Daynton, because he glanced

Mark's direction. Mark wanted to do so much more to this guy who had made Katty and Bea's life miserable. Of such were horror movies made.

Guy averted his eyes. He knew. Mark didn't have to blurt out how he felt right now. His partner knew. They'd never even talked about love. About marriage. Oh, Guy talked about getting frustrated with his wife once or twice. But he was always respectful and kind. Loving.

But this.

Mark couldn't keep his eyes off of them—Katty and Bea.

Thank God for Clarence.

"Why don't you sit Daynton over there by your desk, Mark." Sheriff directed the process. "Chantelle, please bring the test kit for him."

The three men moved as one. Daynton sat on the chair beside the desk, with a deputy standing on either side, a hand on each shoulder.

Bea had quieted, but sat stiffly upright on Clarence's lap. Watching. Eyes wide but glued to the kit, the process.

She knew.

"Open wide." Chantelle held the swab, ready.

Daynton snickered. "Just like the dentist's office."

No one laughed.

Or smiled.

He opened.

Chantelle swabbed the inside of his cheek, then slipped the swab into a prepared sleeve and sealed it. She took a new swab and swabbed his other cheek and sealed it inside another sleeve.

"Just so you all know. I filled out an envelope with Mr. Daynton's name and … future address, his social security number. We will get the results here first, though. The lab gets this back to us within twenty-four hours—rarely forty-eight."

Mark swallowed.

Katty looked green. Her chin quivered. She tried to look away, but met Mark's eyes. A tear slipped down her cheek.

Bea's eyes had not left Daynton's face. She watched every movement Chantelle made. Didn't miss a thing.

Mark was thankful for the man Sheriff was. He looked grim.

No one in the room was looking forward to Bea's turn.

Except Daynton.

"When did you say you get the results?" Daynton sounded almost giddy.

Chantelle paused on her way to where Clarence and Bea sat. "I said. Within twenty-four hours—at the least." She turned to the sheriff. "From there, I don't know."

Sheriff released his hold on Katty and turned to face Daynton. "When we get word, we'll make sure you get the results before you're escorted to prison." His voice sounded tight. He cleared his throat. "That's the way it works."

He nodded at Chantelle to continue.

She moved her kit to where Clarence and Bea sat.

Bea watched every move again.

Chantelle took her time.

Mark thought of the times his mom had ripped bandages off fast—so it wouldn't hurt.

It always hurt.

Katty moved closer.

Sheriff hovered, ready.

"Okay, sweetie." Chantelle held up the swab. She sucked in a deep breath.

Mark felt Daynton tense.

Everyone on guard.

Bea was quiet.

Chantelle held the swab in front of Bea's mouth. "Open wide." Chantelle had a small son. She tried to sound upbeat, almost happy. But she failed.

Bea clamped her lips together and braced.

"Bea." Clarence rubbed her cheek. "Sweetie, you have to open your mouth." He held his mouth open. "Like this, so she can rub that swab inside your mouth." He did it again. "It doesn't hurt. Open like this."

Mark's whole body tensed. He realized he was holding his breath. Not good if he passed out.

Daynton started to say something, but Guy flicked Daynton's ear to shut him up.

Clarence yawned. Faked it.

Bea didn't.

For some reason, she reached down as if she was holding someone's hand. Like she held her fingers around someone … else's. She blinked away tears.

Chantelle hesitated. "Look. I'll try Clarence first. Okay, Clarence?"

He sat up and nodded. "Look, Bea. I'll try it first." He opened his mouth wide. "Ahh."

Bea watched intently. She mimicked him and opened hers.

Chantelle quickly pushed the swab into Bea's mouth.

Bea bit down hard, cracking the swab.

Mark almost laughed. Almost cheered. Not appropriate for a deputy.

"God. I hope she didn't break a tooth." Chantelle still held onto the swab.

Bea didn't let go, but her teeth were small, so she still had spaces between some.

Chantelle gently slid it out of Bea's mouth. "Got it all." She held it up. It was bent, but in one piece. She looked up at Sheriff.

He shook his head and bit his lip. The man was firm and almost cold with criminals. Little girls, not so much.

Mark wanted to just forget it and tell Daynton too bad. But the judge had ordered it.

Chantelle opened the last swab envelope and held it up. "If we don't get it with this one, I have more."

Katty squirmed, but Sheriff held firm. Black mascara ran down her cheeks. She sobbed silently.

Clarence started to tickle Bea.

She opened her mouth to laugh.

Chantelle was quick on the draw and swabbed the inside of her cheek.

Bea blinked and stared at Chantelle.

Then at Clarence.

Something dropped into the atmosphere of the room and sucked the air right out. The air exploded back in and slammed against the walls.

They all visibly felt it.

Physically. Emotionally. Spiritually.

A depth of reality from heaven to the pit of hell. And back again.

Injustice.

Betrayal.

Chantelle choked. "I'm sorry, Bea." She dropped the stick into the sleeve and sealed it. "I'm so sorry." Her voice cracked. She stood and rushed to sit at her desk, her face in her hands.

Bea's chin jutted. Her eyes accused, tried and convicted Clarence and the others. She struggled to get down, then ran away from him. She turned to each person in the room, seemed to ask for help—for justice. Stomped her foot, then ran to the exit, and tried to open the door—to get out—but couldn't.

Finally, she crumpled onto the floor.

Mark started, but restrained himself. God, to run to that little girl and hold her. All he wanted to do right now. The crappy part of his job: show restraint and discretion.

Daynton chuckled. "That's my girl."

Guy decked him. "Shut-up, jerk."

Sheriff caught Katty just as she slumped to the floor.

Clarence's head fell back, his eyes closed, his mouth tight.

"Bea." He turned to find her and held out his hands. "Bea. I'm sorry. I had to—"

Mark couldn't stop himself. He rushed to Bea and tried to pick her up.

She kicked and screamed. "No! No. Put me down." Until she saw who was picking her up. Not Clarence, her deceiver.

Mark.

She jumped into his arms.

This child. This little girl.

She was shaking, sobbing.

He didn't care if she used him to get back at Clarence.

Mark didn't care.

Sheriff cleared his throat. "Daynton, you are responsible for any costs. You pushed for this test and it will not be on the taxpayers to pay for it."

Daynton laughed. "Right. Blood out of a turnip."

ELEVEN

Bea stomped up the steps to the trailer house and opened the door. She gagged and turned back to face Mommy, who was lugging boxes out of the car. "Mommy!" She pointed behind her. "It stinks in there. What happened?"

Mommy shoved a couple of boxes onto the deck and went back for more. "We are homeless now." She opened the trunk and pulled out more boxes. "I don't think we'll even need any boxes. Not keeping anything."

"Mommy!" Bea stomped her foot. "We can't go in there. It's bad." She pinched her nose and shook her head.

"Well, we have to, Bea. If we're going to get anything out of there before tomorrow. They're tearing it all down. To-morrow." She looked behind their trailer. "Looks like Mrs. Nosy is all out. Wonder where she moved to." She slammed the trunk and the car doors and stood looking at the trailer house, then at Bea. "What?"

"We can't go in. It stinks in there."

"I know." Mommy stepped past Bea onto the deck and pushed the door open all the way. She waved her hands in front of her as if trying to wave out the mess. The stink. "I'll go inside and open the back door and maybe we can get some air moving through the whole trailer. Maybe that'll help." She hugged Bea. "You stay here and I'll see if that helps."

Bea sat on the bottom step of the deck when Boy appeared. "Hi Boy. What are you doing here?" Bea glanced around. "Are the angels here, too?"

Boy nodded slowly. "They're always here." He stopped. "Hey. I'm an angel. I'm always here." He smiled. "Not like Jesus is. He's always with you. He never leaves you. Didn't you know that? Didn't Mrs. T tell you that?" He crossed his arms over his chest. Pretty smart boy. He knew all of heaven and all the angels. "They stay with you all the time—no matter where you go."

"I don't see them now."

"Gotta open your eyes."

Bea blinked her eyes closed and open several times. "My eyes *are* open. I still don't see them."

. "No, silly." He patted her chest. "Those eyes. People can see with their heart." He looked around them. "Like the angels see. Like … you can see through your heart."

"Who are you talking to, Bea?" Mommy reached for a couple of boxes. "It's not so bad with that back door open." She turned to go inside, but backed out again. "Who were you talking to?"

Bea pointed. "Boy. Boy's here today."

Mommy stopped with a box in her arms, squinted, and slowly shook her head. She didn't believe her. She had that funny look on her face. Nope. Mommy didn't believe she could see angels. She looked back and forth outside, then inside. Back outside. "Well, I don't see him. Why don't you come inside and help me clear your room?"

Bea stood. "Boy, you can come inside, too. Help me pack my stuff."

A pickup truck drove into the trailer court and honked.

"Who's that?" Boy shoved his hands into his pockets. "Do you know who that is? We should call the cops, so you're safe."

Bea jumped. "It *is* a cop! It's Depdy Mark!" She yelled into the house. "Mom! Depdy Mark Scott's here!" She jumped up and down. "He brought his truck to help us!"

Depdy Mark Scott pulled in behind Mommy's car and opened his door. "Hi Bea." He stood up and held out his arms.

Bea jumped and ran to him. "Depdy Mark Scott! What are you doing here?"

He laughed and picked her up. "I came over to help you and Mommy with packing and moving. Is that okay?" He hugged her and set her down.

"Sure. That's okay with me."

After he put Bea down, he reached into his truck and came back with a pretty sack all decorated with—

"Daryl & Dumpty!" Bea clapped her hands. She started to reach for it, but stopped. "Is that for me, Depty Mark Scott?"

Depdy Mark Scott leaned over to hand it to her, and his head dropped to his chest.

"You okay? Did I hurt your feelings?" Bea reached out and touched his cheek.

He looked up at her, grinning, laughing, shaking his head. "Of course it's for you, Bea." He glanced behind her. "You are the only person I know that is crazy about Daryl & Dumpty."

"Mommy. Deputy Mark Scott brought me a sack with Daryl & Dumpty all over it!" Back to Mark. "Your face is all red. Are you sunburned? Have a fever?" She felt his forehead. "You're hot, but you don't have a fever."

Depdy Mark Scott stood and blew out a breath as he looked up at Mommy. He held the sack up to show her. "Is this okay? To give to Bea?" He shook his head. "I guess I should've asked first."

Bea jumped up and down, clapping her hands. "It's okay, Mommy. Right?"

Mommy sat down on the top step of the deck and nodded. "Sure. Sure it's okay, Bea." When she looked at Depdy Mark Scott, her face changed. *Her* face turned red.

"Mommy. Your face got all red. Just like his. Do you have a fever?" Bea started to take a step up.

"No. No, Bea." Mommy shook her head, pushed Bea away. "I'm fine. Just … hot from going inside that stinky house." She looked at Depdy Mark Scott. "Thanks Mark. You didn't need to—"

"Can I see it? It's a pretty bag. I could color it like on TV. Daryl's shirts are pretty colors." Bea held out her hands.

Depdy Mark Scott picked her up and sat on the step beside Mommy. "Open it."

Bea peeked. "Oh, there's stuff inside?" She pulled out striped paper. "Pretty! So pretty!"

Depdy Mark Scott jumped. "Wait! Don't break it." He held his big hands under a balled up piece of the pretty paper. "Here. Let's unwrap it together." He slowly opened one side and then the other.

Inside sat Daryl & Dumpty. "Oh. Just like on TV."

"Look." He unwrapped a long cord with a plug and held it up. "It's a lamp. So you can plug it in … in your room. And turn it on at night. It lights up." He chuckled. "I played with it last night to make sure it worked. It's really cute."

"Ohhh. In my room?" But she stopped. "It's not my birthday." To Depdy Mark Scott, "Not even Christmas."

"We should plug it in." Depdy Mark Scott glanced up at the trailer.

"Oh. There's no electricity here anymore since they're tearing the trailer down." She smiled. "That's so cute. We'll have to try it when we get back to Noell's. Okay?"

"Can I hold it? I'll be careful."

Depdy Mark Scott gently handed it to Bea, his hands under hers.

"I'll be careful. I won't drop it." She looked up at him. "But can I take it home?"

"Umm." Depdy Mark Scott looked at Mommy. He opened his mouth, but closed it right away.

Mommy tapped the lamp with her fingers. "She, uh … Bea hasn't ever had a grandparent—except for Clarence. And Clarence hasn't ever been a grandpa, either." She swallowed. "He gives us stuff. Helps us out." She patted the deck they sat on. "He had this built."

"Yeah. The other one fell down."

Mommy shook her head. "And to be honest, I might buy her a new box of cereal, or—"

"Peanut butter!" Bea clapped her hands. "Noell bought me some yesterday. I love peanut butter."

"Shh." Mommy tapped Bea's lips. "She never asks for anything. She watches all the Daryl & Dumpty shows with all those toys and never whines for them."

Bea knew why. She *knew* better—whether Mommy was in a bad mood and drinking or not—Mommy's hand was quick and painful. Bea traced the colors on the lamp, keeping her eyes down. She knew mad. She knew drunk. Bea knew when to duck. She peeked up at Mommy, at Depdy Mark Scott. Back down to the lamp.

Depdy Mark Scott reached his hand to touch hers. "Bea." He lifted her chin so he could see her face, so she could see his. "This is a gift. A present. From me to you. For you to keep forever. No matter what."

Silence.

Bea's heart hurt. She didn't feel scared. She didn't know what to do with the way her insides felt. She wanted to cry. She wanted to jump and run and laugh. And she wanted to cry some more.

Back to Depdy Mark Scott. "I love it." Back to the lamp. "It's beautiful." To him again. "Thank you."

He wiped a tear away and gently bopped her nose.

Mommy covered her mouth with her hand. "Where'd you learn that, Bea? To say thank you?"

"Boy taught me." Bea nodded. "And I'm pretty sure he knows everything because he hangs out with all those big angels." She paused and scanned the area around them. "Like them." She tried to point, but both hands still held the lamp. "Over there." She smiled. "I don't know their names yet. Boy is over there with them." Back to Mommy. "Boy taught me to say please and thank you." She nodded. "Mrs. T did, too."

Silence.

She caressed the lamp. So cute. The bag and paper. So pretty.

She glanced up at Mommy and Depdy Mark Scott. They stared at her, eyes big, and mouths open. Like on TV when Dumpty surprised Daryl. That wide and open.

"What?" She patted her lamp. Boy sat beside them and smiled.

"They don't believe you but they'll see." Boy seemed sure. "Someday they'll see."

Bea nodded.

"Bea." Mommy wasn't mad. She wasn't scared or drunk. Bea knew drunk. "Bea." Mommy nodded toward where Bea had pointed. "You see something ... over there?"

Bea nodded. "Yep." She smiled and nodded again. The big angels smiled back and waved. "Yep." She listened. "Boy says they were with me yesterday at the 'partment, but I couldn't see them."

More silence.

"Well ... shall we ... get to work?" Depdy Mark Scott stood. "Do you want me to wrap that lamp back up for you?" He held out his hands. "We can put it in your car so we don't break it."

Mommy seemed to wake up. "Yes. We can put it in your car seat so it doesn't get broken."

"Okay."

Depdy Mark Scott re-wrapped the lamp very carefully and slid it into the bag.

"I like that paper. So pretty." She jumped up and hugged him around his neck. "Thank you Depdy Mark Scott."

He blinked several times and hugged her back. "You are so welcome." He shook his head. "And so cute."

A dog barked from far away.

Mommy sighed and smiled. "Well, I need to get inside and start digging to see if we need anything out of here." She stood and rubbed her hands off on her jeans, turned, and stepped inside. "Here were go. I didn't think we'd need gas masks, but we might."

Depdy Mark Scott laughed on his way back from her car. "I could get some from the department." He stepped in after Mommy. "Oh!" He pinched his nose.

Mommy stuck her head back outside and sucked in a deep breath. Blew it out. "Bea, stay outside. This is bad. I don't want you breathing this in."

"But Mommy. I have to get my stuff."

"I don't think there's much left. I'll check. You have all your books and clothes, remember?" She sucked in air and rushed back inside.

"I have my Daryl & Dumpty blanket. I have my books." Bea checked the car. "I have my lamp." Deep sigh. She jumped. "Mommy! Don't forget my rocker!"

Mommy said a bad word from inside the trailer and came back outside. "Bea. Why do you want the rocker?"

Bea stared at Mommy, then at the ground, and immediately up at Mommy. Mommy was gonna get mad. Bea knew mad.

Depdy Mark Scott looked at Mommy, then at Bea. "I-is it heavy? We can put it in the front seat beside me." Back at Mommy. "Can't we?"

"But where will we put it at Noell's, Bea?" Mommy shook her head. "It's not our house."

Bea blew out a big breath and hung her head. "But what if I need it?"

"Need a rocking chair?" Mark shrugged. "Doesn't Noell have one you can use?"

"Sh-she …." Did Mommy look mad? No. Maybe. Was she gonna cry?

Mommy turned to him. "When I used to be gone out … all night? Like in drinking and partying all night, Bea used to hide under that rocker."

"Ohh." He nodded. "I remember finding you once, under the rocker." He nodded. "But Mommy doesn't do that anymore, right?"

Mommy glanced at him. "We'll go in and check it out, though. If it still looks okay, we can take it. We can maybe store it in Grampa's shop, or somewhere. Okay?"

"Thanks Mommy." Bea breathed. "Thanks Depdy Mark Scott."

He stuck his tongue out at Bea and stepped inside the trailer. He made all kinds of silly sounds, groaned, made like he would throw up.

Bea giggled. "Depdy Mark Scott is funny." She nodded and turned to Boy. "It does stink in there, though. You better stay outside, too."

TWELVE

"Yes, Sir. God had a plan. A plan that Pharaoh didn't see." Jasper followed Jerahmael down the hallway into Katty's old bedroom at the trailer. He chuckled. "There have been several plans Satan didn't see."

Demons lined up against every wall in the bedroom. Evil yellow eyes followed as the angels walked into the room. Each demon hissed and spit at them. Some kind of party.

"Oops. They didn't like that. What'd you just say?" Rael faced the demons, not to attack, but out of pure curiosity. The demons' eyes sparked, their fangs dripped. Stringy, sparse hair on their heads fell over their shoulders and covered dirty strips of fabric that barely hid bare bones. "It's okay guys." Rael pushed his hands at them. "Stay! Settle."

"Heh. They're not dogs, Rael," Jasper held out his hands to the demons like he would give a dog a treat, but thought better of it and stood up. "I just said that several times all along history, Satan has missed God's plan—like he didn't see it coming."

The demons growled at that.

Jerahmael poked his thumb toward the demons. "So, what's

with these guys? What do you think they're doing here? This place is getting torn down tomorrow."

All three angels faced the mob of demons, hands folded across their chests. All it took was for an angel to take notice of a demon, and all the demons acted out by hissing, spitting, and growling. Something held them in place, though. Not one attacked. Not one flew at the angels. Each one was ready for a ruckus, but seemed tied down.

Jasper spoke first. "Something's up in paradise."

Jerahmael chuckled as he watched the demons, the backdrop of the destroyed trailer behind them. "Yup. Something's up."

One to always keep the plan moving, Rael pointed at the rocker. "So, back to the chair. What's the plan?" He grinned at the demons.

Jerahmael smiled and nodded. "It's a good thing to take the rocker." He remembered his little Bea hiding under it many a night when her mommy left her alone. "It would be a good thing to have, no matter where they end up moving." He sat down on it and rocked. "This rocker holds a special place in Bea's heart. It's her sustainability, her comfort, her solace, her peace."

"But they said it might be in bad shape, maybe broken?" Jasper, Katty's angel replied. "Is it? Maybe Mark can fix it?" He leaned over to examine the legs and rockers as Jerahmael leaned back and forth.

They all watched as Katty walked into the bedroom.

Jerahmael rocked a few more times and stopped. Oh-oh. Had she seen him move the chair? The angels froze.

Seemed like she was open to the invisible realm more and more. She had seen Jasper's big boots a while back. Bea was always talking to Boy in front of Katty, even Mark. All the angels wanted the humans to become as the sons of God and become a total part of both realms. But today might not be a good day for that to start in the midst of the demons.

They held their breath and watched as Katty seemed to pause

and look at the chair. She turned white and gagged.

"Back to the chair." Jerahmael grinned. "Feels okay to me. I like rocking chairs. Do we have them in heaven?" He took note of when Katty turned to look and where she faced, stopping and starting to rock again.

Jasper grinned and crossed his arms across his chest. "Pretty sure Mrs. Roosevelt has one. Maybe others do, but I've never focused on rocking chairs before. Now, that's all I'll see! And, if it's broken, Mark now has tools from Uncle Ted." He turned to Rael. "Isn't that right? Mark has those tools, right?"

Rael nodded. "Yep." He tried to move out of the way as Katty stepped around the room. "And they could put it in … um." Rael stepped forward and opened his mouth to speak. Then he closed it.

"What?" Jasper turned to face Rael, directly. "What do you want to say?"

"Well, first of all, aren't we just letting little Bea put her faith in a rocker, rather than—"

Several demons landed amid the three angels and Katty. Many others landed around the outside of their circle. These demons didn't speak. They didn't hiss. They almost stood as statues in a museum. Two circles of demonic statues.

Jerahmael smiled, despite the presence of the demons, as if they had not appeared. He spoke, "I'm sure Father has a plan on how to apply the rocker to her faith, her life." He glanced at each angel. "Don't you agree?"

Rael relaxed. "Absolutely. He has a plan for each one of his humans."

One demon snickered. So … maybe not statues. Jerahmael continued the conversation as he left the room, ignoring the demons. "Just like when Moses walked this earth, this realm. God's people might have escaped the Pharaoh and his army. But how could millions of men, women, and children swim across the Red Sea?"

THIRTEEN

There was still stuff in Katty's own room that, of course she remembered, but seeing it now, in the light of having lived at Noell's, it all looked like crap. Even with all the hoarded stuff that Noell hadn't even gone through yet. The stacks of boxes and totes still looked better than Katty's old room.

And there was the rocker. Still draped with old blankets, so when Bea hid under it, she could pull them over the rocker and feel safe.

Wait. Had the rocker moved? Rocked back and forth? She blinked. She wasn't drunk. She was stone sober. Movement layered over movement. Woah. She held out her hands and braced against the chest of drawers for balance. She should've eaten. Smelling the rotten contents of the trailer was making her dizzy and sick.

She shook her head. Awful. Tears welled up, not only from the stench, but in realization of the life she had dragged her daughter into. She was raising Bea to live the same lifestyle and habits as she herself had been raised in.

She wiped her cheeks as she pulled up the bedspread, knowing what she would find, but still shocked at what flipped out. Little bottles. Little empty shooter bottles. Under the bedspread. Under the bed. In the closet. In the back of a drawer. Even one stuck in the window. Empty.

She gagged.

The sight of the putrid mess, the bottles, what her life had been, made her gag. Breakfast came up.

A hand reached around her waist and another held hair away from her mouth.

Mark.

"I can't believe—" She choked. "I can't believe how bad … I can't … "

He breathed out. "Come on. There's nothing in here you need. Except the rocker."

She nodded. Blinked. Swallowed. "I need—" Gagged again, but kept it in. "I need to make myself … make myself really see." More strength now. She straightened up. "I must never forget how bad this was. I can't ever forget this stink. This what?" She stomped her foot. "This sickness. No. This sin. For my sake and for Bea's sake." She puked again.

"Come on. Let's get you some fresh air. This isn't my stuff, but I can't see much of anything you need out of here." He held out his hand.

Just the sight of him holding out his hand stirred emotion in her. If only Katty had found a guy like Mark when she ran away from home back then. But no. She ran into Phil and forever changed the direction of her life. Bea's life.

She grasped his hand and tripped over the rocker.

An odd sensation rushed over her as she touched the rocker. A shiver of something in the air that passed through her.

"Woah." Mark rubbed his arm with his free hand. "What was that?"

"You felt it, too?" She steadied herself and intentionally breathed in and out. "I thought it was just me—you know, getting sick from the smell in here."

"Yeah. It was like a jolt of electricity or … like when you walk under high-voltage power lines, right? You hear the hum, but you almost pass through a … whoosh of power?"

"Let's get this done and get out of here. Bea is seeing things. We are feeling things. It's time to get out and let this trailer fry." She shuddered. "Even feels kinda scary. Let's go."

Mark dragged the rocker and lead her out to the living room.

They both stopped.

The wall. The painting. Shocking in the midst of the mess and stench.

Mark stopped her in front of it. "This is the only thing going. Again, it's not my stuff." He chuckled. "And if you'd go inside my house right now, you might … well. I need to get rid of stuff."

Go inside Mark's house?

Whew.

One step at a time.

She nodded.

The painting. Babies floated on clouds. The tree with that old treehouse—her only sanctuary growing up. Dark clouds. Red drips that she didn't remember. With what had just happened by the rocker in her old bedroom and now this, something in Katty finally broke. The pain of what her life had been. What she had done. All blatantly painted before her. Nowhere to hide. No way that Katty could avoid what she'd done. Yes, Phil had been the one who had lured her into the bloody evil, but she'd been there, too. She maybe … maybe could have run away. She swallowed and breathed out. She guessed she had run away—with Bea still in her belly. She had Bea. She'd saved one.

Crossroads.

This moment was a crossroads in her life.

She knelt in tears.

"I'll go … I'll go check Bea. For a minute." Mark released her hand. "I'll take the … "

He didn't finish what he was going to say. Or maybe he had, and she was so deep into another zone, another realm, that she didn't hear what he'd said.

When he was outside, she leaned over and sobbed. Threw up and sobbed some more. "Oh Jesus. Help."

A cool, damp towel mopped her tears, her face.

Silence.

She sat up. Mark moved to the side, next to the painted wall. He waited, eyes downcast.

All she did was nod. And nodded again. "We need to remember." She'd said "we." She'd included Mark in that thought. She wiped her face with the towel again. "Yes."

Tools clattered in front of the wall.

She raised up, wiping her face again.

Bea stuck her face inside. 'Mommy. Can I come in now?" She had a towel, too.

Oh, Mark.

He raised the chainsaw at the same time that he raised his eyebrows. "Ready? It's gonna be loud."

This man was going to bat with his chain saw for her weird painting on the wall. Never had she felt such validation, such approval. No. Such acceptance. Phil had always made fun of her art. Mark would give his … well …

"Ready." She stepped back and grabbed Bea close to her. "Cover your ears!"

Bea hid under Katty's arms and covered her ears. She peeked out and watched.

Mark pulled the cord and began outlining the painting. The sound rattled the very paneling. It was so loud that the empty bottles Katty had thrown into the kitchen sink earlier clattered together.

Katty checked Bea's face. Her eyes were wide.

A cupboard door popped open with the last roar of the chainsaw. A memory popped into Katty's mind of not too long ago, when an old, evil man had threatened her with his chainsaw. She shivered. She hadn't thought of that in a long time. She shuddered and hugged Bea.

Then Mark used his crowbar to lift the old paneling from the wall. Nails gave way with a screech and there it came off. All in one piece.

Katty supported it upright until Mark put down the saw.

Together, they lifted and carried it outside to his truck.

"Just fits."

Katty chuckled. "You knew. You measured, right?"

"Yeah. I guess I did." He closed the tailgate. "I didn't want to leave it behind." He patted the paneling. "This is important."

Those green eyes. And right now they were filled with such … admiration and … was that love? She'd mistaken something in another man's eyes for love.

She blew out a breath. Nodded. "I, uh, I—"

"Mommy. Depdy Mark Scott." She held up a small piece of paneling. "You forgot a piece." She showed them. "A baby." She held it like she might hold a baby, rocked side to side.

It was. It was a piece from the wall. Part of a baby was painted on it. Little eyes and curly hair.

Bea held it. Bea, with her big, beautiful, brown eyes and curly, messy, brown hair, held it like she would … a real, live baby.

Katty shook her head and stole a glance at Mark.

Mark shook his head, his hand at his jaw, as he stared at his phone.

Those green eyes looked into hers. Those eyes were serious.

"What, Mark? What's wrong?"

He glanced at Bea, then shook his head. Hesitated, then shoved his phone inside his pocket. "What are we going to name this art, Bea? People name their art, right?"

Good diversion, Mark.

FOURTEEN

Phyllis stood at the kitchen sink and sipped, savoring the last drop, before rinsing her coffee cup. She shut off the hot water and watched through the window as the wind swished the trees in her backyard.

The sky was dark.

A gust of wind bent the branches right and left. "I hope they are strong." Branches snapped all the time. She was forever gathering twigs and sticks from her yard. "Old trees." She shook her head and sighed.

She leaned to see more of her yard, left then right. A limb dropped as she looked. "Yup. That's what I get to do later. I guess it's good exercise and good to get extra fresh air." She loaded her cup and bowl into the dishwasher and clapped her hands. "Well, day. What's in store for me?" She tilted her head as if to hear what it said to her. "Hello? Day?"

Some days dragged on—too quiet, too empty. Too alone.

Thunder rumbled. Well, so much for the quiet part. At the back sliding door, she watched the wind whip through the trees, the wires, her American flag. Phyllis wasn't afraid of storms. In fact, she embraced them. If there was a storm warning at night or in the evening, she prayed, enjoyed the pelting of rain, and then rolled over to go to sleep. If a storm woke her, she did the same thing: prayed and rolled over, soon back to sleep.

Only once did she stumble to the basement, and that was when Mark called her from his car. He'd been weather watching with a guy and witnessed a tornado on its path toward Osceola. He called to tell her to get to the basement, and she had followed his orders.

That had convicted her a bit and made her more careful, but she still rolled over and went to sleep. "If I go, I go. I know where I'm going."

She chuckled as she imagined angels pulling her from her blankets, rushing her to what looked like the storm clouds in her mind, but breaking through them with her and bursting into sunshine.

"Is that what it's like, angels?" She always talked to them like they were right there with her. She was never sure. If she thought she was wrong, then she imagined she was talking to the Father in heaven. That was even better. "So Father in heaven? Is that what it's like?"

Thunder answered her.

"I think we need church tonight. Something's up." She checked her phone calendar. "Why not? Looks like I'm free." She shook her head. That again. She was always free. She never had people over. No one ever invited her to their house to eat. No one ever invited her to even go out to eat. Well, except when Mark came over for a meal. He did offer to buy her a burger when they delivered boxes to Mrs. Gelda's store. She always refused.

She should call him, but when? Didn't matter—lunch or supper. Even breakfast would be good. She loved bacon and eggs. She never cooked that for herself.

She nodded at the bowl in her dishwasher and closed it.

In her living room, she picked at a thread on the sofa, then walked to the front window.

She should call Mark to come over for lunch. Was he working? She shook her head. Still on nights, she was sure of it. She pulled her cell phone out of her pocket and tapped the screen.

"Hi Mom. What's up?"

"Hi son. I was just thinking." There was giggling in the background. Little girl giggling. "Well, sounds like you're busy."

"Kinda. I headed over to help Katty and little Bea here move out of their trailer since it's being torn down tomorrow."

"Oh. That's nice of you." Were they moving in together now? Had it progressed that far between them? "Well, I won't keep you. Just thought if you weren't busy, you could buy me that hamburger you're always talking about."

"Oh, Mom. I'm sorry. Probably not today." He hesitated. "This could take a while."

Giggles again in the background. Another voice too. A woman's voice.

"Oh, that's okay, Mark. Another time."

"Just a minute, Bea." He must have stepped away. "Are you okay, Mom?"

"Oh, I'm fine. Just hadn't seen you in a while, that's all." She'd seen him just last week—not even a week. "I'll let you go. Nice of you to help." She needed help, too.

"Okay, Mom. Bye. I love you."

A little voice said, "Bye." Then, "Who was that?"

Click.

Silence.

Where had all that come from? Phyllis blinked tears away. What on earth? She knew Mark better than that. *Were they going to move in together now?* Even if they did, it was none of her business. None of her business what her son did. He was an adult now and had his own life.

The giggles replayed in her mind. Over and over. That little girl.

So Mark was helping that woman and her daughter. When would he help Phyllis again? In spite of herself, she let her thoughts wander that direction. She knew better than to go childish. But she couldn't help it. Mark was probably helping get all her stuff out of that awful trailer park and he'd take them over to his house. It wasn't very big, but that's what people did nowadays.

Move in with each other.

They didn't get married anymore.

She guessed doing that wasn't any worse than what she'd done. She'd gotten married against her parent's wishes. Dad had a premonition that Carl was lying to them all about his drinking. Dad always said Carl was no good, but Phyllis couldn't see it. She married Carl anyway and paid a terrible price. The only good thing that came out of that marriage was Mark.

The ring. And maybe that. When Dad and Mom saw that ring, they'd softened a little. They must have seen dollar signs, or a better future for their daughter, than they had when they first met him.

They'd been right all along.

Oh Mark. Make the right choices.

Her fingers burned to call him again. She picked up her phone and tapped it on.

No, no, no. She put the phone back into her pocket and a visual of the ring flashed in. That ring. Where had Carl gotten the money to buy that thing? She'd always wondered that. It had to have cost $3,000 or more. It was huge—three carats or something close to that.

She sat for a couple minutes, then walked to her bedroom. She'd found it not too long ago. Now where had she put it?

She'd found it before, she'd find it again. She stood in the center of the room. Not a big room. Nice size. Good size for an old lady like her. The bed took most of the space. She didn't need much room or, for that matter, she didn't need much of anything.

What she wanted most of all was time with family and friends. Well, she had her Bible study friends. And they were a powerful group of ladies. But time with Mark. She sensed she was at a transition in her life—a different season where she would have to give up time with him, as he might have found a family of his own.

Where was that ring? She could remember thinking that she may need to find it again, and soon.

Breathe.

As soon as she let the breath out, she remembered. She put it right back where she'd found it—in that vase—only where had she put that vase? A vision popped into her mind.

She blinked as a beautiful landscape opened up in her imagination. Green leafed trees. Potted flowers at the base of the trunks. Better than any plant store sporting every potted plant and flower in the world. Several people stood in a group under … under an arch of some sort … a canopy over them. All beautifully decorated with more vines and flowers.

"Lord, what is this? It's beautiful. I want to be there."

A couple—a man and a woman stood—facing away from her. The man was neatly dressed in pants and a white shirt with a vest of some sort—maybe Western style. The woman had on a simple white dress.

Phyllis gasped.

A white dress.

The woman's hair was pulled up in a topknot, with tendrils fluttering in the breeze.

A tiny girl in a long, white dress, with a netting skirt, stepped between the man and woman to look at … her? She can see? Precious, pretty little girl … looked so familiar.

The girl waved.

Phyllis stumbled backward, her legs bumped the bed, and she sat.

Could that … K-Katty's little girl? What was her name? Bumble bee. Birdie?

Phyllis patted her chest, tried to breathe, and shook her head. Couldn't be. Couldn't be seeing that little girl with—

The man turned toward the woman, and she turned to him.

Gasp.

Mark.

An-and that woman was Katty.

The little girl had to be … Bea. That was it. Her name was Bea.

FIFTEEN

Mark sat in his squad car outside. He could see inside the department through the windows as the day was getting dark and streaks of sunlight illuminated the inside of the building.

Katty and Phil seemed to be having a dispute or something. Mark guessed that it was probably about Bea.

He touched his phone, remembering the alert from the department earlier. This would not be good. Not to act childish, but it wasn't fair. Phil Daynton should not have the right to push for blood tests, just to prove he had the same DNA. Monsters have different DNA.

And there was Bea. Right there inside with everyone, hearing every word.

He shook his head again and almost teared up. That little girl deserved a better daddy than Phil Daynton. He was evil in human form. Every cell oozed darkness and evil. And little Bea would have to live under that garbage for the rest of her life.

Just like … Mark guessed he had.

And just like he was sure, Katty had.

Awful how relationships circled around and repeated in the

next generation. That evil blood ran through every person from the way back, till now.

What if … what if there was a way to stop that crap for good?

What would it take to make a better way?

A better pathway?

A better life?

From the looks of Katty's red face inside the department, things might be heating up.

What about abuse? What about the words people spoke to others? Things like stupid, trash, wicked. His own father had spoken those words to him. His mother even, before she started back to church.

That was the difference, for sure. Jesus.

What if he could make a difference in Bea's life, in Katty's? What if … they knew Jesus, prayed to Him, like he had?

He tapped on the steering wheel, when Katty and Bea started for the door.

Uh, no.

He backed out and parked around behind the building. He should have known that was her car.

Stupid, stupid.

Stop. He was doing the same thing to himself. Reverse those words. "I'm not stupid." He let them land and something magical happened. Something in him changed. Maybe not everything, but a spark had come to life.

Again. "I'm not stupid." He stretched to see himself in the rear view mirror. "You're not stupid." He tapped on the mirror and his green eyes looked back at him. "You, Mark Scott, are not stupid." He straightened and grinned. "In fact, you are a pretty smart guy." He glanced at the building, then back at the mirror, and he pointed to himself. "You will ask Miss Katty out on a date. Bea, too."

Someone knocked on the window. "Hey Mark. Saw you

looking in the mirror a lot. Your hair isn't quite right. You need my comb?"

Mark dropped his chin onto his shirt.

Dang.

Guy.

Caught.

Caught red-faced.

Mark needed to hide somewhere. Anywhere.

But his partner opened the car door. "Let me help you with your door, Pretty Boy. It might be too hard for you to open after time with your mirror." The enormous man swept his arm out wide. "Here. Let me help you out."

Mark shook his head and chewed on the inside of his cheek. "Jerk!" A man needed to check his rear view mirror to make sure his hair wasn't all messed up. And to speak truth to his reflection. That's just what he'd been doing, and he'd gotten caught. He wanted to crawl out or maybe crawl under his squad car, but instead, he slid off the seat and stood. He stretched and stood tall, but still only came to Guy's shoulder. Dang. His mom was short and his dad had been shorter. No hope of growing taller, either. He was stuck.

Well, shit.

Phil shook his head and tried to scratch an itch that really wasn't there.

After sitting through the judge reading every entry on his record, they had ushered him back to the county jail. Hearing names like Daniel—buddies from his past—at first made him grin, until the judge looked up and drilled Phil with his eyes. There was not any question as to what the judge had been thinking. Phil had seen evil in people's eyes many times before. This was not evil. It was pure and simple truth and righteousness. Justice. He didn't have a chance with that judge.

One other name the judge had spoken was his father's name —which Phil would never speak aloud with anyone. Just hearing it out loud after all this time was jarring.

And that old jerk, Daniel and what's his name—both drunks. They had tried to horn in on his parade with Katty and Bea. Had actually broken into Katty's trailer and tried to come on to her and Bea? They really did that? What were they thinking? They all went back years and years—years of drugging and drinking and partying in ways that would make them all blush today. There was a protocol to this whole thing. You didn't step into some other man's claim.

Well … even though he himself hadn't even known about his daughter until Daniel—yeah, it had been Daniel who had spilled the news that he had a kid.

Phil stood straighter. He might be headed for prison today, or soon, but he was still the kid's dad.

"See ya Daynton." Daniel walked behind Phil, his hands cuffed behind his back. Evidently, the guy had been in and out of jail since the day he'd broken into Katty's trailer. He was like the weather—sunny one day and rainy the next.

Phil didn't answer. He knew enough about rules and protocol in a sheriff's department to know that speaking to other prisoners meant more time in solitary. In a small jail like Polk county, it didn't mean they'd stick you in a hole somewhere outside like in a third world country, but it did mean there was no speaking to the prisoner—whether they were being served meals or trans-ported. It was almost like they had leprosy. Don't speak. Don't touch.

The deputy tapped Daniel on the shoulder. "Nuff said. No talking to other prisoners." He pushed Daniel out the door.

Phil looked across the table at Bea and smiled as Daniel and his buddy were ushered outside to the squad car. Gon-dae for good-ae.

He could hear her thoughts even before he saw the expression on her face. "Naughty Daddy. Bad Daddy." She hadn't missed a thing. She's seen Daniel speak. She remembered Daniel from the break-in. And now she connected Daniel with Phil. Smart kid. Another strike against him.

Bea was looking at him, only it didn't feel loving. Not even curious. Not even cute. Oh, she was pretty. What was she thinking about, to make her stare at him like she was now? Her expression was blank. No. Her eyes wanted to dig holes in him, throw daggers at him. Her mouth wasn't turned up in a smile—it was … mad. She was angry. Even though she was only four? She wanted to kill him right now.

He could almost hear her thoughts. Was she … did she know how to send thoughts? Maybe. She was his daughter.

He guessed she might be remembering when he'd thrown her against the wall back at the trailer before the accident. He'd thrown her pretty hard.

Well, she deserved it. She'd peed on his arm. Damn brat.

She wasn't smiling back. Pretty certain she hated him. Why was he even getting involved with them?

Screw them all. He was her dad. Exerting his rights. And she was sweet and fresh and pure.

Down boy. Not here.

Those brown eyes weren't looking away.

"Naughty Daddy." Her thoughts came across loud and clear. He had perfected reading people's mind when he tried to come onto a woman. Came in handy then. Now, not so much. Bea's face said it all. She had definitely mastered sending thoughts his way.

He guessed it'd be a few years before he'd see his daughter again—if he ever got out of jail or prison. She'd be all grown up when he finally got out. Even though he wasn't the fatherly type, there was something he was experiencing right now, even as she stared at him. And what he was experiencing would not win him Father of the Year awards.

Knowing what she was thinking made it all too clear.

"Mommy." Bea tugged on Katty's sleeve.

Katty dropped her arm down to the counter and looked over at Bea.

Katty didn't look good. She wasn't quite to that level of used-upness like when Phil had left her, but she was almost there. Tired-looking. Dark circles around her eyes. Almost a haunted look to them, which made him wonder if she was using again.

She had been so self-righteous about the fact that she had quit before the accident and when Clarence—that old guy from prison—seemed to be helping her.

Phil had heard that the old guy married some bitch from the nursing home. Almost laughable. Two old people … no, he couldn't go there. Nasty. That was way above his imagination.

He looked over at Bea again. No, that freshness, newness.

Down, boy.

Bea shook her head. "Bad, bad Daddy." This time she said it out loud, or he thought he'd heard it out loud. Maybe she was getting really good at pushing her thoughts at him. Or maybe she'd really said it.

The dispatcher walked past into the sheriff's office. Her, too. She was fresh and inviting. But Phil could tell by the way she paused behind Bea that she guessed what he had been thinking. He didn't need to read her mind. She had that momma wolf expression on her face and she was about to show her fangs.

Mark entered the department from the back entrance.

Katty glanced up, but quickly looked away. Bea saw him and started to jump up, but her mother restrained her.

Daynton seemed to growl, without any noise. He was one evil man and by the way he was looking at Katty and especially Bea, Mark might need to be restrained himself.

He glanced at Katty again, but she wouldn't look at him.

What did Daynton really think he could accomplish by forcing this? Did he want to adopt or legally make Bea his child, even though her last name was not his? The saliva tests came back inconclusive. Did he want to do a blood test to prove she was his? To prove he was the man, the conqueror?

Mark knocked on the door to the sheriff's office and stepped in. "Hey Sheriff. What's up with the prisoner? What do we need to be doing?" He closed the door behind him.

Sheriff Dennison looked up from the paperwork on the desk in front of him. He tapped on the paper with his pen and he seemed to be thinking of what to say. He took a breath. "We are doing the blood paternity test here this morning. Then Daynton goes to prison."

Mark glanced behind him through the glass at the three sitting at the table. The jerk was going to push his legal rights with his daughter? It felt like the air had been sucked out of Mark's chest. Like a balloon had been untied, and the air was escaping.

"There's no way to put it off? No way to just get him to prison and not do this today? Or ever?" Mark looked back at the Sheriff. "You can see the woman and girl ..." He shook his head. "Stupid to say it that way. You all know I like her—them." He started again. "It's obvious Katty and Bea don't want it. Don't they have any rights in this case?" He swallowed. "They've already been put through enough with the saliva test."

"I'm afraid not, Mark. It's the only thing Daynton pushed for in court and the judge complied." Sheriff signed a paper and looked up. "I'm sorry. It might be the worst thing for that little girl and her mamma or it might turn out to be the best thing, too." He stood and tucked in his shirt and adjusted his belt. "These things are out of our hands." He stopped and looked directly at Mark, glanced behind him into the central office, then back to Mark. "As time passes and as people are absent, or … an old building can be torn down to make way for the new. Something new might be planted when the old crop is plowed under— never to grow again." He closed his mouth and thought for a minute. "I'm not saying this very well."

"No. You're doing—"

"There's a verse." Sheriff glanced at the map on the wall. "Something like, 'All things are new in Him.'" He shook his head. "Something like that. I just mean, there's new stuff coming. This season has been brutal for Katty and Bea. Hard on you, too. But there's new stuff coming, and it's good stuff." He pointed into the central office. "Old things are dead—well, not really dead. But you know what I'm trying to say."

Mark stared back at the Sheriff and slowly his eyes roved from Sheriff's face to the window behind him and outside as he caught the full meaning of what had been said.

Guy opened the door and held out his hand. Sheriff handed him the paperwork, and he walked into the central office, giving them to Chantelle.

Sheriff cleared his throat. "Patience, son." His voice was soft, meant just for Mark. Sheriff's eyes were soft, too. His whole countenance was understanding and compassionate. "Things have a way of working out." He walked into the restroom.

Mark sucked in a deep breath and let those words surround him, holding onto a moment that he realized wouldn't happen again.

A visual of Uncle Ted surfaced. Uncle Ted had been lecturing Mark about taking care of his old ramshackle car, the only thing he had to drive to school. Mark had left the windows open and there had been a downpour. Even the floorboards had become little lakes. Mark said something immature like, "It's just an old junker." Uncle Ted flipped out and replied, "If you take care of the small things, the old things, even the bad things, when they die, God finds a way to bless with the new."

For such a time. "Things have a way of working out." He repeated Sheriff's words so only he could hear them—just loud enough so his ears could catch the sound. He nodded and walked out to the central room and to the table, not looking forward to blood tests, needles in tiny girls, and test results.

Phil tapped his foot against the metal table leg. Hurry up, people. He'd been sitting there on the receiving end of Bea's darts for too long. He tried to stretch, but the shackles prevented much movement.

The entrance door burst open when a short, chunky woman with shoulder length blond hair, black-rimmed glasses and red lip-stick burst inside, lugging a huge leather case. "Hey Chantelle. You ready for me?" She eyed Bea and Phil. "These two?"

Chantelle nodded and waited as the Sheriff walked into the central office. "She's ready for us, Sheriff."

Sheriff Dennison seemed to take his time coming into the room.

Did everybody hate Phil? Did everybody here know his fatherly intentions toward Bea? Well. He guessed they'd all had access to his record.

The sheriff cleared the table top free of paperwork. "Yeah. Della, set up over here." He glanced at Bea and back at Della. "We need to wait just a minute for Clarence. He's on his way."

He'd barely gotten the words out of his mouth when the old man walked in. Phil shook his head. The old man looked younger than Phil himself did. He didn't get the usual welcome from his girls. Probably still mad at him for tricking Bea during the saliva test. He slid along the wall to stand beside the sheriff.

With the nervous energy surging in the room, this ought to be good entertainment. And Phil had a ringside seat.

Della dropped her heavy case onto the table, opened it and stretched on latex gloves. She pulled out a couple of needles and medical paraphernalia and spread her fingers on the surface of the table. "Which one first?"

Katty unconsciously moved closer to Bea. Bea hid under Katty's arm. "Mommy?"

Phil leaned forward. "Oh, be a big girl."

Bea took one look at Phil and crawled under the table, then under Katty's chair.

Katty wasn't much help.

Chantelle bent down and gathered Bea into her arms and held her tightly. "We better act fast. Kids are quick." She walked over to where Della stood. "At least my son is. Took him to the doctor for his shots and he was out the door before I could grab him."

"Shots?" Bea screamed and reached for Katty. "Mommy! Mommy, help me." She squirmed in Chantelle's arms, almost hit her in the face, but Chantelle was stronger. She grabbed one of Bea's arms around her tiny body and then the other one around the opposite way in a straight-jacket hold, gripping her by the wrists, in spite of Bea's wriggling. She'd done that before.

Katty seemed immobile. She slowly stood beside her chair but didn't reach for Bea or offer to hold her. She almost acted lethargic.

Phil guessed she was on something right then. Visions of her when they'd first met rattled around in his memory. She was still pretty, but boy she'd been a knockout back then. How he'd ever gotten so lucky to get her, he did not know, except he was probably the first guy to offer her an escape out of her beast of a mom's house.

Bea screamed as Della stuck her. Chantelle had a tight grip

on her, but Bea wormed her way out of her arms. Blood dripped onto the floor, but Della had it under control "Got it." She capped the vial and dropped it into the wire holder.

Were those tears in that dispatcher's eyes? Damn, these people were all righteous. He didn't have a chance.

The short deputy, his name tag said "Deputy Scott," stepped inside. There had been so much commotion in the office that no one had seen him. Except Bea. And Phil.

Bea reached out to him, and he took her in his arms.

"You done with her, Della?" He cupped her head against his shoulder.

He'd done that before. And Bea knew it. It seemed familiar to her, too. Something close to bile rose in Phil, and it took him by surprise. A low growl escaped from his lips before he could check it.

For once. Katty almost came to. She glowered directly at him and stood, stomped around the table and slapped Phil across his face, hard.

His skin stung and burned. "What was that for?"

Clarence moved to contain her, but she shrugged him off. "Katty. You don't want to get yourself in trouble."

She didn't even hear him. "You creep." Katty's voice rose. "That was for every time you touched me and beat me. For every baby you killed. For every time you hurt me. For every time you drugged me so I'd black out." She swung her hand back for another crack at him, but Clarence caught her hand in mid-air and restrained her.

The sheriff moved to her other side, catching her other arm. "Katelyn, you don't want to do that. He's already in handcuffs and headed to prison." He slowly and gently released her hand. "Listen to Clarence. Don't get yourself into trouble, too." He pointed at Bea. "You have your daughter to think about."

Startled, Katty rubbed her wrist. "You called me Katelyn."

"That's what's on your paperwork."

"I haven't heard that name in a long time."

Della looked at Phil. "Next?" She pointed at Phil, then looked at Sheriff. "This the one, Sheriff?"

"Yes. Then we'll need to transport him." He glanced over at Deputy Scott, but seemed to think better of it. "I'll call in Roger to transport him."

The deputy carried Bea over to where Katty had sat down again and tried to give her to her mom, but Bea wouldn't have it. She struggled and kicked. "Bea. Settle down."

She jumped at the sound of the deputy's voice.

Phil guessed he had never talked to her that way. Good. She needed to keep her distance from him. She was all Phil's. He winced as Della poked him with the needle and drew blood.

Blood confirmed and covered it all.

All his.

SIXTEEN

How could a day go from one so perfect to the next day so evil? How could life turn itself around like that? Katty hadn't done anything to change it. She'd just been inside her day. She hadn't tried to make the day better, good, or bad.

From sweet time at the stinky trailer house—which should have been bad, but wasn't—to awful blood tests at the Sheriff's Department. After that saliva test, they'd had to do a blood test, too?

Even Sheriff Dennison had quietly commented that a day had its own plans. What had he meant by that, except—

Bea followed Katty from the car. "Come on, Bea."

Katty held out her arms.

Bea stomped right past her.

Oh God. Help. Now she hates me.

"Bea. I didn't know it would be like that." Katty stopped and stood still. "I didn't know."

Noell met them at the door. She tried to smile as she pushed the door open. Bea slumped—just stood there in front of Noell. Noell leaned over and slowly, ever so carefully, put her hands under Bea's arms, and lifted her up into her own.

Katty tried to say something. She paused in front of them and opened her mouth. Then shook her head. She might explode, either with tears or with screaming, but no tears came. No screaming. She'd never felt so drained, like the day her kettle had burned dry on the stove. It had sputtered, and by the time she'd figured out where the sputtering was coming from, it exploded.

From that morning at the trailer house, sobbing in front of the painting that was now in Grampa's shop, to time at the sheriff's getting Bea tested for that evil man to find out he was legally Bea's father. How a day could turn. How time could become evil. How a person could become evil.

So many times in a day, God had shown Katty the differences. Good or evil. And she knew it was God. It was too real. Too powerful to not think it was from Him instead of coincidence.

Mark wanted her to always keep the painting from that smelly trailer house. He loved her art.

Phil would have painted it over himself. Even nailed new paneling over it.

She patted her pockets. She couldn't help it, it had become a saving grace habit, and she wanted a drink now so bad.

But what about Bea? She hadn't spoken to Katty the whole ride home. She'd almost broken the lamp Mark had given her, but Katty caught it just in time. That would have broken more than just the lamp.

What happened now? Phil gets shipped off to prison—Sheriff had said as much before they left the department. But then what?

Phil would have his day. He'd have proof that he was Bea's father. But what would be the result of that? She'd heard about visitation of a father with his kids after a divorce. That was common these days. Probably half of the marriages ended like that. And the kids suffered. Almost as much as she had growing up. Definitely as much as Bea had.

But now Phil had his proof. Katty had no doubt that the blood tests would come back, showing he was Bea's dad. So what? He was going to prison. Locked away till he rotted in there. And that was what he deserved. Let him rot.

She walked into the kitchen and sat down. She didn't want to look at Noell, but she didn't want to avoid her either. None of this was Noell's fault. She'd lived through her own hell.

This was hell on earth.

And what about Clarence today? If Katty let … no, *made* herself think about it, Clarence was only doing what the courts had demanded. He'd tried to help Bea do what they needed her to do. But why did she feel so betrayed?

A big cup of coffee appeared on the table in front of Katty. She caught a whiff.

Noell and Bea sat across from her. Noell sipped from her own mug of coffee. Bea had a favorite glass painted with little white snowflakes all over it, filled with milk. Noell slowly looked up at Katty. "Bad?"

Katty nodded, just barely keeping it together. "Bad."

"Bad." Bea rubbed her arm. "It hurt, bad. And Phil looked at me. Scary looks. He's a naughty daddy." She snuggled onto Noell's arms. "He's a bad daddy."

Katty teared up. "Bea, you were so brave." She shook her head. "And I was no help." Deep breath. "I'm so sorry this … day, all that happened." She couldn't help herself. She remembered the past, and she was responsible for all the pain that Bea was experiencing. "I'm so sorry he's your dad, Bea."

Bea sat still on Noell's lap, looking down at the mug of coffee in Noell's hand. A tear dropped into the coffee. And another. "Mommy?"

Katty leaned closer, her own cup of coffee untouched. "What Bea?"

"Can I have my rocker?" She patted the table. "Can I have it in here? In Noell's house?" She leaned against Noell. "Can I, Noell?"

Noell raised her eyebrows, questioning Katty, and nodded her head.

"Sure Bea." Katty stood. "Let's go get it."

Noell grabbed the keys, and all three stood and found their way to Grampa's shop.

Inside, there the rocker stood, right beside Katty's painting from the trailer house. Katty paused. "It was the right thing to bring it. To bring them both." Thanks to Mark. She nodded, sure now more than ever. The painting stood against one wall. Even though the light from outside was dim and the inside lightbulbs needed a stronger wattage, the painting glowed. The babies glowed. The tree house appeared to have brighter colors than before.

No one spoke at first.

"Mommy, look at the painting, your painting. All the colors are pretty. Bigger than they were at the trailer."

Katty touched Bea's head, then her hand. "Bigger?"

Bea grasped Katty's hand. "Yeah. Bigger. Like bigger or louder."

Noell nodded. "Do you mean that it looks brighter?"

"Yes. But it needs to talk. It needs to talk to us." She tilted her head as she looked at it. She didn't take her eyes off the painting as she climbed onto the rocker. She started rocking back and forth. "It needs to tell us something."

Back and forth.

SEVENTEEN

Bea followed Mommy and Noell toward the house. Jerahmael, Bea's angel, hung behind them a short distance, walking with the other angels, Jasper and Noell's angel, Uriel, and many others. All three listened to the hearts of the humans they guarded. All three felt the sadness and oppression stemming from the recent blood test at the Sheriff's Department.

"Lovely home." Jerahmael observed. "A definite improvement over the trailer." He checked the other angels, Uriel, especially since he usually stayed at Noell's house with her. "You've seen the trailer, right?"

The others nodded. Jasper nodded, but had an obvious questioning expression on his face. He tilted his head, but just nodded.

"The trailer was, from the beginning, not a safe house to raise little Bea in, but Katty made it work."

The others nodded again.

Jerahmael continued. "It's important to keep our humans safe. Especially the young ones like Bea."

Jasper stopped him. "Are you alright, my brother? Is everything okay with you and your charge?"

Unaware of the angels' conversation, Noell opened the back door. "Since Gamma hoarded so much stuff, there wasn't room for lots of furniture. Makes it easier to bring Bea's rocker in." She held the door while Katty carried it inside. Bea held onto the armrest, helping. "We have more room for it. Especially now that I've cleaned out a few things. Well." She glanced around the room. "There's still lots to get rid of."

Jerahmael nodded. "Yes. All is well and all shall be well." He checked Bea's arm where they withdrew the blood at the Sheriff's Department. The woman had been quick. She seemed to know what she was doing. But the bandage, er the band-aide, was loosening on one end.

Jasper spoke up, continuing the angel's conversation, his eyes on Jerahmael. "This definitely is an improvement for all of them."

Uriel nodded. "Noell was growing lonely, since her gamma left this earth, but especially since her mother drowned." He rested his hand on Noell's back. "Now she has family and friends. Both."

"Where do you want it, Noell?" Katty set it down in the kitchen.

Jasper tapped Boy on the head. He'd just about sat on the rocker, but Jasper shook his head.

"Hmm. Well, not in here." Noell thought a minute. "Although, it'd be really comforting to have a wood stove or fireplace in here. Then the rocker would be so fitting."

"A fireplace?" Bea checked the room. "That'd be cozy." She hugged herself. "Warm."

Jerahmael chuckled. "That's my girl." He hovered his hand over Bea's band-aide.

Noell grabbed an old towel as they walked into the living room. "I think it'd look great next to Gamma's red leather sofa, right?" She dusted the sofa and stood back.

Angels and humans all nodded at the same time.

Bea jumped on the rocker seat and started rocking. "Fits here just right. It's perfect with the little red leather sofa."

Katty did laugh then. "Little. Little, red, leather sofa?" She spanned her arms wide. "It's huge."

Jerahmael laughed with her. "Good to hear her laugh. She's been very closed lately. Probably because of having to test, but also because Bea's dad is evil." He was thankful that the human females didn't know the depth of how evil he really was, that they couldn't see the beings attached to him. "Hard on a mommy to have to put her child through those tests."

Hard on an angel to watch what their humans sometimes went through. Many of the host of angels nodded.

Boy checked with Jasper before he sat on the rocker with Bea. "I just want to sit with her. I won't get wild."

"It's okay, Boy." Bea patted the seat. "You can share my rocker." She slid over. "There's room."

Boy waited until Jasper nodded okay. Good boy.

Noell tilted her head. "Boy?" She finished wiping the chair down and watched Bea lean forward and back. "I used to have a rocking chair. Or maybe Mom did." She glanced around the living room. "I wonder where that went?" A pause. "Anybody want supper?"

The angels waited, listening.

"Nobody? Popcorn?"

"Maybe later?" Katty turned toward the doorway leading to Gamma's room.

Jerahmael knew Katty seemed lost. She had patted her pocket three times since coming back from the Sheriff's Department.

"Yeah. Maybe later." She blinked. "But you go ahead, if you want. I might be hungry later."

"Bea? You hungry?"

Bea watched her mommy walk out of the room into Gamma's room. "Can I have some cereal? Instead?"

"Sure, Bea. We just bought some, didn't we?" Noell walked into the kitchen.

Uriel followed her. She seemed to be working hard at staying happy and positive. Trying to perk everyone up. He knew what she'd been doing while they were at the Sheriff's. Checking her cupboards and pantry. Trying to think of something—anything—that she might use to cheer everyone up. She definitely experienced her own pain and problems throughout her young life. She hadn't talked about her nights lately, but Uriel knew the nightmares.

Katty, followed by Jasper, entered Gamma's closet and sat on the floor.

Bea slipped off of the rocker and stood. Boy remained beside her. She glanced at him, then pointed toward the kitchen. "There? Cereal."

He shrugged. "I'm not hungry. I like your cereal, though." He patted her back. "Did it hurt?"

She nodded slowly.

Jerahmael breathed with her. On her. Slowly. He placed his hand on her back. "Rest, little one. Peace."

Boy watched him and tried to imitate every move. He patted her back. "Peace to you, Sister Bea." He breathed onto her, a tiny drip of saliva escaped with the breath. He wiped his mouth with his sleeve, then wiped Bea's cheek.

"You've never called me sister before." She caught his hand as she glanced toward where Mommy had gone. "If she is your mommy, and she is my mommy, then … I guess I am. I guess I am your sister." She hugged him tight and patted him on the back. "It's really nice to see all our angels here with us, right?"

"Yep. Like a family."

"It helps to have you here." She nodded again and shyly peeked up at Jerahmael. "You, too. I love you."

He took boy's hand and hers. "I love you, too."

Boy nodded. "Me, too."

"I should go check on Mommy. She feels bad." She chatted with Boy on the way to Gamma's room. "Why didn't Clarence help us?" She shook her head. "I don't understand. I know he loves us."

Boy checked Jerahmael's face, then back to Bea. "He does love you, but I think there are rules that even he has to follow." Wisdom from above. Wisdom from the mouths of babies. "Just like when you come inside after playing in the mud—out in the garden. You have to wipe your shoes. That's a rule."

She nodded. "I guess. He's so smart, though. He's a law guy. He knows everything." She paused before going in the room. "I guess even Clarence can't do everything."

Boy nodded, checked Jerahmael's face, listening. "There's only One Who can."

"You can come in, Bea." Mommy patted the floor for Bea to join her. Bea did sit beside her. But after a little while—maybe a few minutes—she grew restless.

"Mommy?" She whispered. "Can I go?"

Katty seemed to be in her own world. Jasper knew she was not drunk. She hadn't had a drink since living with Noell. "Sure Bea. But stay out of trouble." She hugged Bea tight. "I love you."

"I love you too, Mommy." Bea patted Mommy's back. Boy stood behind Mommy. "Boy loves you, too, Mommy."

"What?" Mommy smiled as she let Bea go. "I don't know what you're talking about half the time." She pointed to the dining room. "You can color if you want. Or your paints are there, too."

Interesting. Jerahmael remembered that Bea had been the one who kept things together when her mommy was drunk. Bea had followed her own routine and knew where things were. She knew the rules, but also knew when she might be free to follow her own rules. Jerahmael smiled remembering a few. Always put the lid back on the jar of peanut butter and put it back in the cupboard, so the mice wouldn't get it.

Back in the kitchen, Bea finished the cereal and slurped the milk out of the bowl. She had been hungry. She quietly picked up the bowl and carefully placed it in the sink, but the spoon clattered out of the bowl and hit the side of the sink. Loud. Too loud. Mommy might come running. Or Noell.

Bea stopped and listened. She'd never stood so still. Nothing. Nobody yelled. Whew. As she turned back to the table, she tripped over a grocery bag full of cookbooks on the floor. Clunk. She landed on the floor—not hard—but it surprised her.

Noell peeked in the kitchen. "You okay?" She glanced at the bag. "I'm sorry. I left that in the way."

"It's okay. I'm okay." Bea stood. Noell had moved all her art supplies onto the kitchen table. Something about needing to clear out some of Gamma's cookbooks, but wanting to spend time with Bea.

"We both can do our jobs, then." Bea arranged the crayons and colored pencils. Reds by the pinks. Blues by the greens. "Noell. We need a fireplace in here."

Noell laughed. She glanced around the room. "Where would we put one?"

Bea pointed by the back door, then shook her head. She giggled. "We don't have room for one. It'd be nice though." She played with the crayons, then opened her paints. "You can use my rocker, Noell. Anytime."

Noell leaned in and hugged her. "Thank you." She stood. "What are you going to paint today?"

"I don't know. I'll let God tell me."

Noell stopped.

Uriel smiled. A good moment. Noell learning from Bea.

Bea picked up the sack that Depdy Mark Scott's lamp had been wrapped in. So pretty with Daryl & Dumpty all over it.

"Huh. I can color this. So many lines." She tapped the sack. "They forgot to paint the colors in, so I can."

Noell had her head stuck inside a cupboard and probably didn't hear.

Okay. Bea carefully colored the pictures. As she colored, new ideas came to her. "Boy, how do you paint the place where Jesus lives?" She listened. "Boy? Where'd you go?"

She scratched her arm. "Ow. I forgot." She slumped. Tears.

Jerahmael hovered. The day all came back to haunt the little one. Time at the Sheriff's Department. Her dad and how she spoke the truth about what he is. Being held down. Betrayed. The pain of the shot. The pain of betrayal and evil lies almost hurt more than the pain of the shot. He picked up a crayon and tapped the paper.

Boy sat down. "I'm right here, Sister Bea." He watched Jerahmael with the crayon and picked one up, too. "Jerahmael is here, too. He wants to color, so what do you want to color?"

Bea stared at Boy, then at where the crayon moved. And on up to Jerahmael's face.

Her chin crumpled. Her lower lip stuck out. Big girl. He smiled.

She smiled back—not a happy smile—but a smile through her tears that said thank you for seeing. She sucked in a deep breath and picked up the red crayon. Then a blue one. "Can we color together?"

Jerahmael nodded.

She passed out paper and started coloring the sack that the lamp came in. Bea colored the wrapping paper in perfect stripes.

Coloring. With Jerahmael's little human. And with Boy. The best. It beat every other thing he'd been called to do in the Kingdom of God.

He glanced at Bea's paper and blinked. Her drawing resembled … it looked like … the throne room. How did she make it look like the Glory? The Wonder of the throne room?

He forgot to color and just watched her.

She drew and colored a perfect flower with petals all around. As soon as she finished it, it drifted into another realm of the heavens—like a gift for the Father. She drew another and watched it float upward, her eyes wide, her mouth open in wonder.

Jerahmael helped Bea color. He drew another flower and pushed it to her to color in.

"I don't know how to draw flowers." Boy laid down his head.

"Boy. You can help us." Bea tapped his head. "Jer-Jer-Jerry? What's your name?"

He smiled and shook his head.

"Oh well. Jerry will draw the flower. I'll color it. And you can blow it into heaven for … Him." She pointed and stopped.

Even Jerahmael was captured. The Wonder of Heaven.

They all three watched in awe as the flowers floated up into the heart of the Father.

EIGHTEEN

They didn't waste any time transporting Phil to prison. They'd rushed the paternity blood tests back and packed him off. No vacation back at the Polk County Jail. Just kick him out. Drive him to Lincoln Pen. On to bigger pastures—prison.

The building. He'd never been at this building.

Last time he had been in a prison, he'd been in charge. Well, under the Warden, or maybe under several guards. Phil had served under their reign for a couple of years. Long enough to know that the Warden—he used to know his actual name—was a mobster. He literally was king over his own kingdom of corruption and evil.

They'd ruled together. Well, Phil thought they had at first. Until the warden locked Phil up in a cell just to prove his point. He had ordered his guards to shackle Phil and drag him to the torture cell.

Warden was king in that realm.

When he'd released Phil, he laughed and said something about making a mistake. That he just meant to test Phil.

He'd tested him alright.

That day, Phil knew he was at the bottom of the mob team.

Oh, he still had his place at the table and bar, and an occasional woman was saved for him, but he knew where he stood in the line of importance and wealth.

Heh. And now, here he was. Walking into another prison, his arms pulled tightly behind his back, his wrists in handcuffs. A guard on either side, their hands locked through each bent elbow. Even though his legs weren't in irons, his whole body felt shackled. Like in a movie where the main actor had been locked in some sort of medieval irons and chains. Vests with chains running from the back, to the chest, and around the midsection.

His whole body felt heavy, almost unable to move a foot in front of the other. Didn't make sense. Handcuffs. No shackles.

Phil played it cool, just glanced at bars out of the corner of his eyes, and kept on walking. But something was up. He had been used to the aura of evil his whole life. And this was no different. Every prison was unique, he guessed, but they all had a different level of evil.

Even the guards who escorted him inside seemed a part of it. Phil stole a glance at one. His eyes narrowed, mouth and jaw jutted out as if he was going to yell. The guy's body was tense—ready to burst out in violence. His grip on Phil's arm tightened and became painful.

When they checked him in, Phil signed more papers than at the Polk County jail back in Osceola. They issued him the newcomer duds, the brightest color available—orange. No hiding here. He had hoped to blend in, to remain anonymous. No chance. He knew what happened to newbies.

They walked past cells in the cell block and the inmates living there whistled in a soft, low tone. It would have been better if they had yelled. The soft tone made Phil's skin crawl. Something was going on.

Each prisoner focused on Phil, stared at him as if assessing him.

Of course he knew that stuff went on—he'd been a part of it, back then. But now they directed it at him.

The smells were different, too. Usually in places like prisons, jails, and institutions, Pine Sol overwhelmed the olfactory. There was a bit of that, maybe some soap, but actually, there was the stench of emotions mixed with testosterone. Evil mixed in there, too. Overall, it was a greasy, sexy, fearful stench.

Phil braced himself for what was to come.

NINETEEN

Katty watched through the enclosed porch window. It wasn't quite time for Mark to be there, but as far as she was concerned, he could take all day, or two days or the week.

She was nervous.

Noell was so good to them. She knew Katty was scared shi … scared to death. And she was keeping Bea inside, reading books to her, tickling her so Katty could breathe.

Both Katty and Noell were nervous about the day. Katty's insides trembled and shuddered. Noell had seen Phil's stuff, what he'd done. That time she picked up things he'd touched after he broke into her house. She'd seen everything he'd done, heard his voice, all through that gift or curse of hers.

Seeing Phil anytime—whether it was him trying to attack her or kidnap Bea, or today in prison—anytime terrified Katty.

Totally the opposite of when they'd first met.

Opposite.

She knew Phil was her knight in … she couldn't even think of it right now. In that way, after all he'd done to her. To them. How had she been so stupid, so naïve? Katty had been sucked in.

She tapped against the window.

Sucked in by his good looks? She couldn't even imagine right now because the evil had morphed his looks into … a dragon. A monster.

What had she seen in him back then? It couldn't have totally been his looks or his charm, because he could shut that stuff off with the blink of his eyes. What had it been?

Something from Gamma's journal to her stirred. She'd said something or written something …

Katty started back into the house to grab the book, but Mark pulled up. He'd driven the squad car?

He got out. He was wearing his deputy uniform? What on earth? Why didn't he just wear jeans and a shirt? He had dressed in full-dress uniform, complete with gun, camera, the works.

She didn't have time to run get Gamma's journal. "Bea." She held the door open for him when he reached the front steps. "Hi." She didn't back away, though. Just stared at him. He was so cute. But. She glanced at his uniform, then back to those green eyes.

He patted his chest. "I know. The uniform." He looked away, still patting his shirt. "The sheriff wanted me to do this. He said then it could be on department time." He shook his head. "But he said that it might appear to be more business-like. To protect you and Bea."

Katty shook her head. "I don't get it. But whatever the sheriff thinks." She shrugged. "I know he's just been doing what the judge set up. He's … he'd never want to hurt Bea." She glanced toward the car. "And this? Saves us … er me paying for the gas. Right? I would have to drive us there and back—what, how many miles from Osceola to Lincoln? Saves us money." She held the door open. "Come in. I'll get Bea."

He slipped inside. "Does she know?"

Katty shook her head again. "No. She'd never leave the bed

if she knew where we were going or especially who we were going to see. She'd live the rest of her life in bed, or in a tree. Never come out or down." She looked at her shoes. Why she looked down at her shoes, she didn't know. If she looked at him —at Mark—she'd come unglued. She'd fall apart. Because if it were up to her, she'd stayed in bed herself. Maybe she'd said that about Bea because that was exactly where she herself wanted to be right now.

She glanced at Mark. Well …

Whew.

Katty wanted to just stay in bed today and avoid all acknowledgment that Phil even existed. He shouldn't even exist. Why had God allowed him to live? To even come to earth, or however that happened? Someone that evil shouldn't be allowed to even be born.

Mark tilted his head. He was so cute. Those eyes. "Think we should get on the road?"

She let out a breath. "Only if there is no way of escape. Maybe call in and see if Phil no longer lives on this earth. That would be nice. Then we wouldn't have to go. You could go on to work or—"

He shook his head. "This is my day off. I'd just go change clothes and … I don't know."

She opened her eyes wide and raised her eyebrows. "What? You have to do this on your day off?" She turned to face the rest of the house. Without realizing that Bea was standing right there.

"Mommy?" Bea's brown eyes popped wide when she saw Mark. "Depdy Mark Scott!" She started to run to him, but stopped. "Wait. Are we in trouble?" Her eyes obviously took in his uniform. "Are you going to 'rest us?"

Mark chuckled and leaned down to Bea's level. "No, little one. I'm here on business." He lifted her up and hesitated. "How would you like to take a ride in my cop car?" He glanced at

Katty. "A very long ride. You could bring your books and your crayons and paper."

"Crayons. What's a crayon?"

He let his head drop to his chest, then looked at her. "Colors. Bring your colors. Do you have a backpack? Or some sort of bag to put stuff in?"

Noell spoke up behind them. "I remember seeing it in the dining room. I'll check." She held up her finger. "Just one minute and I'll be back." She turned to go into the house.

"Like a school backpack?" Bea looked at Katty. "My Daryl & Dumpty one, right Mommy?" She squirmed to get down and started to follow Noell. "Where is it, Mommy?" She stopped. "Wait. Are you going with me and Depdy Mark, Mommy?"

Katty nodded and reached for Bea. "Yes, I am. It's a road trip clear to … Lincoln, right?"

Mark nodded and stepped to the door. "But we need to get going so … we won't be late." His eyes searched Katty's. "So we have time for lunch on the way." He still watched Katty while he talked to Bea. "We need to get going to be able to eat lunch at someplace."

Bea jumped up and down. "At MacDonald's?" She clapped her hands.

"Maybe."

Noell rushed in with the colorful backpack. "I found your colors and paper. Some books. Is that okay?"

Bea checked inside the backpack. "Yup. Looks good." She checked it again. "Is there enough paper? I like to draw and color. Is there enough to last all … all day?" She tilted her head to see Mark's face. "Are we gonna be gone all day? All night? Back tomorrow?" She bounced up and down. "Stay overnight?"

Mark shook his head and laughed. "No, little one. Not overnight. You will probably fall asleep on the way back home." To Katty. "Should we take pillows for her, maybe even you?"

Noell left the room again.

"Good idea." Katty held Bea's jacket up. "Get your jacket on so you're ready to go." She helped Bea get it on and strapped the backpack over the jacket. "This is going to be fun. Like a little adventure. A road trip. A lunch out."

"Why are you talking so loud, Mommy?"

Katty blinked. "I didn't think I was."

Bea looked at her, then at Mark. "You were Mommy. Are you okay? You haven't had one of those little bottles."

Katty's face burned. Bea had seen too much, and in her honesty, brought truth every time. "No Bea. No bottles. Not for a long time."

Noell came back carrying three pillows. "Just in case." She gulped. "Didn't mean to make a joke." When no one laughed, she continued. "Pillow case. Case. Just in case."

"Oh. I get it now." Mark chuckled. "I was thinking of something else." He gathered Bea up in his arms. "Ready? Ready to hit it?" He opened the door and looked back at Katty. "Ready to hit the road?"

He stepped outside and down the steps.

"Hit the road? Do we have to hit the road? Do we have to hit the car?" Bea battered him with questions. "Hit the driveway?"

They walked down the sidewalk to his cop car, chattering. His answers stirred up more of Bea's questions, making him laugh again. Questions and answers. More questions. More answers.

Katty breathed in a deep breath. Shook her head. An arm circled around her waist. Warmth hugged her. Love hugged her. All through Noell hugging her.

"It'll be okay, Katty. Even if it's not okay." Noell leaned her head against Katty's. "Even if it's not okay. You'll get through this. There is always another side or another … well, there is always a reason and sometimes we never know that reason, but sometimes we don't know that reason until much later."

"You're nervous, too, aren't you Noell."

"Why?" She hesitated. "Was I talking too much? Too fast?" She sighed. "I guess I'm nervous too."

"What is this going to do to Bea? Seeing that bastard." Katty shook her head. "I'm sorry. Seeing Phil. It destroys me every time I think about having to walk into that prison with her, and seeing all that … I don't even know. But seeing him there as her father."

Mark had set Bea down outside the squad car, opened Katty's car and retrieved the car seat from it, then installed it inside his squad car.

She shook her head. "It seems so natural to see him do that, doesn't it?" She checked Noell's face. "Am I crazy to even hope? Even dream? Am I crazy?"

Noell hugged her tighter around her waist. "No. One verse Gamma always pounded into my thick head? Something like … God makes everything possible. Or with Him everything, anything is possible." She released Katty and turned to face her, pulling a tendril of hair away from her eyes. "I'll look it up while you're gone today. I'll find it." She visibly swallowed. "And even if you three have to go to the prison every week."

Katty flinched.

"Er. Every month. Once a year, it will be fine. It'll work out."

Katty shuddered. Then remembered all Noell had shared about her *own* life, what *she* had gone through, when her mom drowned and she witnessed it—almost drowned herself. Her Gamma died—well, her Grampa died first. Then her Gamma.

Katty glanced behind Noell. Yes, she had a fantastic house and … lots of stuff, but Katty had seen the amount of mail that came in almost daily, always followed with an expression of confusion and fear, until Noell could get to Clarence, who helped her sort it all out. Noell was worth millions, maybe.

And here Noell was, hugging her and speaking Gamma's words, sharing her house, food, her whole life with Katty and Bea.

Maybe Katty really did have a true friend. Well, they were cousins, real cousins. And for an eternity, Katty had never felt a camaraderie with anyone.

Until now.

TWENTY

The angels had been alerted to the possibility of travel with Mark, Katty, and Bea.

Even though it might seem easier to watch over their charges when they were at home or in their usual habituation, when the humans traveled, any attack on them was more obvious. When the humans were at their own residence or usual place of work or rest, the attacks seemed more subtle and often more powerful.

Angels on alert.

Jasper loved the fact that the Father knew all things. Even if he himself didn't, Father always judged any attack or blessing and either allowed it or broke it off.

Jasper also loved the fact that they all knew the Father didn't need any of them to complete His plan for humanity. He had all the power that was needed. He created and included other beings because He loved them and wanted an intimate relationship with them. Jasper shook his head at the thought. So great, but humble a God, who relished the relationship to the point of letting the other beings, even the humans, receive the acclaim for a job well done. And most times, rightfully so. There were humans and beings who deserved the praise and those were the ones who gave the glory back to the Father … mostly.

Jasper smiled at Katty's comment after seeing Mark switch Bea's car seat to his squad car. Yes, it seemed natural to Jasper, seeing that too. Like it was meant to be.

Again, whatever the Father's plan.

He found his place behind Katty, along with Jerahmael and Mark's angel, Rael. Humans would have thought that it was crowded in the squad car, but as he moved his shoulders up and down, the space felt quite comfy.

"What?" Jerahmael scooted over. "Need more room?"

Jasper chuckled. The angels hovered above the car, heads outside. But somehow they found a way to change their structure to fit within the confines of the car. He shook his head. Crayons and papers covered each angel's lap. "You have this all the time, dear Jerahmael?"

"Yes. All the time." He picked up a crayon and tapped it against the completed artwork.

Bea glanced up at him and grinned. "Like it?"

He nodded. "Love it." He pointed out an area. "Especially the colors right there." He tilted his head. "Reminds me of … of the garden in heaven. The Garden of Eden." He gave her the crayon back. "Have you learned about the Garden of Eden, Bea?"

She slowly shook her head. "No. Is it a garden like Noell's?"

<h1 style="text-align:center">TWENTY-ONE</h1>

Mark transferred the wrapped and boxed food from the tray onto the table and sat down.

"What is the prize in my meal?" Bea tapped the colorful box. "Are my chicken nuggets in there?" She sat across from Mark at their table in the fast-food restaurant. She was excited. Even Mark could tell, for she was swinging her legs back and forth, kicking his legs with every swing. Not hard. Just enough to feel it.

"You must be starving." Mark grinned as he inspected the meal box. "How do you open these things?" He spun it around to check it out. "Smells good, right?"

Out of the corner of his eye, running shoes appeared, then a long sweater over jeans and a T-shirt. Mark glanced up. Katty stood a couple feet away from their table, a sweet half-smile on her face. Back to Bea. Then to Katty. "How long have you been standing there?"

She shook her head. "Long enough to see … uh." She walked to the table, slid onto the bench beside Bea, and gently removed the box from his hands. As she slipped her fingers under the flaps and shoved it over to Bea, a gentle smile was still on her lips.

What a beauty.

Bea picked up a nugget and started to open her mouth. She stopped. "Mommy, did you potty?"

Mark bit his lips together. Little kids were so open and transparent. No shame or embarrassment there.

He glanced up at Katty. Her face was red. She wouldn't look at him. Time seemed to stop.

"Shh, Bea. Eat your nuggets." Katty opened a box. "Is … is this one mine?"

"Yep." Mark pushed her fries to her. "Right? You had fries, right?"

She nodded, slipped one into her mouth, as she glanced up at him.

Those brown eyes. Big, beautiful brown eyes. Her dark hair was loose today, curved around her shoulders and covering her … chest. Back to her eyes. She might have on some makeup—like mascara or liner, but did she even know how beautiful she was? Her skin glowed. He'd seen her skin glistening with sweat from drinking too much. This was different. This radiated from within. A beautiful glow from within.

"You're staring at me." She smoothed her hair. Looked down and checked her zipper. Pressed her hands against her sweater. "Is something wrong?"

He just smiled. "No. Nothing is wrong." He shook his head slowly. "Everything is just right."

Now she visibly blushed, her cheeks a beautiful rose color. God's make-up, maybe.

"Wanna bite?" Bea held out a nugget to him, then to her mom.

"Heh. I guess we should eat … so we can be on time." He totally forgot why they were even there in Lincoln, eating together.

Katty unwrapped her burger and took a bite. "No, you eat yours, Bea. We have our own. Eat your nuggets. You need to be strong." Something in her stiffened, somehow. She straightened after she said those words.

Mark sensed it in himself, too. They all needed their strength for what was ahead.

Phil.

Bea did not know. They had just told her they would take a car ride together, maybe get some lunch somewhere, and back home. Like a play date. But both he and Katty knew that today would be a possible play date from hell. How to tell little Bea the truth—to prepare her—without alarming her into refusing to go at all? The judge who had ruled in Phil's favor for him to have visitation rights at the prison was either a stupid idiot, or he had bought into the corruption and evil.

Heck of a first date with Katty, too.

Katty dipped a fry into the ranch dressing, tapped it against the edge of the container, and paused.

Something was definitely going on. Katty seemed to be quieter, more pensive, thoughtful. She kept tapping her fry onto the ranch container, her eyes on the French fry, watching herself do that.

Movement behind Bea alerted Mark. The silhouette of an enormous person—a huge what? A person of some sort appeared behind her. He flinched at the sight, but Bea was focused on her prize toy since they had told her she had to eat her nuggets before she played with it. She busily ate nugget after nugget, her eyes on the prize.

Katty was eating her fries slowly, one by one. As Mark watched her, something rose behind her, too.

Mark froze, but for some reason didn't reach for his gun.

Not a person. A being? Was this an angel like Bea was always talking about? Like Mom talked about? She was always saying that she wanted to see an angel. She wanted to know more about them.

Were these their angels? He'd started reading the Bible—keeping it to himself—not wanting to stir up his mom. He just wasn't ready to share that with her—get into huge religious debates with her yet.

Something or someone put pressure on his own shoulders and back, almost like a person had leaned into his back, but he knew it wasn't human. He felt it, but it was different from an actual human. It had a different energy or vibe that Mark couldn't describe. A definite tingle or goosebumps.

"Mark, you're not eating. Are you feeling okay?" Katty bit into her cheeseburger and chewed, searching his face, then down to his food. "Is your food okay? We can get something else. We have time."

Mark shook his head and picked up his burger. "No. It's fine." He took a bite. "I'm fine. I just like watching people sometimes."

Katty chuckled. "Must be the cop in you, right?"

The being behind her smiled at him, and he almost choked. He coughed and cleared his throat, sipped on his soda. The being closed his eyes and at the same time he felt something press into him from his back again. A surge of peace overwhelmed him. A sort of strengthening, like when his mom told him she was praying and if he paid attention, he felt it. Felt new strength, more peace, a better direction for what he was dealing with.

The being behind Bea closed his eyes and Mark wished he could turn around to confirm if there was one behind him and if *his* eyes were closed.

Bea chattered about her meal box and toy. She lined up her nuggets all in a row and was now eating them, one at a time. "Daryl & Dumpty had a—"

Mark didn't hear the rest of her song because a mist filtered over everything. Over Bea. Over Katty. The only things he could see were those huge beings. They seemed to rise up, grow bigger and bigger, towering over them. He somehow knew that the one behind him was rising as well.

A powerful sensation of strength overwhelmed him. The mist parted and an impression of hundreds of wings beating made the air throb and vibrate. The sound was like multitudes of bees, or winged creatures flapping their wings, pulsating, pounding until the sound became tangible. Heads became visible, hair flowed with the vibrations. The wind of their wings rustled their robes around their huge bodies. Huge swords and other strange weapons glistened in the light. Trembling horses stomped their hooves, seeming to vibrate as other angels saddled them, pulled the reins around and tethered them to other angels mounting the horses. The angels mounting them and the horses they rode almost seemed to become one as the vibrations connected them.

An angel who had just mounted his horse saluted … saluted … Mark?

Mark glanced behind him and shook his head. The mist cleared.

"What?" Katty grinned. "You don't want your cookie?" She chuckled and glanced at Bea. "She would eat it if you don't want it."

Whew.

"Well, she'll have to fight me for it." He shook his head again and laughed. What on earth just happened? He still sensed the angels, or beings, or whatever they were. They still surrounded them at the table. The air vibrated, but they didn't appear as clearly as just a moment ago. But they were still there.

"She'll have to win at arm wrestling to get *my* cookie." Mark held it against his chest.

Bea's head popped up. "Arm wrestle? I could do that. What's arm wrestle?"

TWENTY-TWO

Angels gathered around the table as Mark and Bea opened and ate their food at the fast food restaurant.

Jerahmael and Rael, Mark's angel stood behind their charges, always alert, always listening to their conversation and all other humans sitting or moving about them.

Interesting. Food wrapped in paper and boxes.

Jerahmael checked Rael's face. Rael's head was cocked at an odd angle, then tilted back to the other side. He looked up at Jerahmael with a questioning look on his face. "What is this food that they eat out of paper?" He checked the food on the table again and back to Jerahmael. "Is it fresh? What is it made of?"

Jeralmael grinned. "I once questioned that myself when Bea was born. My charge, Katty, fed her food from a jar." He shrugged. "And that seemed okay with the baby. My former charges found their food from the Earth, the ground, or directly from one of God's creatures. Fresh, like you said."

"I see." Rael clucked his tongue. "Do the humans exist well on this … food?"

Jasper laughed as he walked up to the table with Katty. He punched Rael on the shoulder. "They seem well, do they not?"

Katty stayed a little way away from the table, observing her daughter and Mark.

Jasper stepped behind her as she sat.

"And, what's this arm wrestle?" Rael shook his head. "I get wrestle." He pushed Jasper. "We wrestle all the time in God's kingdom. But what … or should I say, how do they wrestle with arms? Would it be arms like this?" He held up his sword.

Jerahmael laughed. "Maybe. I think some humans do it that way." His eyes darted outside. A swarm of small birds swooped down outside the windows of the restaurant, actually slid along the glass, and rose as one cluster, over and above the squad car, and back along the restaurant glass.

Each angel quickly stepped behind their human. Angels guarded the squad car outside. The tall and wide restaurant windows provided the perfect opening by which the angels could keep account of the car. Several battalions of angels had been added to their mission with Katty, Mark, and Bea. All unknown, or for the most part, not sensed by the humans.

On guard.

Alert.

As the swarm of birds flew to the car, the angels didn't move but guarded the vehicle and protected any unsuspecting humans that might have walked past. The longer the swarm rose and fell, each bird transformed into a demon. Heads first morphed. The bird-like beaks elongated and teeth emerged into fangs. The feathers changed into scales.

A true horror movie in the supernatural realm.

A child being carried by an adult who happened to pass the car screamed in terror. "What? What's the matter, buddy? What happened?" The adult checked the child. "Your diapers pinching? You have a tummy ache."

The child quit screaming as they moved away from the swarm, but when a demon cut away from the swarm and flew right at the child, it screamed again.

Ornery demons.

An angel raised his sword at the demon so the adult could walk into the restaurant and into the restrooms. "You need a diaper change, buddy?" the dad asked.

The child's wild eyes never left the demon or that angel.

TWENTY-THREE

Phil started to stretch without even thinking of what had transpired the night before. No guards had rustled him for breakfast or outside fresh air duty. No one had called him.

He was all alone.

All the better to think about his future plans.

He stretched again, and the pain reminded him of what truly had happened overnight. A couple of days before, there had been the usual check-in, issuing the usual rookie inmate orange duds, getting escorted to his new digs. The cell needed paint. The window was cracked. Other than those things—the combo toilet and sink were still the same. Flushed millions of times over the years.

No, the pain reminded him of the normal new inmate greeting and hazing. Just like in fraternities. Just like in cults. You wanna be a part of this wonderful, violent group of people who worship Satan? You gotta pay. They always paid in flesh and blood. Yeah, some cash. Always cash too.

Interesting that they waited until he'd been incarcerated for a couple of days. Probably figured to create a sort of tension. Because it was well known how initiations in prisons went.

There had been five of them. All different races and colors. The usual grinding and bumping. The yeses of those men revealed their turn master. Same evil. Same master.

The night had turned from something that could have been devastating to someone else—to a newbie—but to Phil, it had turned into a swinging orgy. All in all. All in.

At first, the men were angry that Phil didn't seem terrified of them and what they were about to do. The tide turned when Phil embraced the evil. Then it just became one giant sexual free-for-all.

Hence the pain this morning. Phil rolled over to his side and stretched. The other side and stretched. He knew he had bruises. But he knew they had bruises, too.

And they also had a plan.

He stretched again and rolled up to a sit. If they hadn't come up with any sort of plan, Phil knew he'd be overcome with depression. This cell. This building, the regimen, the services or lack of them. Everything would drive a man crazy. Into deep depression, making a person abusive and angry. Ready to rise with aggression and abuse.

But they had a plan, and it began to rule Phil's heart and mind.

TWENTY-FOUR

Jerum stood guard at the cell entrance.

His charge, Phil Daynton, was waking up after sleeping in. The night of foul sex still left an aura in the cell's atmosphere. The evil had a stench all its own.

The man sat up on his bunk.

The angel knew Phil had a private cell for a reason. Designed by the minds of the spiritual rulers of this prison realm. There was a definite plan, and it was never for good. Especially since this ruler was under Satan. Satan had many levels of workforce, of angels and demons under him. All fully trained in manifesting fear, wounds, and anger, amongst other things. They knew how to manipulate, how to stir, how to trigger to get the needed results.

In fact, there were five demonic rulers circling Jerum—breathing, spitting, slobbering. They all knew what Jerum could do all by himself. But they also knew that Jerum would not budge unless the Father commanded him to do so. It gave them no actual power to stand there all cocky and such, but they enjoyed it just the same.

They swayed their heads and shoulders as they mocked

Jerum. They raised their horns high and poked their swords into Jerum's ears, into his shoulders.

He didn't flinch at all. This was child's play, and they knew it. Jerum knew it. It was like when a fifth grader got caught unaware of bigger kids who had been discretely following him home, and they finally closed the circle, but hadn't seen the big brother and his friends in the trees above, until it was too late. If it gave the demons power to taunt and poke at Jerum, then let the games begin. Let the fun begin. Because it made no difference in the outcome. It made no difference in the end of the Book. They knew it. He knew it.

A guard stomped onto the walkway of the cell block and paused in front of Phil's cell.

The demons immediately hissed and spat at the guard.

Jerum recognized the guard. He had been one to help clean the prison up after an assault on staff. Cleaned it up with a broom and cleaned it up with a prayer. Things had been different since, although there were still strongholds of Satan that ruled.

"Daynton. Time to rise and shine." The guard brushed at his arm, like he might have brushed away a fly.

Phil glanced up and shrugged. "I'm up."

A demon traced the guard's arm with the tip of his sword. The others grinned and tittered as the guard swatted at the disturbance.

"Daynton, we received paperwork from Polk County Jail that your daughter is being brought to see you."

"Yeah." Phil slid off the bunk to a stand. He walked to the toilet, unzipped and relieved himself.

The guard turned away, but still stood outside the cell.

The demons laughed, knowing how rude that was. They never even spoke a disrespectful word in front of their master or their rulers. They knew that if they did anything like that, they'd be melted by Satan's breath.

Phil zipped up and walked close to the bars.

The guard never backed up. He had respected Phil's privacy —even though Phil didn't care at all—but the guard never backed down to Phil's act of disrespect. "Today. Your daughter is coming here to see you. You are scheduled for a shower in thirty minutes, escorted by fully armed guards. She will be here in … " He checked his watch and swatted at his arm again.

The demons were having a riot, laughing and pounding each other on the backs.

Jerum stood his ground, his sword still sheathed. There wasn't anything they could do that would trigger Jerum to lose control of his senses and his emotions.

"She will be here in a couple of hours, so you need to clean up and get ready to see her." The guard began to fume. "Have some respect, man. She is coming a long way and you need to step it up for her."

Phil rushed the bars and growled. He seemed to know that he had an audience.

The demons applauded, stamped their taloned feet, and growled along with Phil.

The guard jumped back without falling, his hand on his Taser. He came to his senses and stepped forward, his eyes direct. He wouldn't back down, either.

Jerum knew the guard wouldn't back down. He could see the God spark within him as he stood there in a face-off with Phil. No backing down. Jerum knew he had an advantage in being able to see into the spirit realm, plus being able to operate in the physical realms. But he also knew that humans could do that, too. They obviously could operate in their own physical realm, but through the Spirit, they could learn to operate in the invisible realm as well. Took time with a bit of practice, but it was possible. One Other had done it and left His mark on eternity.

Phil slowly shook his head as he stood next to the bars. "You just wait, Mr. … Mr. Tate Grissom. Don't get too cocky with me or my kind today. Watch your back. It's gonna get … well, you'll find out."

"Threats will get you nowhere with me."

Phil slowly blew on the guard.

Tate blinked and stumbled backwards against the bars lining the upper deck of the cell block.

Phil blew again, but the guard jerked straight upright and stepped forward. "You have no right to try your witchcraft on me." He swept his arm in an arc between them both, then clapped his hands loudly.

Jerum was impressed. The handclap was loud enough to break off anything in the invisible realm. It broke whatever his charge, Phil Dayton, was trying to stir up.

He knew Phil had the ability to stir things up in the invisible realm, but he'd not seen him practice it for a long time.

Until now.

TWENTY-FIVE

Katty followed Mark as he led Bea, holding her little hand in his. The prison loomed over them. Minimal landscaping tried to soften the fact that this was a prison that was meant to lock up all kinds of people who had done all kinds of bad things.

So many windows. Katty felt exposed. How many prisoners were watching them walk up the sidewalk? Something moved inside. No. Just a reflection.

"Is there a playground inside, Depdy Mark Scott? Is there a big slide inside like at home in our town—at the park? Will we get to stop and arm wrestle for cookies on the way home? I ate all my chicken nuggets." She pointed at the landscaping. "Why is that guy hiding in those bushes?"

"What?" Mark tried to see. "He's—"

The wind blew the overgrown bushes, like a gigantic hand brushed along them. Creepy,

On to the next question. "Why does that cloud look like a pig up there in the sky?"

"What? Where?" Mark was in deep. Bea had him at every question.

Clouds above the entrance … wings? Flapped like wings.

Katty glanced at Bea, but she was deep into explaining to Mark something from Daryl & Dumpty.

Even though the reason for coming here was grim, Katty couldn't stop wanting to chuckle inside as she listened to the two ahead of her chatting back and forth. Questions and Answers. The answers brought out more questions. They'd hopped on a big merry-go-round of questions, then answers, then more questions. More answers.

Almost to the big entrance door. *Breathe. Breathe.* Katty glanced at the windows again and gasped as a hand, not a human hand, but long fingers with long nails, slid along the glass. The nails screeched against the glass, even from outside. Katty lunged and bumped into Mark.

He turned to make sure she was okay and caught her shaking her head. "What?"

She shook her head again and tried to smile. "Nothing. Just trying to find something good about today, that's all. And I think I found it, er them." She hesitated, avoiding looking at the windows. "I wonder what was wrong with that kid back at the restaurant? He was really screaming."

"Maybe the baby saw the scary angels." Bea didn't miss a beat, asking Mark another question. He laughed as Bea asked another, before he could answer her last one.

"Why are the doors so big here?"

"Well, I suppose to let big people like us inside."

"Why are those guys way up high in the sky? They get to see everything from waaaaay up there." She pointed to the guard towers. At least the guards didn't show any weapons. Not yet. Bea waved. No one waved back.

Katty swallowed. *Breathe.* She wasn't drunk. She'd never seen stuff like that when she was drunk. She'd never been in prison. Just jail. Polk County Jail was all. That was enough. But this felt ominous, evil. Scary, even.

Maybe it was just her. They were here for Bea's visitation

with Phil. The law and the judge demanded it. His blood demanded it. His blood spoke of the evil inside of him. His blood flowed in Bea's veins, too. Did that make her evil, too?

An awful thought flitted through Katty's mind. *Should I have aborted Bea, too?*

She stopped mid step. Awful thought. Where had that come from? Bea was her only reason for living.

She glanced at Mark and Bea. Maybe now, not her *only* reason, but knowing she had to take care of Bea kept Katty alive —maybe not lucid or sane or sober—but she knew each and every day that she'd have to drag herself out of bed, buy food, make sure Bea was clean or as clean as a four-year-old might be. Provide for her. Even though, thankfully, the last year or so, Clarence had provided a job and paid her too well. He had purchased cars, rebuilt the crappy trailer house that was now— probably by now—being torn down.

But it had been home for a few years. Better than living in a car, like she had for a while after Bea was born.

So thankful Mark had convinced Katty to take the art wall with them. It fit in Grampa's shop so well. If he could come back from heaven and unlock his shop door like he used to, what would he say about the wall between his window that faced the garden and where he hung his leather apron? Katty's painting fit perfectly. Babies, treehouses and clouds in his woodworking shop.

Could Noell really mean what she'd said that day? That Katty could use his old shop for her art studio? She'd never even dreamt of having her own art studio before. Would that even be possible? Well, she guessed she could have called the old tree house in that tree behind the neighbor's abandoned house her art studio. She'd only been a little girl then, but it was her escape, her sanctuary, her refuge. Because her mom had never found it, she never realized or suspected where Katty escaped to. Mom never cared to find her.

Even here, entering a prison, the wonder of that little tree house and how it had appeared on her art wall, and then in Gamma's closet, was magical. Unbelievable.

Mark definitely knew his way around these places. She blew out a breath, relieved that the sheriff had approved him to drive them to Lincoln, to the penitentiary. It would have been horrible to come here, just her and Bea. Even in Mark's street clothes, he walked in commanding authority and power, but now in his cop uniform he exuded a presence. She *was* protected.

They waited by the window while a woman checked their identification cards with her file. Thankful Clarence had been able to post a legal birth certificate for Bea. Katty could only guess what trouble that might have caused in not having one. They wouldn't get in—a whole bigger set of problems.

"Do they have a playground in here like at that big store that sells guns?"

"What? Guns?" Mark shook his head while he signed them all in. He handed Katty's ID back to her, giving her a quizzical look. "You've been in Cabela's?"

Bea shook her head. "No. Just saw it on TV. They have guns. And toys, and shoes, and a playground. It's cool."

Mark smiled as he finished the paperwork.

"Here you go, sir." The woman pressed a button, and the door clicked open. A guard met them inside.

"Wow. They have cops in here, too?"

The guard smiled. "First time?"

Mark nodded.

"Okay. The restrooms are there—men and women."

Bea piped up. "And girls?"

The guard couldn't help himself. He tried not to grin, but did anyway. "Yes, for girls. In the women's restroom." He pointed to a short hallway. "That's where you will meet your family."

"Family?" Bea didn't miss a thing. "I'm with my family."

Mark shushed her. "Listen to the man. He's telling us where we need to go … and other stuff."

"But first you get to walk through our scanner or metal detector." He held out his arm to direct them to it. "You have emptied your pockets, correct?"

"Absolutely." Mark looked back at Katty.

"Yes. Nothing in my pockets. No purse. No phone." No booze. She patted her pockets and walked through first, passing Mark and Bea.

Quiet. No beeps. No alarms. Whew.

"Okay. This is fun. Like a ride on a—"

Beep!

Bea jumped back.

A man and a woman moved in front of her and grabbed her from Mark.

"Mommy!" She let out a shriek and clawed for Mark, for Katty.

"Shit. What'd she do?" Katty patted her mouth. "What did she do?"

"I need you both to step away from the child and we'll figure this out." The female guard kept her voice low and reached for Bea. "We just need to see what triggered the detector." She tried to defuse the atmosphere and bring the emotions down a level. "Little one, I am going to check your pockets. Check your buttons."

"Her buttons?" Mark stepped back, but was fully engaged with them. He wasn't afraid, but startled. At the least.

The woman nodded. She squinted at Mark. "Don't I know you from somewhere? You look familiar."

"I'm a deputy with the Polk County Department." He nodded. "I've transported prisoners here several times.

Katty could tell he'd been there before. Thankful.

"Thought so." She removed Bea's jacket and poked into each little pocket. Nothing. She looked up. "Are you Mom?"

"Why do you want my jacket?" Bea folded her arms across her chest.

The woman glanced up at Mark, then Katty.

"We have to make sure you're safe. That you don't have anything that could hurt you or others, that's all." The woman waved the metal detector across the jacket. No beep. She handed the jacket to Katty and waved the wand over Bea's body, from her socks on up.

Katty nodded. All she could do was swallow and try not to pace back and forth. Stay calm.

Beep!

What if … what if this didn't work out? Breathe. Maybe she should just give in to this … this craziness. Maybe she didn't deserve this man who had driven them to the prison. Maybe she should just give in to a life with Phil. Was it for Bea's sake? Was it for her sake? Was he all she deserved?

Katty blinked. Where were those thoughts coming from? She hated Phil.

Bea giggled. "This is like on Star Wars. Those light saver things." She glanced up at the female guard. "Only yours doesn't buzz like in the movies."

The woman paused, nodded, and half smiled. "You're right, Little Ma'am. Only we don't hurt people with these. We just scan them. Make sure they are safe." She scanned Bea again.

Beep!

"What on earth?" Katty rushed to Bea, but the woman stopped her.

Mark stepped closer to Katty, his arm out to her.

"We'll get this figured out." The woman slowly scanned from Bea's shoes. Nothing. Up her legs, her chest. At her head.

Beep!

"You don't have earrings. No nose rings."

"Nose rings. What's a nose ring?" Bea wrinkled hers.

Beep!

"Here. Can I remove the little scrunchy thing around her hair?"

Katty nodded and held out her hand.

The woman scanned Bea again and no beep. "That was it." She held out her hand for it and felt inside of it. "May I pull it apart? We have to figure this out." She pulled on the stitching and two pennies fell out. "What are those doing in there?"

Katty shook her head. "We bought it at Mrs. Gelda's store." She glanced at Mark, then at the woman. "She runs the thrift store in our town. She said some lady had made them and brought a whole basket of them into the store for little girls." She pointed. "Like Bea."

"I've never seen anything like it. But the mystery is solved." She put her hands on her hips and looked down at Bea. "You're all clean. You're good to go."

The male guard waited for them to put their shoes back on and then ushered them into a large room with tables and chairs. A few families were already there with their inmate.

Katty blew out a breath as they walked into the room. She kept looking to Mark for assurance, but also for direction. She couldn't even decide which table to sit at.

Bea had no problem. She just romped up to an empty table and sat down on the small chairs. "This is cute. Is this where we get to have our snacks"

A chuckle behind them made them all turn to see who it was.

Bea shrieked and backed into the guard. "Not him." She pointed at Phil. "Not you." Her eyes darted from the families already well into their visitation, to the guards, to Katty and Mark, and back to Phil. "Did we come to see him?" She backed away toward the door, turned and ran past Mark, past the guards, and slammed into the female guard.

"Oh, no you don't."

TWENTY-SIX

Bea pushed hard against the big woman. "No, no!" She looked back into the gathering room and there he was again. It wasn't her imagination. She had really seen that bad man. "He's a bad daddy." She didn't even wipe away tears. She looked at the lady guard. "He's a bad daddy. Is that why we're here? There's no playground? No clowns or cake?"

Depdy Mark Scott and Mommy caught up with her.

She took one look at them and stomped her foot. Then the other foot. "You!"

Depdy Mark Scott leaned down. "Bea. If we had told you what we were doing here—that we were coming to see him— would you have come inside with us?"

"No!" She screamed, and stomped her foot again. "No! I thought we never had to see him again. He's a bad Daddy." She looked into the gathering room again. "He hurt me. He hurt Mommy." She burst into a wail and slipped away between the female guard's legs. She made it all the way to the exit door before Depdy Mark caught up with her.

"Bea. We have to see him." He tried to pick her up, but she slapped his hands away. He knelt down in front of her.

"You tricked me. Just like back at the 'partment."

"What? The apartment?"

"No! When Clarence tricked me, to open my mouth." She slumped to the floor, sobbing, her fists balled at her eyes.

Depdy Mark Scott leaned his head back and blew out a breath. "The saliva testing at the sheriff's department."

Mommy walked up behind him and bent over. "Bea. It's the only way."

"No!" She kept peeking around them and Phil was still there at that little table on a little chair. He ugly smiled and waved at her. "He's naughty."

The female guard walked up behind them. "Excuse me, but if she doesn't go in today, you'll have to come back tomorrow. This is on the judge's orders."

"We know." Mommy said it loud. She backed away. "I'm sorry. We just didn't expect this. Expect her to—"

"No. Mommy, you didn't tell me we were coming to see him." Bea used the power rising in her chest. "Not fair. Not nice." She glanced at Depdy Mark Scott. "Not nice."

Depdy Mark Scott let his head drop to his chest and shook it back and forth. "You're right, Bea. Not nice. We should have told you. We knew that you'd never get in the car if we told you who we were coming to see." He thought a minute. "I will not bribe you."

"What's bribe?" Now, everything to Bea was suspicious. Were they lying to her about everything?

"Bribe is when I promise you something you want, to get you to do what I want you to do."

"That's not nice." She stood up. "This isn't what I want to do."

Depdy Mark Scott stood up and held out his hands to Bea.

She finally let him pick her up.

"See. We didn't want to come here, either."

Bea popped him on the shoulder. "Then why are we here? If you don't want to and I don't want to, why did we come here?"

"A judge made us come here."

The guard walked to them. "You only have ten more minutes."

"Good. Then we can go home." Bea hid her face in Depdy Mark's shoulder.

"Bea, we have to go in there and see him, talk to him. If that's all we do, this time, then—"

"This time?" Did they think she wasn't listening? She heard those words. Like they had to come back? "This is the last time, okay? Never again."

Depdy Mark shook his head. "Bea … let's just go in and get this over with. Then we can go get some snacks and go home. Okay?"

Bea growled. She didn't want to be mean. She loved Depdy Mark Scott. She loved Mommy. Why should she do something that hurt? Something that didn't feel good. Didn't feel right. Why would they make her do this?

Depdy Mark put her down and took her hand.

Bea saw him look at the jail lady. She was not mean. Bea could see her eyes. Her eyes said she was sorry. Her hands on her hips said she had to do it. 'Dults have to do things they didn't want to sometimes, too.

Deep breath.

But one step toward Phil made her flinch. Those eyes that moved funny. He was smiling, but his smiles never made her smile back. His smiles were icky—slimy and greasy. His eyes always had something else inside them, moving, swarming.

And today, there was something behind Phil.

Those bad angels.

TWENTY-SEVEN

Boy peered into the prison visitation room from behind Jasper, Katty's angel and Jerahmael, little Bea's angel. Rael, Mark's angel, was right behind him, his hand on Boy's shoulder.

There were a whole lotta devils in there, mostly surrounding Phil. "That's not right. He's my daddy, and he's got more demons around him today than anybody else in here." He tapped Jasper's leg. "Is it because there's more demons here at the prison? He's my dad, and he's the worst?" He blew a breath out in exasperation. "And those demons are bad—real bad."

Jasper nodded and patted Boy's head. "I know that's what it looks like, Boy. It looks bad."

Jerahmael was so huge. When Boy looked up at him, his head almost touched the ceiling. Wait. It did touch the ceiling. Sometimes his head disappeared through the roof. They all were that big. All except him.

Boy was short. Very short. He guessed that was probably natural—since he was a kid. But still. He knew more about being an angel that any other kid, than even his sister Bea did. Didn't that make him bigger?

Bea flinched and put her brakes on when the deputy and

Mom tried to get her to go into the room. He didn't blame her a bit, because he had seen every time their dad had hurt her, thrown her. He'd even seen Dad tie her up on the big slide—wrap her with that silver duct tape, clear up at the top, and light a fire below in the weeds.

Boy guessed maybe it was better to be where he himself was —a young angel, an aborted baby—than where she was. Bea was never free from the abuse, the fear, or the anger.

It was easier to know what he knew because of where he was. Because of who he got to hang out with.

Boy looked up again. The angels were huge and magnificent. There was a sort of sweet smell that was always with them. A light shone from inside them, all around them.

The demons in the room didn't have any light. They didn't have the beauty that the angels did. More demons slithered into the room from the ceiling, through the walls. Boy shivered. He bumped into Jerahmael and grabbed his hand.

As they dragged Bea closer to Phil—er, their dad—the demons growled and hissed. They were so ugly. He'd have to ask Bea sometime if she could see the demons, too. He knew she could see the angels. She could see him.

But maybe not today. Maybe she was just extra scared today.

He wandered beside her. "Hey, Bea."

She glanced at him. "Boy!" She searched the rest of the room. "What are you doing here? Don't you live in my town? How'd you get here?"

Mom leaned over. "What Bea?" She couldn't see him or the other angels. "Who are you talking to?"

"Mom wouldn't understand." Boy looked up at Jasper and saw him nod. "She can't see me or the others. Be strong, my little sister." Out of the corner of his eye, he saw Jasper and Jerahmael nod. "Be strong. It won't always be like this. You can do this."

"Well, hello Bea. Hello my little girl." Phil's voice broke in and sounded echo-y, like he was speaking through a microphone. His voice spoke in many realms that Boy knew a small bit about. The angels had just started to teach him.

Bea froze as she stood and eyed their dad.

"Say hello, Bea." The deputy tried to help, but Boy knew that it would take more than a few kind words to get her to respond.

Boy touched her shoulder. She stared at him a minute, then bowed her head. "Jesus, make me strong in You. 'Tect us from the bad angels. 'Tect us from evil Daddy."

Something shifted, like big revolving doors moved him into another realm. Boy almost fell, but Jasper caught him. On the other side, in the other realm, was Mrs. T in her room at the nursing home. She reached for him. "Boy, help me pray for Bea." Then swoop. The doors rotated again. Boy and Jasper were back in the prison.

More demons flew in behind and around their dad.

Something was up.

Something big was up.

TWENTY-EIGHT

Katty wanted so badly to go back in time. Live her life over. Make better choices. Relive her past, so that her little precious Bea wouldn't have to go through what she was going through right now.

Bea visibly trembled. She could hardly walk.

Katty herself could hardly walk. Was it super cold in this big gathering room, or was it just her? She couldn't stop shivering. She had to bite her lips together to stop her teeth from clattering. She pulled her sweater close under her chin.

Thankful Mark had been freed by the department to actually drive them. Thankful for his escort.

Because if it had all been up to Katty, she never would have made it past the check-in. Past the parking lot, even. Especially after what she'd seen when they walked up the sidewalk.

Driving up to this formidable building—knowing what it held or who it held. She never would have made it. She would have driven the other direction. They'd been somewhere by North Platte, Nebraska by now. Or … in Iowa. In Kansas. If she could tap the heels of her tennis shoes together, she'd wish to be back home in Gamma's bed, snuggled in with Bea, and anticipating a cup of coffee with Noell. Instead, they were at the Nebraska State Penitentiary in Lincoln, Nebraska.

And she was watching her four-year-old daughter walk the plank to her certain—

"Mommy, take my hand." Bea held out her little fingers.

Katty clasped her hand. Bea's hand was clammy, almost wet. "We're in this … together Bea. We're here with you. We can do this."

Katty didn't even believe her own words. She wanted to run away just as much as Bea. Without Mark here, she might have. She might have been the one running to the exit door. Why not? What would it hurt? Screw the judge.

She glanced behind her.

The female guard stood in their way, watching them, her arms folded across her chest.

Nope.

What would be the big deal if they didn't do this? If they pleaded that it was too dangerous for them both? Wasn't the judge supposed to be on the children's side? Always putting them first, against the abusive parent? Because every time they'd seen Phil, it had been dangerous for one of them or both. Why couldn't that be enough for some dumb judge to make this go away?

"Hello, baby girl."

Shit, just the sound of his voice made Katty cringe. Tears brimmed without her realizing. Had something, some smell, or cleanser made her eyes burn? No, just the sound of his voice brought tears.

She couldn't look at him. Bea glared at him. Katty wished that arrows could be shot at Phil through that little girl's eyes, because she was deadly right now.

Phil held out his hands to Bea, and she immediately backed away.

The female guard cautioned him. "Why don't you be happy

with just a face-to-face greeting today? Maybe next time—er, maybe some other time there can be more of a handshake."

She couldn't look at him. But she couldn't not look. Was Bea seeing what Katty was seeing? Phil's mouth morphed into a long snout. Horns grew up from behind his ears and his belly bloated out. Scales covered his skin, and a tail circled the chair he sat on? A tail? Phil was sitting there on that baby chair, but a dragon sat there too?

Katty backed away, rubbing her eyes. Her very nerves, her bones, felt like they were being crushed or shattered right now. She'd never felt this much evil in one place before. She blinked her eyes, rubbed them again. The dragon was gone, but that didn't in any way lift the evil she felt or saw in Phil.

Bad, bad vibrations in this room. Even the jail at the department in Osceola hadn't felt this brutal, this cringy, this evil. Even abortion clinics hadn't felt this bad. She had her share of experience.

Her eyes flitted from Mark to Phil—back and forth. One, a righteous warrior who had already saved her life, who would go to the extreme to do what was right and good, who had outwardly admitted to his faults. The other, a demonic, egomaniacal dragon who would stop at nothing to kidnap their daughter, to abuse and assault them both at every opportunity.

They stopped right at the table where Phil sat on those funny little kid chairs. He was almost folded up. Looked entirely out of place with the evil toxicity she was sensing from him.

"Two minutes left." The lady guard was timing them. She knew they wanted this over. She must have known that they were wondering how much longer.

Mark was super tense. On alert.

Katty knew that this was hard for him. Katty knew he loved Bea. Maybe he even loved her as well. And to have to bring them to see her ex and Bea's evil dad, to actually experience

Bea's emotions first hand, must be hard. But Mark was really tense—really agitated, too.

Bam!

They all jumped, except Phil.

Prisoners swarmed from every corner, every door, roaring—the sound deafening in the large room. Like someone had shot the go gun, and the race was on. Many waved weapons—real and homemade—bats, guns, bars, chairs. One even kicked the bottom of the drinking fountain and a gun fell out. A plant … from when? Even with all the activity, Katty couldn't take her eyes off Phil. He just sat there. He didn't jump up or move. He just sat there, grinning. What was he—their king? Their ruler? Their god?

Bea screamed. Mark reached for his gun. He was armed?

Katty ran toward Bea.

Phil jumped up and rushed behind Mark, his arm in a choke hold around Mark's throat.

The female guard stepped in front of Bea, her gun drawn.

Blam! Blam!

More gunshot.

Mark fell.

Bea screamed again, her little hand wrenched from Katty's.

Someone grabbed Katty. "Mark!" Katty screamed as someone dragged her over him. Blood pooled behind his shoulder onto the floor. His head. His green eyes open —seeing—

"No!" Katty heard someone scream his name. "Mark! No!" She threw back her head and screamed to the heavens. "Help! God help!"

A huge, hairy arm gripped her around the neck and dragged her out. She couldn't see him, but he was gurgling and laughing, growling. He stunk. His arm was tight around her neck. She gripped his sweaty arm and tried to breathe.

Where was Bea? Her little voice screamed over and over. "Mommy! Mommy. Where are you? Help me!"

"Bea! Someone help us. Bea!" Again, Katty screamed to the heavens. "God, help!"

Katty slapped at the man's hand. He was hurting her arm, her neck. She kicked at his legs and stomped on his foot.

He punched her, and she stumbled.

One last look back. The female guard was down. Mark was still down.

All Katty could think of was that his green eyes were open, staring up at … was he dead?

"Stop fighting me or I'll kill you." The man hooked his arm around her waist, lifted her, and trudged on. "Daynton told me to bring you, but if you were too much trouble, to kill you."

If he killed her, who would rescue Bea?

Where was Bea?

Was Mark dead?

Nothing else mattered.

Something ran down on the side of her head. Blood. The guy had decked her pretty hard.

Where were the guards? Inmates flooded the room, then all at once they burst out of the doors, broke out the windows and escaped outside. How on earth?

Even the fresh air from outside smelled rancid, moldy, awful, burning.

She wrenched her arm out from the guy. She twisted to see.

Fire poured out of one window and smoke rose above the building.

"Oh, shit." The last visual. Mark lying on his bloody back, his eyes staring up, unseeing. "Oh God, help."

"Shut up." The guy dragging her jerked her arm hard. Wrenched it till it popped. Oh ow. She blinked out.

Something else in her popped. She slapped the man with her

other hand. "Stop it! You're hurting me. Stop! I have to find my daughter."

"Oh, I know where she is. She's in good hands." He motioned up ahead where most of the escapees were running.

There. Phil had her.

Katty screamed. "No!"

Bea was draped over Phil's arm—probably unconscious. Head flopped wildly as he jumped over someone's legs. Someone had fallen. Phil kicked the body to the side of the parking lot.

"Bea!" Katty screamed for her. Anything to know if she was alive. "Bea."

"Shut up." The man backhanded her on the mouth.

TWENTY-NINE

Outside, prisoners swarmed across the parking lot and over the grass yard. They acted like a bunch of monkeys. Definitely animals. Horrible noises. Grunting. Growling. The air, the whole atmosphere stunk.

Katty, Mark and Bea had walked over this grass and concrete on their way into the prison—just minutes before, but there had been no stench like this. The stench was overpowering. Unbearable.

"Ow. My arm." She tried to pry the big man's fingers open, bending them back, so she could free her arm at least. "That hurts."

He only growled. Was he even human?

Monsters.

Katty couldn't see Bea. She was alive. Katty could hear her little voice screaming over all the other noises. Oh God.

At a certain point, the guy dragged Katty. Her foot bounced once in a while. Ow, her knee. Her arm. He was gonna break it. Maybe he already had.

Oh, God help!

"Put me down!" She kicked at wherever she could reach. The guy was huge. Punched with her free arm. Clawed with fingers.

Pounding across the grass with the convicts was like running in a herd of horses.

She blinked.

A herd of … mixed in with the escapees were creatures, monsters, down on all fours. Hands and feet, but loping, running. Like monkeys? Like a horse? Like part human, part monkey, part … demon. Yellow and sickly, bloody skin. Huge horns grew out of heads above the ears. Horrible, yellow eyes.

As Katty stared, one looked over at her and roared, growled. Grinned.

She cowered under the man's arm.

He laughed and roared with the monster.

They loped across a road to where several trucks had been parked.

"Oh God. No." If she and Bea were loaded inside one of those, there's no telling what could happen inside or where they might end up.

"Oh God, help." Katty glimpsed Bea with Phil. She didn't know if that was comforting or—

The man hefted Katty up and tossed her inside the cab of the truck, beside a driver, and then he crawled in after her. Pushed her over to sit between them. The driver was just as scary. A ball cap pulled down low over a bloody mask hiding his face. Thuds and pounding from the truck box behind the cab. More prisoners loaded in there. She and Bea didn't have a chance.

Bea screamed from somewhere. Katty began to sob. "My baby."

The driver shushed her and when someone pounded on the back truck box, he shifted into drive.

"No! Where are you taking us?"

The big lug next to her slapped her hard across the face. She gasped for breath. Almost blacked out. God, please protect Bea.

Katty could take anything—well, almost anything—but Bea was just a little girl. Please God. Katty had been scared many times when she lived with Phil and his druggie buddies. But she'd never experienced gripping terror like now. She shuddered, shivered like she had been buried in a frozen lake, between two monster demons.

She reached up to wipe her mouth and got hit again. Harder.

"Sit still. Be quiet." The man rolled down the truck window and waved at the truck beside them. "Move out. Why aren't they moving out?" He reached inside his shirt and pulled out handcuffs and clamped them on her. "That'll keep you from hitting me again." He chuckled. "The guard won't be needing them anymore."

Katty shivered. "No. No." What if she never saw Bea again? Or Bea alive again?

The man yelled again for the trucks to follow them. His voice echoed in the truck cab.

She'd never see Bea again.

Or Mark.

Still. She had to pray. She had to stay strong. She had to stay alert—even though she had suffered several blows to her head. Hard enough to black out. The monster was big and brutal. He didn't care who he hurt. Or who he killed, for that matter.

Where was help? Where were the police? Where were the guards in those towers, or had they been decoys, infiltrators?

Tears threatened, but Katty swallowed, keeping them inside.

Jesus, help us. She swallowed again. *Jesus, I don't know how to do this. But Bea believes. And I believe. You are here.*

Help us.

THIRTY

Boom!

Every realm where Jasper had jurisdiction and rights exploded at the same time. Heavenly realm exploded. Earthly realm exploded. His sword came out of its sheath without him even grasping for it—all on its own. It stood and positioned in front of him.

Ready.

Every realm shifted, every heaven, and all the earth shifted. Layer upon layer shifted at the same time, making a visual impact of every piece of history, every part of the future of humanity, every moment of time past, visible. Each moment of time could be glimpsed as layers and layers of glass, open windows over more windows, over multitudes of windows, revealing all—every moment of every human event, all across time.

If his human charge hadn't caused the explosion, Katty's cries for help, Jasper might have thought the Lord Jesus was blowing the trumpet to come back to Earth. But Katty sat right in front of him. He heard her heart cry to the Father, and the Father had moved all of heaven and earth in response to Katty's cry. Her prayer.

Angels landed into every space, every quantum moment of space from the physical world to the invisible world.

Father heard. He answered. He moved. He moved all for His daughter.

Angels lined up and surrounded Katty.

Demons hissed and kicked at angels. They knew they had already lost, but it didn't stop them from entering the battle.

Each angel that was packed into that space lifted weapons. "Holy. Holy. Holy to our Lord and King. To our God be the Glory. Glory be to Yeshua, forever and evermore!" The sound waves of praise burst into every dimension, shifting the physical and invisible worlds. Affecting every human who was entwined with the Spirit, one with Him. They heard. They saw. They felt Him. Felt the shift. They felt the cry of one who was lost.

Every creature, every being, each and every host and all the saints joined in worship of the King, Who was slain from the foundation of the world.

Suddenly, silence.

No one breathed as the Judge and Conqueror of all issued judgement. He saw all. He knew all. He was King and Ruler over all.

Jasper knelt in submission to his King. All around him did the same.

Righteousness. Righteous Judgement on behalf of His children—His daughter.

Jasper knew Katty would overcome. But the total outcome of this day might not be what she would hope. Only the Father knew.

All Jasper knew was just this moment. He knew the Father had made him long, long ago—ages really—for such a time as this. He'd served many humans during his life, but this time, this moment, felt like his true mission.

He landed on top of the truck carrying Katty, switched his legs so they hung down in front of the windshield as he sat on the cab, his feet on the hood of the truck. He knew the humans couldn't see him, so he wasn't blocking their vision. He was big enough to see over the trucks in front of theirs. He could see the entire line of about five or six trucks.

The inmates had to have planned this a long time ago. They would have needed tremendous help from outside the prison to commandeer this many trucks, fill them with gas, line them up, ready to jump into—all without alerting the prison staff. Maybe some of the staff were in on the prison break. A sort of coercion of all evil—in-mates and out-mates. They all seemed to be mates. Some were just trapped inside the prison.

He chuckled at his joke. In-mates and out-mates.

A demon slid down beside Jasper. His stocky legs and taloned feet landed on the hood of the truck.

"Hello." Jasper wasn't intimidated. He knew stories. He *had* stories! The Spirit had put them in The Book. He knew not to be prideful, but he also knew the end of that same Book.

The demon only growled. Its clothes appeared filthy and torn, barely covered any privates—as if the demons cared. The stench was always there—a mix of dead everything, of rotten meat, and dung. That smell was always there, but the lower level of the demonic that Jasper guessed accompanied the hairy man who had grabbed Katty, had a peculiar blend of sweat and blood mixed in, too. Nasty.

"How's your day going for you, mate?" Jasper loved taunting the demons.

It only growled again, but something from below in the cab made Jasper back off. Katty was fighting back. She needed to get to Bea and would do anything to get there. Anything. Jasper had to tread lightly, so the demon didn't stir up the monster man.

Another demon slipped down on Jasper's other side.

Jasper glanced at it, and then at the one on the other side. "Twins?"

It flinched and lunged at Jasper until someone or something slammed an enormous fist on both demons's heads. What? Where? Jasper stretched his neck to see behind him.

A magnificent angel stood on top of the truck box. He was gigantic and amazing. Layered armor edged with metal and rivets covered dark, muscular skin. He had kind eyes and a lopsided grin. He waved.

Jasper laughed.

One big happy family.

THIRTY-ONE

"Shh-shh."

What? Whenever monster man yelled, there was a sort of shushing. The truck over heating? Boiling over so that it sounded like shh? They weren't even off the prison grounds.

By now Katty was afraid to move, to speak. She leaned back into the seat cushion, just to stay safe—out of the way of the big man's huge hairy arms. Her face was wet with tears and her eyes burned, but she didn't dare reach up to wipe them. She tasted blood, but she forced herself to swallow. She'd swallowed worse things in her past of drinking and drugging.

Monster Man was still waving to the other trucks. Great. Katty got kidnapped by the ring-leader, the one in charge of this insurrection.

"Shh."

Katty breathed out, slowly, quietly. Listening.

"Shh." It was the man next to her—the driver. Great Monster Man was brutal, and the driver was having a panic attack. Two very dangerous opposites.

She leaned back into the seat even further, trying to get a better look, without getting clobbered by the big hairy one.

Monster man was loud and busy, but their driver, he was shushing her? She pretended to be interested in the monster man and what he was doing and saying, but checked to her left at what the driver was doing. Or saying.

"Shh." Keeping his head straight ahead, he seemed to concentrate on driving, but his eyes flickered toward her. He glanced her direction out of the corner of his eye.

Breathe. Was he an infiltrator? Was he on her side? A cop plant?

Oh God, if that could be true.

The first truck in line up ahead turned onto a street. There was some heat in the cab, but still Katty shivered. The cab stunk with the man's body odor, but more. She knew the foul smell of evil from back in the days with Phil. He'd taken Katty to some rituals. She hadn't thought about those for a long time. Like she had pushed them out of her mind until now.

"Why are we slowing down?" She peeked out of the corner of her eye at the monster man. Why didn't he fall asleep? Why was he still awake? If only his head would nod like he was sleeping. He must be too pumped up to sleep.

She was too. If only she could see what was going on with Bea. Dear Lord God, what was going on with Bea? Mark? *God help. God protect them.*

The truck ahead of theirs swerved—the right tires ran off the road for a few yards. Back on the road, only to abruptly cut way over the center line. Back off the road.

"What the?" The monster man next to Katty cussed, leaned forward in his seat. He patted his pockets. "We need phones. Damn." He pounded on the outside door in frustration. "What is going on?"

The truck stopped abruptly. The brakes squealed against the pavement.

Katty breathed in and out. *Slow down breathing. Keep calm. What was going on? Bea. Baby Bea.*

"Shh."

What was that about? Monster man yelled, opened his truck door, and jumped out.

"Shh." Katty stole a look at the driver beside her.

He lifted his shirt to reveal a gun.

"Shit. You gonna shoot me?" Katty scooted away from him.

He shook his head. Leaned forward, then backward.

From the truck in front of them, Phil jumped out of the passenger side with Bea. She was pounding him on the face.

Katty jumped forward in her seat, stretching the seat belt, her hands still cuffed. She couldn't help it. She tried to wiggle side to side.

"Shh." That's all the driver would say. "Settle. No matter what. Stay here." He hardly moved his lips.

But she heard him. Softly.

Back to Phil and Bea. He popped her on the head and she was out. Slumped over his arm. He hopped back into the truck, still holding her.

Katty choked. "Bea." Her chest wanted to burst, and she realized she was sobbing.

"Shh." The man next to her still rocked forward and back. "Shh."

Monster man ran back to their truck and jumped inside, pushing Katty against the driver. "Let's hit it. Stay right behind them. This isn't going as planned. We're not even off prison grounds." He punched Katty. "That little shit of a kid. Phil's fault if this goes all wrong. We never should have let him in on it." He stopped, then looked down at Katty. "Wait. You're the kid's mom, right?" He burst out laughing. "I'll bet that was fun watching him beat on her just now." He threw his head back and roared with laughter.

Katty gulped.

"Shh. Shh."

Katty blinked. This was a bad dream. A nightmare. Between

Bea getting grabbed and beat up by Phil and Monster man kidnapping her. And whatever was driving the truck.

Phil was the monster. Phil was the demon—he was the worst dragon in any fantasy. He was the demon in a horror story.

"Okay. Let's go." Monster man pounded on the door. "Get on the road!"

Just as the trucks started to pull out, squad cars screeched in front of their truck on both sides, followed by a couple of armored trucks blocking the truck escape route. Cops suddenly rushed the truck ahead—guns raised.

"Damn."

Several more surrounded their truck on each side and in front of the truck.

The driver drew his gun and in one fluid movement, pushed Katty forward, reached around behind her, and cocked his gun against Monster man's head. "Don't move or I'll blow your brains out."

Breathe. Katty couldn't breathe. He had pushed her over, her face at her knees. Her hair tumbled down to the floor. All she could hear was her breathing. Was Bea crying? Oh, God help. Dear God, help. So far, not a shot fired. Katty felt Monster man suddenly push with his arm.

Blam!

Katty screamed. And screamed. Blood spattered everywhere. And screamed. All she could see was the floor of the truck cab. Blood. Brains.

"Shh. Stay where you are." The driver shot Monster man, again. "We'll get you out, but not until I know the truck ahead is secured." He tapped Katty's shoulder. "You hearing me?"

She tried to nod. "Who? Uh—"

"I'm a cop. A plant. I'm not leaving you. Stay down where you are."

She tried to nod, but her whole body trembled She shut her

eyes. No more blood. No more blood. "My daughter. Can you see her?"

Blam! Blam! Blam!

Someone was screaming. Loud.

A door opened and monster man slid off the seat and outside the truck, onto the concrete. Cops surrounded the body.

Katty puked. Someone screamed again. Loud.

The driver shushed her. "Almost over. Hang in there." He bounced up and down. "I see your daughter. Still unconscious."

"Is … is the driver in that truck a cop? Are you really a cop?" She started to raise her head, but he pushed it back down.

"Yes, I'm with LPD. We got word … someone on staff, a woman, heard inmates talking one day. She put herself in danger to get word to the department."

Immediately, Katty thought of the woman who had checked them in. Was she okay? She'd gone down. Was she shot? That brought on another visual of the man down right beside her. Mark. Tears flowed all over again.

The driver seemed to relax, just a bit. "Okay. They are giving the all clear. Ma'am, you can lift your head up. I'm going to slip out of the truck and down and I will reach up and help you out." He reached over to her seat belt.

Katty shoved him away without thinking. "No. No." Then realized he was trying to unbuckle her seat belt.

"Don't move until I reach for you. Okay? Shh." He unhooked the seat belt and unhooked his own.

Katty silently wept. God had put her in the truck, right next to a cop plant.

His door opened from outside and he gently slid off of his seat, his hand never leaving her side. "Okay. All is okay." He pulled her out like she was a baby and held her close in his arms. "Wait. Just stay here with me. I'm not leaving you. I need to make sure all is safe."

Never had Katty felt so cared for, so safe—even in spite of the dangerous situation. "Is Bea …?"

"She's free of him. I'm just making sure there are no more surprises. No more trucks behind us. No more escapees that we might have missed."

Katty felt him nod.

"Okay. I'm going to … we'll go find your little girl." He set her feet on the concrete, but still held her close around her waist. He unlocked the handcuffs and walked with her slowly toward the truck in front of theirs.

She could finally see. She wiped her face and wound her hair to one side of her neck.

Suddenly, there was a tussle. Inmates appeared from every direction: backs of the trucks, from inside the cabs. Prison inmate uniforms surrounded them. They swarmed all over the truck, just like in the prison when it all had started.

Katty screamed. "Bea!"

In the scuffle, Katty got dumped beside Phil as he knelt down with Bea.

With Bea dangling from one arm, Phil's other arm raised a gun in the air. He fired several shots up and turned to Katty. He gloated, the sweat poured from his body, his clothes were wet and he had that stench she remembered from years ago. That stench of evil and death.

Rage rose in her. She wanted to kill him. Needed to kill him. He didn't deserve to live.

"Hey bitch. I got my little girl." He straightened up, almost unnaturally tall before her. "You can do whatever you want to, but she is mine. You can come with us or not." He smirked as other in-mates jostled them. "Either way, she is mine."

"Damn you!" Rage burst from Katty. All the years of abuse, his evil accusing words, the brutal slaps of his hands, the plunging to the very center of her being with his murdering hands—all broke loose. She grabbed at the first thing her hands fell on. She pulled his hair with one hand and yanked his ear with the other. Hard. Hair came off in her hand, in clumps, and the other hand held … an ear.

Phil screamed.

Bea roused.

The truck driver suddenly appeared beside Katty. She yanked the gun from his holster.

Bea screamed. "Mommy!" She struggled to get free of Phil's death grip. When he wouldn't let go, she bit him on the hand.

Blam! Katty fired the gun at Phil's other ear and was knocked off her feet.

An in-mate rushed them, reached his huge hands to grab Bea from Phil.

Blam!

The inmate stopped, his hands just about on Bea's shoulders. His eyes crossed and glazed, and he fell to his knees. A cop standing behind him grinned at Katty. "Got 'im."

Behind the cop, more men dressed in swat clothes rushed toward them, swarmed over Phil and other inmates ahead. Handcuffs clicked.

The truck driver cop eased Phil's hand out of Bea's mouth. "Let go, little one. You are okay. We are here."

Blood dripped from Phil's head where his ear had been and where Katty shot him.

Katty glanced down at her hands. She had a death grip on Phil's ear with one hand. She raised her hand to fling it, when the cop grabbed her and stopped her. "Evidence." There was a gun in her other hand. She had become oblivious to even grabbing it from the truck driver.

Oh-oh.

"You're not in trouble. You saved your daughter's life. And yours." He gently pried her fingers open and lifted the ear from her hand. "I'll take care of that."

Another cop peeled the fingers of her other hand from the gun, keeping it pointed at the ground.

Katty leaned away and puked. She'd seen too much blood in her life, but never Phil's. It made her sick to her stomach to even touch his blood, much less see it drip from her hand. She threw up again and wiped her hand on Phil's back. "Take that. Wiping your blood on you. You are evil. I hate you and you will never see Bea again. Ever!"

Phil growled, but the cops popped him on the head, and he blacked out.

Katty wiped her hands on the grass again until one cop pushed a rag at her. She did not want any of Phil's blood on Bea when she picked her up. The cop seemed to understand that.

A man held Bea in his arms. For some reason, the man reminded her of Clarence. She choked. "Who's holding her? Is she safe?"

"He's an undercover agent with our department." The driver chuckled. "And a grandpa. He knows."

The agent walked toward Katty and the driver. Another agent rushed to Katty with some towels. 'Let's not let the baby see her mommy like this." He wiped her face and side. "I'm not being fresh. Let's just make sure the baby doesn't get scared seeing you like—"

Bea blinked her eyes open. Her face crumpled when she saw her mommy and she began to wiggle and whimper.

Katty slumped to the ground, her arms went slack. "Baby Bea." She tried to stay strong. "Bea. Are you … are you okay?"

"No. Mommy." She held her head. "He hit me." She checked her arms and her legs.

The agent holding her slowly set her down beside Katty.

Katty crumpled as Bea slumped against her on the ground. She touched Bea everywhere she could, checked her legs, her arms. Her head. A really big bump. She hugged her, afraid to hurt her, but needing to hold her tight.

"We'll get you both to the hospital as soon as we have the scene cleared of … Ma'am, are you hurt?"

Katty looked up at the driver. "I … uh, I don't think so."

But—what about Mark?

"Shh. We don't know." Did he also read minds? Was he an angel? "We have ambulances coming in just—"

Sirens screamed.

One ambulance stopped at the prison building. Drivers jumped out and opened the back doors. They pulled a long gurney from the back and raced inside. It was minutes before they raced back outside with … Mark on the gurney? Katty couldn't see. They pushed it inside the ambulance, one got inside, and the other slammed the doors shut. The ambulance swerved and drove back the way it had come.

"Mark!" Katty sobbed into Bea's hair.

THIRTY-TWO

Phyllis now knew why she had almost fallen to the floor. She had been overcome by fear, but someone or something was wrong. Something was happening, and she needed to pray.

Whatever was going on was life-threatening. She'd had no idea at the moment what it might be.

But she knew now.

She continued to pace back and forth in the hospital hallway. Mark was in surgery. Phyllis wiped her eyes.

When news of the prison break reached Phyllis, she didn't think too much about it. She knew Mark had taken that man—Bea's father—to prison, but that had been last week, sometime? There was no reason that she should be worried about Mark today. He was in Osceola.

It wasn't until a big brown-skinned deputy rang her doorbell that she realized it must be about Mark. The man told her to hurry, get what she might need for a couple days and that he was going to transport her to Lincoln, Nebraska, to a hospital there.

Mark was alive.

Even now, as she walked—er, paced—she could still hear

Guy's voice say that. "He's alive." What? Like he shouldn't be? Like he was serious? Like he was dying?

Where were the tissues? There should be some in this little waiting room. People died in the hospital all the time, right? Their families wept here every day.

Her tears would not stop. Mark was all she had.

A little hand reached up to her. Phyllis could just barely see through her blurred vision.

Tissues. An enormous box full of tissues.

Phyllis took them, wiped her eyes, and looked into the most beautiful little face in the entire world. Bandages and all.

"You need some more? I can get you more." The little girl pulled her by the hand to where a young woman stood weeping, holding a box of tissues. "Mommy has some. She can share."

And there she was, the woman Phyllis had despised, holding out the box of tissues to share. The woman—no Katty—her eyes were red, just like Phyllis supposed her own were. Her face was bandaged, her arm in a sling.

She took the box. "Thank you." To the little girl—Be-Bea. "Thank you, little one. We need to sit." She swallowed. "I need to sit."

Katty nodded.

They both turned to see Bea crawl up on a chair between two empty chairs. The babies leading the blind.

Bea tapped Phyllis' hand. "Are you Depdy Mark Scott's mommy?" Bea's beautiful brown eyes were wide.

Phyllis couldn't help the sob that escaped. "Yes. He is my boy."

Bea sniffled, then let out a wail. "I love Mr. Depdy Mark Scott." She climbed onto Phyllis' lap and put her arms around her neck, her head on her shoulder.

Startled, Phyllis stiffened, but soon found herself relaxing and hugging this little girl. This tiny girl who she had ignored and probably despised. Her hands patted Bea's back, her cheek against Bea's curly head. She closed her eyes. "Oh my Lord. Why didn't I see?"

"Bea, you need to sit down on your chair and leave Phyllis alone." Katty sniffled and wiped her face. "She is—"

Phyllis reached over to Katty and pulled her onto the chair Bea had vacated. "She is so fine, right where she is." Phyllis stretched behind Katty and pulled her close in a hug. "Did I hurt you? Are you okay?"

Bea lifted her head. When she saw her mommy getting hugged, she reached to hug her, too. "Group hug."

Phyllis chuckled. "Yes, you precious little girl." She raised her head to look at Katty. Looked directly into her eyes. "Group hug, you precious woman."

All three sat that way for a long time as Phyllis rocked them all back and forth. Her heart wanted to burst—with grief for what her son might be going through, but with true love for these two. Somehow, they were going to be friends. Phyllis blinked, remembering the vision. Maybe even family.

All of a sudden, Bea scrambled out from her arms and knelt on the floor, her head down, her hands folded on Phyllis' lap. "Jesus, please help Mr. Depdy Mark Scott feel better. Please help him." A tiny sob escaped her as she breathed. "Please make Mr. Depdty Mark well again."

"Oh, dear God in heaven." Phyllis shook her head. She hadn't prayed. But this dear child set the standard, convicted her own heart to pray for her own son. Phyllis choked.

Katty, in turn, reached out and held Phyllis. Her hands covered Phyllis'. Bea's hands found both women's hands. They all bowed their heads.

Phyllis started to pray, but a sob stopped her.

A tiny voice broke in. "Dear Jesus. Please help us be strong —as strong as You were when You did the cross thing."

Phyllis' eyes popped open. This was a child. How could she pray better than she herself could?

"Dear Jesus. Could you please help the doctors and nurses? Could you get Mrs. T to pray for Depdy Mark, too?" Bea released a deep sigh. "And Mr. Father in heaven, howdy be Your name. Your kingdom come, Your will be done."

Phyllis found herself following along with little Bea.

Katty, too.

They finished that prayer, all together with amen.

Bea's sweet words were almost funny. Howdy. God's new name was Howdy. Phyllis released a deep sigh. She guessed God would like His new name, especially from such a sweet child.

Tears welled again.

She'd been so wrong. So wrong to judge these two. She'd totally ignored them and missed the beauty she could have shared with them. She'd been terribly critical. Maybe they weren't who she herself would have chosen for her son, but here they were. Both beautifully made by God Himself. He had chosen them for her son. Who was she to think any differently?

"Excuse me."

All three looked up at the same time.

A nurse stood before them. "The doctor will be out here shortly. Do you need anything?"

Phyllis glanced at Bea and then at Katty.

Katty shook her head, no.

Bea, on the other hand, even though seconds ago had become the Prayer Warrior, jumped up. Despite her wound, she had spunk. "Could I have a ... a ...." She glanced at her mommy. "I'm hungry."

The nurse chuckled. "Well, we have a cafeteria just down the hall." She was cute and obviously liked kids, because she knelt down to Bea. "They have hamburgers." She must have realized that she might be leading the child down a path of causing trouble for her elders. "Um. They have vegetables and fruit and milk."

Bea jumped up and down and clapped her hands. She wobbled just a little.

Six hands reached out to steady her.

"Calm down, little one. You don't want to shake off your bandage. Does your head feel bad? Does it hurt?"

Bea immediately slumped. She gently touched her bandage. "Yes. It hurts. Bad." She perked up. "But I'm still hungry. And I love bech-tables. And fruit. Bananas?"

The nurse stood. "I can show you the way, but maybe you should wait and talk to the doctor." She glanced behind her. "He should be right out."

Phyllis wiped her eyes. *What was to become of Mark? How badly was he hurt? What would his life be like after all of this? Would he even live?*

Tears threatened.

A woman tapped Katty on the shoulder. "Ma'am?"

Katty jumped. "Oh. You're the guard from the prison." She stood.

"How is your man?" The woman grabbed and hugged her.

Phyllis flinched.

Katty glanced at Phyllis' face before replying. "He is still in surgery." She motioned over to Phyllis. "This is Mark's mom, uh … Phyllis?" She shook her head. And to Phyllis. "This is the guard that checked us in …"

Bea stood. "From my bad daddy. He's naughty." She hugged the guard's legs.

The guard pulled her up into her arms. "I'm so glad—so thankful that you are okay." She patted Katty on the shoulder. "It's a miracle."

Katty patted her shoulder. "Are you okay? I saw you fall."

Phyllis pointed to a chair nearby. "Can you sit with us, join us?"

"Yes. Thank you. Just for a bit." To Katty. "I'm sore. Bruised. But I'm fine. They're sending another guard and board member here to check on you two—make sure you're all right." She squeezed Katty's hand. "But I wanted to come myself." She shook her head. "Now that I look back on it … er, after the fact, like now after it happened, I can remember so many clues."

"Clues?" Phyllis moved closer to hear her properly.

"Yes." She patted her own chest. "I'm sorry. My name is Deputy Shirley Haverson."

Bea piped up, straightened on the deputy's lap. "Depdy? Like Depdy Mr. Mark Scott?"

Deputy Shirley chuckled and leaned her face in, looking at Katty, then at Phyllis. "Depdy?"

Katty blew out a breath, obviously not wanting to upset Phyllis. "That's what she calls Mark, the one in surgery."

Bea nodded. "He's my friend." She pointed at Katty. "He's Mommy's friend, too. She just doesn't know it yet."

Katty's eyes popped wide, her eyebrows raised. Phyllis knew her eyes and eyebrows must be the same.

"Um. Well. My daughter really likes Mark." Katty tried not to look at Phyllis again. "And he … is my friend." Her face appeared to turn red.

Phyllis blew out a breath. Tears wanted to fall. She swallowed, but if they could have seen what her heart was doing at that moment. She had given all this over to her Lord and she wasn't taking it back.

Katty appeared to love him.

Bea reached over to Katty. "Mommy, do you have a fever?" She felt Katty's cheek, her forehead.

"No, Baby Bea." She fanned her face with her hand. "It's just warm in here, is all."

The guard filled in. "Yeah and you have been under lots of pressure, what with the attack at the prison and all." She fanned her own face.

"Right." Phyllis tried to help. "Yes, with all that—especially the stress." She nodded, sure that she'd helped Katty. Oh, Lord only knew how much she needed to make things right with this dear young woman and her daughter.

The deputy patted Bea on the head and lifted her up onto the floor. "Well, Little One, I best be going and get back to my post. Things are gonna be pretty chaotic for a while and we need to stay on top of it." She bowed to Phyllis. "Good to meet you Mrs. …"

"Scott. But please, call me Phyllis." She stood and hugged her. "I'll be praying for you and the prison."

That stopped the deputy. "Oh, please do. We need Him now more than ever." She hugged Phyllis. "Thank you."

They watched her walk down the hall. Just as she disappeared around a corner, two men stepped off the elevator, looked both ways, then one pointed toward them.

"Hello." One man held out his hand to Katty. "Are you Katelyn Randolph?"

Phyllis could feel Katty shrink back in fear.

"I … uh, I'm Katty." She started to shake his hand, but evidently thought not to.

Smart girl.

"Sorry. You must still be on edge." He pointed to himself and the man with him. "I'm Sargeant Killroy and this is Mr. Harry Decater. We are from the prison and need to get a statement from you about what happened there. Do you have some time to talk?"

Katty glanced at Phyllis, like, *save me*.

"Um, she needs to be here with me." Phyllis nodded at the men. "It's my son who got … who got—" She had not expected the rush of emotion. "He's the one—"

"Oh, the deputy who got shot." Mr. Decater burst out.

The Sargent stepped forward and pushed Mr. Decater behind him. "I'm sorry, Ma'am." He pushed his hand at the man. "He is new on the board—new with prison protocol." To Katty. "Ma'am, I'm sorry to bother you, but could you come with us to a conference room? We need to hear your version of what happened. There are a few inmates ... well, we just need to talk."

A voice coughed behind the two men. They parted to see Sheriff Dennison.

Bea backed away.

He cleared his throat, looked directly at Katty. "The man who was injured is my deputy from Polk County and I need them to stay with me." Pause. "If you don't mind. *We* can get the statement from her and her daughter." He stepped in between the men and Katty. "And we would then be happy to send it to you." The sheriff held out a business card for the men. "And we'll be in touch."

"Uh, well ... we can't—"

"Excuse me, sir. I have to see to my deputy." He tipped his head toward Phyllis. "And his family."

His family. Phyllis peeked at Katty. She visibly wouldn't look at Phyllis. Oh dear Lord, Phyllis had a lot of forgiving to do. Forgiving and forgetting. *Lord, please fix this.* Katty had done nothing to her. Little Bea, either. And what had they been through at the prison, with that man ... Phil?

Laughter. Then beeps. Then whirs. Then shushes.

Dang. The sheriff must be bringing in a workshop on new technology, or some new thing.

Beep.

Whispers.

The beeps and whirs might be from ceiling fans. It got hot even this time of year in the department for some reason, even as it got colder outside. It was an old building, so—

Clang.

What the?

Mark blinked. He tried to open his eyes. Man, if he didn't get out of this nap before the other deputies came in, he'd be in so much trouble. They'd never let him hear the end of it. If they had been a bar hopping group, he'd be the next buyer for the next round. Or he'd have to share all Mom's leftover lasagne with those dorks for the next year.

Mom. Her voice, too.

What?

Why was she at the department?

Needed to rub his eyes, but his hands wouldn't move—he

needed them to be at his eyes, but … why couldn't he rub his eyes? Needed to open his eyes.

Barely. Were they taped shut? Had the guys played a trick on him while he napped?

There. Open. Eyes.

Beep.

What was that? This didn't look like the department. The walls were too white. The department was so old—they kept it up and clean and all, but the walls there were kinda off white by now.

Beep, beep.

"He opened his eyes."

Mom? Her voice.

"Son? We're here."

It *was* her. "Mom?" He tried to look around, but he struggled to move. "What's going—" He couldn't lift his head. The pain. The pain. Oh!

A deep voice. "Mark. Good to see you awake."

Sheriff? Mark stirred, told his head and shoulders to raise up. It *was* the Sheriff for Pete's sake.

"Sir." He couldn't raise his head … or even his shoulders. He couldn't feel his arms. His hands wouldn't move. He started to sweat. "What? What happened?" His breathing cut off. He couldn't get a breath. He must have raised up because he flopped back down.

A nurse pushed through and placed an oxygen mask over his face.

"No. No." He tried to move his head right, then left. "No."

"Only until you settle down. Until you relax." The nurse held on. She was strong.

Breathe. The only thing he could do with the oxygen mask on his face was breathe, blink his eyes, and try to scan the room. Mom. And Sheriff Dennison. What happened?

He blinked, trying to remember, and it all crashed back.

The prison.

Phil.

Inmates had swarmed from every corner of the room, every window, every cell. Some had been armed with actual weapons: handguns and rifles. Some with strange configurations of knives and bats.

Right now, as he relived that terrifying moment, awful spirits … demons … swarmed over him along with the inmates. Their eyes evil, their talons clawed and scraped over him. The stench unbearable.

Tears welled up in his eyes.

Oh God. He was still alive. Terrifying vision.

He tried to push the pictures away.

He tried to push the mask away. He tried to see his body. Why couldn't he move anything?

"Sir. Mark." The face of the nurse blocked out everything, everyone else. "You need to try to relax. Breathe." Her calm voice helped settle him. He focused on her blue eyes—so kind and gentle. Was she an angel? Because as he listened to her voice and focused on her eyes, his breathing slowed. He matched his breaths to hers. In. Out. In and out.

"That's it. We need to keep you calm so we can assess the extent of your wounds. Help you recover from the surgery." She licked her lips, reached over to a nearby table, and held up a lip balm. "Okay if I apply this? Your lips seem dry, maybe uncomfortable."

He slowly nodded. Someone else putting on chapped lip stuff? Okay.

A thought slammed in. He might have others helping him do much more than applying lip balm.

She was gentle and careful. Almost hypnotizing, mesmerizing. She moved her lips along with where she applied lip balm on his.

He didn't understand how she did it, but he felt himself slow down, calm down, and breathe. In fact, a deep breath pushed out, almost involuntarily.

Oh dear Lord, what happened? What was to become of him?

He'd seen veterans with limbs missing, or tragic victims of vehicular accidents living life as a paraplegic. Even worse, he'd seen the dead bodies, not very many thankfully, because he hadn't been on the force as long as … the sheriff.

He glanced down at his body, covered with a sheet, then at the nurse who was still close by. She could read his mind, or at least follow where his eyes tracked.

A man appeared behind the nurse. The doctor?

Mark guessed he'd get the low-down now. If only he could be somewhere else and not hear what all had happened. At the same time, if only he just had a headache. Which was doubtful with the expression on his mom's face.

"Hello, Deputy." The man nodded his head. "I'm Doctor White and I have been taking care of you since they brought you here."

Mark struggled to lift his head up, to even look the man in the face.

"We want you to lie flat until we can determine the extent of your body's response to your injuries and to the surgery." Doctor White stepped around the bed to the other side.

Mom switched places with him. She smiled and patted the bed.

Where—?

"So, right now, we know you have a concussion. We did a brain scan, and you held still for us, so it was very clear."

The nurse chuckled—kind of.

Was he making a joke?

The doctor shook his head. "I'm trying to make a joke, to lighten this news." He shook his head again and leaned closer to Mark. "What you went through at the prison, as near as we can determine, was brutal."

He glanced at Mom, then at the nurse.

Not looking at Mom again. She was weeping.

"You took a bullet to the ribs—just missed your lungs."

Blam! The loud blast!

Dr. White shook his head again. "When you fell from the gunshot, you must have hit your head—hence the concussion." He stopped to get his breath. "I will not mince words here, son." Another breath. "As the breakout, er the uprising—whatever you call it in prisons, continued, and as near as we can tell, every escaping prisoner who ran past you, jumped on you. They beat you, kicked you, and with whatever weapon they carried, they bludgeoned you."

Mark blinked. Don't look at Mom.

The visuals of that insurrection hit him like a flood. Men, no. But something else swarmed over him, his body. He felt again every hit, every kick.

"You should not be alive."

Mark shuddered.

"You took the beating that each inmate there deserved and you took it for them."

The sheriff. Look only at the sheriff. Even the nurse was crying.

Mark blew out a breath and chanced a look at Sheriff Dennison. He wasn't crying. Yet. His chin quivered. His eyes were wet. He looked directly at Mark. Some kind of energy was coming from him, even though he looked about to cry.

"Yes." The doctor removed his glasses and wiped his own face. "Yes. So you see, Deputy, you are a lucky man to be alive. Again." He replaced his glasses and continued. "Aside from the concussion, the bullet in your chest, both legs are badly bruised but only broken in one place, your right arm is broken and several ribs are bruised or broken." He blinked and shook his head. "I know that it's a lot, but I want you to try to move your toes—your feet."

They all shifted their gaze to the end of the bed. Mark could hardly bend his neck enough to see for himself.

Nothing.

Mom choked.

The nurse hugged her and led her out of the room.

"Wait. Wait. I know I can move them. I've always been—"

Nothing. Not one little quiver of the sheet.

Sheriff stepped up and pulled the sheet away. "The sheet was just … go ahead, son. Try again."

Felt like Uncle Ted had come into the room. The sheriff's voice. But Uncle Ted's voice.

Mark closed his eyes. *Please God.* He even pictured his toes like they had been taught in some visualization workshop years ago. "Come on toes. You can do this. Wiggle. Move." He didn't even look down at his toes. He just watched the sheriff and Dr. White's faces.

Nothing. No …

"What do I need to do? I can exercise and do what … physical therapy, right?" Mark tried to nod. "It just needs time."

Sheriff Dennison was the first to recover. "Yep. That's the ticket. It just needs time. Right Doc?" He touched Mark's foot gently, like he wanted to move the toes himself. He wanted to help. He wanted to make it all okay. He wanted to fix it.

Dr. White nodded and stepped closer to the bed. "You're a brave man, Mark. And with that kind of attitude—"

Mark cut in. "And with the help of God."

The doctor closed his mouth, then said, "Yes. And with His help. I'm not much of a believer—"

Mark cut him off again. "I am." Emotion began to get the best of him, but he swallowed it down. "I'm learning. He's a good God."

Dr. White nodded and peeked a look at Sheriff's face. He tapped Mark's toes. Tapped his foot. Other foot. "Could you feel any of that?"

Oh, he wanted to lie. But what good would that do? Mark shook his head. He could do that. He could shake his head no.

"Okay." Dr. White folded his arms across his chest. "This is what we are going to do." He twisted his mouth as he gave it some thought. "Every day, multiple times a day, we will—either I or a nurse will move your feet. They're not broken … thanks to shoes." He glanced down at Sheriff's feet. "We'll gently move them back and forth, like this." He grasped Mark's foot and gently bent it up and down. Back and forth. Just a little. Then he took each toe and twisted it slightly, then bent it back and forth.

The sheriff took the other foot and did the same, watched what the doctor did and followed suit.

Maybe it was a release of the emotion from the news the doctor had just shared. Maybe it was the absurdity of his boss rubbing his feet, but Mark started to chuckle.

Sheriff Dennison stopped rubbing, looked at Mark. "This hurt?"

Laughter burst up in his belly.

The sheriff began to laugh, too.

Dr. White shook his head. "Unbelievable."

Mark continued to watch one man at one foot, the other man at his other foot. "Unbelievable."

The nurse peeked in, Mom right behind her. "Is there laughter?" She reached behind her and escorted Mom back into the room. "So this is what our highly trained medical and police personnel are up to." She grinned. "Come on in, Mom. We might still cry, but we will laugh, too."

Mom stepped to the bed and tucked her hand into his. "I love you Mark." She started to say more, but stopped.

He could just about guess what she wanted to say. My Bible study ladies are praying. We all are praying. "It's okay Mom. Please pray. Ask your ladies to pray." He choked. "Ask Katty and Bea to pray. Mrs. T., Clarence." He could shake his head. "Lisha—everyone at the nursing home."

Sheriff cleared his throat. He smelled his hands. "Phew!" He laughed. "I better get back to Osceola." He stepped up and clasped Mark's other hand in his. "We're praying at the department, Mark."

Mom nodded. "And thank you, Sheriff. Small town blessings."

"Thanks Sheriff." Mark swallowed. "I don't know—"

Knock, knock. A dark-skinned man stuck his head in the room.

Guy. Oh, man. *Don't cry.*

He towered over the bed. "Where do I touch you? Can I shake your hand? I don't want to hurt anything." He kind of chuckled, but then wiped his eyes. "Mark." He pushed his chest out like a bodybuilder. But Mark knew. The man was holding his breath, not to cry.

They finally found each other's hands and held on.

"I-I'm sorry I wasn't there for you." Guy cleared his throat. "You've always had my back, and I wasn't there."

Mark shook his head. He tried to raise up. He couldn't talk. His throat closed up.

Sheriff stepped in and saved them both. "My two best deputies. Mark, don't worry about your job, son. It'll always be there for you. Always." Sheriff saluted.

Guy saluted, too. He quickly turned to Phyllis. "You ready to go home?"

"One of us will bring you back when you want." Sheriff Dennison nodded. "The least we can do."

Phyllis nodded and hesitated. She kissed Mark and touched his cheek. No goodbye, just out the door they went.

"Wait." Where—?

The nurse checked her computer. Then she checked an IV beside him.

"We are giving you a mild sedative to keep you relaxed and

it will help you heal." The doctor listened to Mark's heart. "What were you asking the sheriff?"

"Where are Katty and Bea?"

The doctor shook his head as he flipped the stethoscope around his neck. "Who?"

"Uh, my … um, they were with me at the prison." He couldn't collect his thoughts. "Are they okay?"

Doctor White glanced at the nurse.

She shook her head.

So fuzzy. So tired.

He must have blacked out. The nurse was still checking the IV, but the doctor was gone.

There had been one last glimpse … of some guy dragging Katty over him. Screaming. Then Phil grabbed Bea.

Where were they? He should have asked Sheriff, but when he thought to ask, Mom had come back in the room. Where were they?

The last he had seen of them, Phil had them. Had them both.

Had he lost Katty and Bea before they even had a chance? Would he ever see them again?

Were they okay?

So sleepy.

Phil won?

THIRTY-FOUR

"Thanks, uh, Guy." Phyllis tried to relax her shoulders, moving them up and down. "Thank you for driving me there and back."

He waved her away. "If you need another ride, I'd be happy to take you there again." He tapped the steering wheel. "Your boy … er, that man means everything to the department … but he means a lot … to me." He swallowed. "They all do. But he's my partner. He always has my back." Guy visibly swallowed. "And I didn't have his, this time."

What to say? "It happened the way it was supposed to happen. He's alive. That's all that matters."

He stared straight ahead at her garage, sucked in a deep breath, and turned to her with a smile. "I guess you're right. He's lucky to have a mom like you. Not everybody is that lucky."

"I'm blessed to have *him*." Phyllis nodded and fiddled with her purse handle. "He didn't have a father figure. Well, he had a father, but he was always drunk." She peeked at Guy. "You are that friend—that mentor. He looks up to you. And the other deputies. The Sheriff." She nodded as she pictured herself there in the actual department building with every person who worked there, all lined up. "That young dispatcher … Chantelle? She's good, too. Everybody is so good to him."

She'd gone on long enough. Held him up too long. She opened the car door, stepped out onto the driveway, and closed the door.

She glanced at her house and backed away from the cruiser.

But—

The window slid open. "Well, I need to get going back to the department." He shifted into reverse and backed out, shifted into drive, and drove back into her driveway. "And Phyllis. If you need anything. Anything. Just call the department. Chantelle knows how to find us." He chuckled. "And she always finds us."

Phyllis waved as he backed into the street and drove away.

Her house waited quietly. She loved her little house, had remodeled several places that her husband's drunken rants, his brutal angry battles, had destroyed. Every hole fixed where his fist had broken through walls, or kicked in doors. Her little house had been restored through the years by generous carpenters and … her son had helped … some.

Mark had started down that drinking and drugging path, the same as his father. But Ted, Phyllis's brother, had intervened and saved Mark. Ted had saved Mark's life.

As Phyllis unlocked the front door, she had a thought. She was always praying angels around Mark. She knew the dangers, the evil that cops met up with. She herself had been on the receiving end of that evil from her own husband. How she had survived all that was because of God.

She stepped into her living room and surveyed the space. "Angels?" She always hoped she might actually see one. In her house. In front of her. "Angels, are you here?" They were always around her. She read things, books, the Bible. "God, open my eyes, so I can see." She repeated that verse many times a day, even rephrasing it to make it personal. "*My* eyes, Lord. Help me see." She dropped her keys into her purse and slumped onto her chair. She rested her hands on the chair arms and patted them. Her prayer chair.

She leaned her head against the cushioned back of the wing-back chair and sighed.

"Father in heaven. Mark." That was all she could get out at the moment. Tears threatened, but she swallowed them down. If she let herself breakdown, it would be all over. She'd end up a soppy mess on the floor. She breathed in and out several times. In through her nose. Blew out through her mouth. Her trauma-tized heart settled into peace for the moment. In. Then out. If she really knew herself, she'd guess that would last a couple seconds and then she'd be right back into fear. "Lord, what are you going to do about Mark? Please heal him, Lord." Praying in fear and not by faith.

A few more breaths. "Lord, I know you love Mark. You love him and me. And I know you have a plan for him. Not to hurt him, but to help him prosper. Please Lord, heal him. Bring him home a well man. Healed, Lord. Healed."

A vision blinked into her mind. A quick flash of … what was that?

'Need to keep things the same. I need to hang onto my schedule, my habits." Phyllis reached for her notebook and her Bible. "This. I need to keep in the Word. Not let my thoughts get out of hand, or go crazy."

Another flash. She must be having a panic attack. Who wouldn't blame her, having just come from the hospital and seeing her only son in that condition? Who wouldn't blame her?

She knew people who claimed that they had panic attacks but always wondered about their sincerity. She'd had plenty of reasons to actually have them, but now felt like she was having one herself. Like her chest might explode or implode.

She flipped through her Bible, trying to find a verse. "It's … it starts out with … what?" She flipped the pages back and forth. "I can almost see it. I can almost see it on the page in my Bible."

She flipped another page and another. "It's right there." She pointed. It wasn't there. "Lord, where is it?"

Another flash in her mind. Another picture.

This time, she didn't avoid it or disregard it. She actually focused her thoughts on that blink of a vision.

"Lord, what is that? Please show me again. I"m not very good at this." Stories of events like this flooded her mind. "Paul saw things. He saw things. Heard things. Ezekiel had visions." She closed her Bible, then jumped. "John wrote his vision in the last book." She opened the back of the book. "The entire book of Revelation is ... a vision?"

She heard a voice and jumped. She pushed up off the chair and checked the windows, walked to the front door, and checked the lock. Still locked. Nothing. "Who's there?" Holding her breath, she stood very still, listening and tilting her head to the right, then to the left. She had to have locked her front door before even going to the hospital with Guy, because she had unlocked it when they got back. There couldn't be anyone here.

"Huh. Must have been the wind." She pulled the curtains back. "No wind outside."

Back to her chair.

Nope. First a cup of tea from the kitchen. That would calm her down. The tea kettle took forever to whistle, but finally she carried a cup back to her chair, set it carefully onto the nearby table, and plunked down. Her favorite chair. The small end table was on her right side and a hassock in front of her so she could prop her feet.

Hard to sit knowing where Mark was at the same time.

"Find the ring." There it was again. It was a soft whisper at first. *Breathe. In and out. Just breathe.* This couldn't be—

Again. "Find the ring." Louder this time.

Phyllis gasped. Her hands gripped the arms of the chair. She sat upright, her back straight up. Was she having a heart attack? She patted her chest. No pain.

"Go. Find the ring."

"Find the ring?" She repeated what she'd heard. "Find … find the ring?"

A flash in her mind of the ring. That ring.

"Find … that ring?"

Warmth blanketed, hugged her shoulders.

"Lord, I'm not … is this real?"

Another hug of warmth, this time all throughout her body. All through her body. Inside and out.

"The … the ring, Lord?" She waited. "Go get the ring? Find the ring?"

An almost audible chorus in every harmony sang, "Yes!"

Phyllis jumped. Her arms swung out wide, and she knocked over her teacup. She didn't move for many seconds, her arms still up in the air, as the tea dripped off the edge of the side table. Her eyes flitted around the room. Nothing. Nobody there.

But something had happened. She heard a perfectly harmonized chorus of … angels? Was that even possible?

Phyllis needed to potty, as in now. That came on fast. As she hurried to the bathroom, she became distracted by the thought of finding the ring again, but knowing her bladder, she pushed into the bathroom and did her business. But right away, she turned into the bedroom and headed for the vase on her dresser. She pulled the flowers out and dumped the ring onto the palm of her hand. The vase landed on its side on the bed.

Walking to the window, she held the ring up in the sunlight. It sparkled almost more than it should have. Yes, it was in the sunlight. It reflected the sunlight. But the rays of sparkle seemed more than they should have been. She held it so the rays painted the walls of her room with streaks of beautiful white light. Tones of rainbow colors—every color sparked on the walls.

Magical.

She slipped the ring on her finger. It didn't fit anymore. It didn't fit anymore because it wasn't for her. It was no longer for her.

It was for … for Katty.

Phyllis thought of the vision. Katty as a bride and Mark, her groom.

With the ring in the palm of her hand, she knelt beside the bed. "Oh, Lord Jesus. Forgive me of being so selfish and controlling. You have the better plan. You know all things." She held the ring up and rays exploded against every wall. No sunlight hit it. Beautiful colors and white light emanated from the ring itself.

Overwhelmed, Phyllis leaned on the bed. "Lord, bring this to pass. I submit the vision of Mark and Katty getting married to You. If it is your will, please bring it to pass. Please help Mark heal and be able to … whatever, Lord. If he's in a wheelchair, let it be. You know me. I want it all perfect. But Lord, I'm not seeing a wheelchair in that vision You gave me. Mark is walking. He is upright and standing. Lord, I believe for his healing and for their marriage."

Her thoughts strayed to the little girl. "And Lord, that precious little girl. Bea? I used to think that was a stupid name for a little girl. She is so cute." Phyllis paused. "But Lord, what if her name signifies, represents what she is to be? Be." She chuckled. "I don't know. I'm making that up. But she is more than a name." The moment when Bea prayed and Phyllis hadn't. "Little Prayer Warrior."

She sniffled. "Lord, I'm sorry for … being so rebellious. For thinking that I had all the answers, when You had them all along. Please forgive me."

She held up the ring. "Please bless their marriage, Lord."

THIRTY-FIVE

Katty helped Bea out of the car seat in Sheriff's squad car at Noell's. Times she'd ridden in cop cars. Just today. With Mark. *Choke*. And when she'd been so drunk that she didn't have any memory of the equipment that Bea was so excited about.

Bea had chattered the whole way back to Noell's. "What's that knob for? Can you turn on that big, noisy thing?" Otherwise, she probably would have fallen asleep. Nothing to look at. Too dark to see.

"Oh. You mean the siren? The woop-woop thing?" The sheriff seemed to enjoy Bea's questions. Probably made it easier to transport people. Easier to transport Katty and Bea after the prison break. He'd driven all the way to Lincoln to pick them up from the hospital—well, to see Mark, too. The truck driver who had shushed Katty in the truck with that monster man had turned out to be a cop for real, only in disguise. He'd been an undercover agent the whole time and Katty had thought he was one of the evil inmates escaping. Or he could have been someone they had set up from the outside to bring in the trucks.

Instead, he was a true cop. An undercover cop.

Katty realized she had been holding her breath as she let the prison break play out in her head. She blinked.

Mark.

They'd barely gotten to see him. He'd been asleep because they had just given him a sedative. He didn't even know they were there. Bea had almost jumped up on the bed before the nurse caught her. Crushing to not know. Not know if he was … okay.

Thankful that the sheriff kept Bea engaged. He was giving good answers. He must have kids or grandkids.

Mark. She could never forget his green eyes staring up … seeing—

"Mommy. Mr. Sheriff Sir said I can have a ride in his cop car anytime I want." Bea giggled. "Anytime."

He cleared his throat. "Well, if I'm picking up bad guys, then we can't." He glanced at Katty. "Okay with you, Mommy?" He opened his mouth to say something else, but closed it.

Mark. Mark was on all of their minds. Even Bea's.

Katty blew out another breath. She knew he wasn't dead, but if he never walked again, or was paralyzed, it'd be her fault. She and Bea were the reasons he was even at that prison.

Phil.

Phil was the whole reason they had been at that prison. He'd pushed and won paternity rights and made Bea go through all that. The judge had been on Phil's side and not hers or Bea's. The saliva test was bad enough, but they'd had to take Bea's blood, too. His blood. Her blood. Phil had been the whole reason that they had been captured. Phil was the whole reason Bea had the bruises she did. Phil was the whole reason that Mark—oh, her own blood was boiling right now. Still. Even after tearing off his ear and shooting him, she was still angry.

She waved as the sheriff pulled away from the curb in his cop car, almost spellbound, seeing her own hand wave. It seemed to wave by itself. The same hand that had ripped Phil's ear off.

As they trudged up the sidewalk, Noell pushed the front porch door open and light streamed onto the sidewalk. She must have been alerted or just perched at the porch window, watching for them. She rushed down the sidewalk toward them, her arms wide.

She grabbed up Bea first. Tears streamed down her cheeks. "Oh, Bea." She choked. "I'm so glad you're okay." Her eyes locked onto Katty's and she reached out for her.

Katty let herself be hugged. She embraced Noell and Bea. But she couldn't get Mark's face—his eyes—out of her mind. His eyes had been just staring up … he hadn't seen her, he hadn't blinked. They hadn't moved … like he was really—

Katty choked a sob back. God. Dear God. What if he had …

She broke free of Noell's embrace.

"Katty. Please. Let me help."

Katty stepped away from them both. She gasped for a breath. Her chest wanted to collapse in on itself. Her head throbbed. "No. No. He—" She glanced down at Bea and stopped. One more step away and she ran into the house.

The one place she knew that she could be. Just be.

Gamma's closet door was always open. She ran inside. Felt like years since she'd been away, when it had only been this morning?

The front porch door slammed. "Mommy?" Bea was crying.

Katty braced herself for Bea bursting into the closet.

But she never ran in.

Noell.

Noell *was* helping right now. Katty could almost envision Noell sitting down at the kitchen table with Bea snuggled in her arms, rocking side to side, cooing in Bea's ear. Asking her if she was hungry, then reaching into the cupboard or refrigerator for whatever it was that Bea wanted. Spoiling Bea, but Katty guessed she probably needed spoiling right now after what she had been through.

Katty bent her head down and closed her eyes. She tried to dig through today's memories of when Phil had grabbed Bea, run outside, and up ahead of where Katty was being held. She couldn't see her. All Katty could see were Mark's green eyes.

A sob escaped her lips from way down deep inside her chest or her belly. From somewhere in her past. From memories hidden deep inside.

She was next to the door, so she reached and pushed it shut. That door hadn't been closed since they'd discovered this magical space.

In shutting the door, Katty shut out Noell and Bea. She tried to shut out Phil, the sheriff, her mom. She shut out the lies of her past. She shut out those images of her past. It was as dark as a tomb inside the closet, but in that darkness, every word spoken against her, every abuse against her, every pain inflicted upon her rose up.

If Mark never recovered, the only future she had was with Phil. Unless he was dead, too. She had no place to go. The trailer was destroyed. She had no place of her own—even though Noell always assured her that this was her home.

She cracked the door open. A narrow stream of light illuminated part of the wall, the floor.

No Bea.

She felt the floor for her paints and brushes. Leaving the door cracked open didn't give enough light for her to see clearly. She just wanted to paint. To paint over the day. To paint over her thoughts. Her fears. To paint over those … those green eyes that might be … no.

The only color she could seem to daub onto her brushes was dark. Black. Brown. Grays. More black. She swiped the brush onto a wall. Interesting that wall hadn't been painted on before. She glanced at the rest of the walls, even pulled the door open wider, flicked the light switch on and off. Why didn't that work? There was a light bulb in the socket, but when she flicked the switch up and down, nothing happened. It had worked that morning …

Didn't matter. She wasn't painting anything at all. She just wanted to swim in the darkness. Like a snake slithered underwater, along the muddy bottom.

She continued to slap black onto the walls. She coated one entire wall, and then another appeared. Black. Gray. With each slap of the paint, anger spewed out of her mouth. She wanted to growl. She did.

Mom.

Phil.

As soon as she thought of him, a giant, terrifying dragon appeared in her mind. It roared so loud that she dropped her brush. That demon. That dragon could kill her, eat her. It raised far above her and spewed fire and roared. All she could see was fire and death. All Phil ever did was destroy. He destroyed her art, her dreams, her self-esteem. Well, Mom helped with that. They both had destroyed all she had wanted to become and dreamt of doing. Being.

Her life. Her whole life from her childhood on. She couldn't remember a time, a minute, a day that wasn't painful or terrifying.

Each day that she thought of, each memory or visual that invaded her mind got painted over with black. The pain. The suffering.

Death.

All of her hopes. Her home.

Her dreams. All dead.

Her art.

All the babies.

And now Mark. What if—?

She had nothing left.

Nothing but Bea.

The black paint turned to red. She blinked and jumped away

from the red wall. Every paint cube in her paint set had all turned to red. She grabbed the set and carried it to the open door. No Green. No blue.

All red.

She knew there had been all the other colors in that paint set. Right before she started painting, she knew there were other colors in it.

But not now.

All red.

She kept on painting the walls that seemed to keep appearing, seemed to multiply. More and more walls appeared, and she painted them.

Red.

Like the blood. Like the blood of those babies. Like when she had bled, herself. Almost died. Like the blood under Mark's shoulder that spread second-by-second into one big pool.

What it had cost her. Her own suffering, the blood she had shed and that of her babies.

The blood that Phil, that dragon—that demon had shed.

Red now covered them all.

Every wall was a memory, a brutal part of her life. From Mom smacking her, dumping hot macaroni on her, breaking her colored pencils and shredding her drawings. Another wall was Phil and his wooing her, lying to her, drugging her. Another wall became babies.

All red.

Another hand raised a brush and painted alongside hers. This wall. All in red. It startled her, made her jump away from the wall for a minute.

Gamma's hand?

She realized she was weeping. Tears dripped onto the paint brush.

What it had cost her.

A thought entered her mind. What it all had cost Jesus.

All of her life, she'd been robbed of joy, peace, hopes and dreams. Of life. She'd been robbed every minute, every colored pencil, every moment of peace. Every baby.

Robbed.

Jesus had totally given his up … for her.

She never got to choose, never got to keep anything, or to be anything. All *stolen* from her.

He had chosen and *given it all*.

She crumpled onto the floor, not caring where she landed. Not caring if she sat on paint.

Her life had been evil and hatred.

Jesus had given it all. In love.

Hers had burned in hatred.

His had poured out love. What he had sacrificed for her.

Another wall. The hand lifted and painted without hers. As she watched, it painted a bright white light.

She couldn't stand the light, she couldn't stand to look. It was too bright. But she couldn't not look—not watch. She shielded her eyes.

The light flowed into a face. Was that Jesus? The face morphed over a cross. The cross became her own face. Her own face stared back at her. Her eyes appeared red, puffy. Tears dripped from her chin.

The hand began again.

This time Katty watched. Was it the hand of an angel? Was it really Gamma?

Or Jesus?

THIRTY-SIX

Jasper bowed his head.

There were certain moments that Jasper was strong in his calling, in his daily duties. Today was not one. Today was a day when his charge, Katty, might have taken her own life, before.

Before she had quit hiding those little bottles of golden liquid in every pocket and behind the vegetables. Before she had pounded on that cell door. Before she had fallen in love. Before she had quit drinking from those bottles.

Jasper could only worship the Creator. He could see the Father's hand. And he wept at the truth spilling from Katty's heart and her paintbrush.

He always hoped and prayed for the best for his charges. He collaborated with humans who had gone from the earth into heaven. They knew what it was to be human, so Jasper could hear their prayers for his charge and understand more of what Katty might be thinking or going through.

He opened his eyes and blinked. Lining every wall of this very unusual room were angels. Against every wall. This room was like a king's chamber of gold, or throne room full of treasure and gold, but the treasure was Katty. The gold was Katty. And each wall, even ones that magically floated in, were lined with angels guarding his charge.

He shook his head. Tears threatened. His fellow angels banded together to further the Kingdom of God. Each angel here had fought a hard fight. They would never quit the battle.

A demon slithered inside the circle of angels. Gutsy fellow. Stupid fellow.

Another one dropped in.

Jasper wasn't surprised, for the battle within Katty at that very moment was intense and very real. She wasn't drinking, and she was facing those demons. She had identified them, accused them and faced them.

As Jasper watched another demon drop in, he wondered if Katty could see them? He didn't think so. They were gruesome —the worst in the enemy's kingdom. Bea could see the angels and he knew she had seen a demon or two. If humans could see the demons, would it be so terrifying that it might set them right with God?

Interesting how the demons kept dropping in, despite the hundreds of angels lining the room. It didn't matter to any of them, angels or demons, that the walls were out of order and even stacked against each other and against the real, physical house. The walls were mobile, almost alive. Every time Katty covered one wall totally with the paint, another one appeared in front of the last one.

As she painted over anger or fear, she asked God to get those demons out. To get rid of the pain. Just as those words left her mouth, and the paint covered the wall, angels swooped in with small threads, tied them to the roots of the pain in her heart, and yanked them out. Other angels followed with nets of fire, caught the roots and burned them up.

Now it was up to her to remain entangled with her Creator, her Savior and walk with Him in sanctification.

The hand painted beside Katty. The hand. People had made

funny movies with just a hand as a character. Even monster movies. The hand had a role in the story.

This hand did as well.

It was the hand of God. And even though Katty thought at first that it might be Gamma's hand, that was okay with the Father.

THIRTY-SEVEN

Mark groaned. The pain ran so deep.

If Phil had won, Katty was no longer Mark's. She was Phil's.

He started to shake his head. Ow. Ow.

Everything hurt. Every bone. His head. Even moving his head back and forth … hurt.

His heart. His heart hurt worse than the gunshot wound. His heart was breaking.

If Katty was no longer his to pursue—

The door opened, and the nurse walked in with a tray.

"No. No. I'm not--"

The nurse smiled and placed the tray on the over the bed table and paused. She didn't do anything but stand there. She didn't offer him food. She didn't take the tray away. She didn't leave. She just kept smiling that … goofy smile.

"Hey. I'm not ready to … eat." Dang, he couldn't even shake his head without pain. "I don't want to talk or anything."

She wasn't moving. Still smiled. Not a word.

"Is the doctor here? He can tell you. He knows, right? He knows that I'm in pain. That I don't want any company." Mark swallowed. Was she not listening? Was she even real? She was acting like a dummy right now. He chuckled. Yeah. A dummy. "Don't you get it? I'm not eating today." Maybe never. The pain inside was too intense to eat.

She kept on smiling, but something moved behind her. Something moved behind her shoulders. He glanced up at her face. Still smiling. She was beautiful. Her eyes seemed to twinkle … sparkle. White something moved up from behind her and spread up and out like a fan. Impossible. Like wings.

She was grinning now.

But Mark suddenly realized that she was flat chested. He'd thought she was a woman, but she … er … grew taller. Right before his eyes. Her … uh, head and shoulders grew Almost reached the ceiling. The white uniform flowed into robes. Dark hair grew thicker and longer.

Still grinning. "Hello." Deep voice. So deep that it seemed to rumble and shake the tray in front of … him.

Mark couldn't breathe. "I … uh. What? Who?"

"My name is Michael." That a voice so deep, could resonate, that it could cause Mark's own body to tremble. Or maybe he was just terrified. That was it. His very bones vibrated and trembled with fear.

Where had the nurse gone? And who was this manifesting in his hospital room?

Mark was overcome with fear, but with a knowing. A knowing that somehow a miracle was happening before his very eyes. This stuff happened in the Bible, in other countries, but not here. Not here in his hospital room. He'd heard stories. His own mom had heard of them and told him—respectfully, knowing Mark might not be ready to hear that powerful of a testimony.

Today, he was seeing, hearing that powerful of a testimony right before his eyes. Right in his room. Right after being beaten to within a hair's breadth of his life. His very life that now, he wasn't sure he wanted to live it.

Not without Katty or Bea.

If Phil had won them over or somehow kidnapped them so securely that they'd never be free, Mark's chances of ever seeing them free or even alive were zero.

The huge being in front of him stopped smiling at him and withdrew a huge shining sword.

Mark jumped. Gasped. "Ow. Oh." He knew it would hurt to move, but he wanted to jump off the bed and hide underneath. He checked the window. That would work.

Back to the being. Angel? He … uh, it? He was still smiling, but his eyes had changed. The sword still pointed at the ceiling. But his eyes were determined or compassionate.

Determined. There was something … something moving behind the being. Something to Mark's left moved. And to his right. Behind him. Beside the window and now blocking the door.

Goosebumps rose on Mark's skin. Even that hurt. He could sweep his left arm across his chest to try to stop the goosebumps, the pain. Even his skin was painful. But the tinging would not stop in his skin, in his whole body.

At the same time, there was more movement along the walls, the floor, behind his bed. He felt it even though he couldn't see it.

Tears that Mark couldn't swipe away ran from the corner of each eye, down his cheek, and pooled in his ears and on the pillow under his head. He couldn't even wipe away his own tears. That made more spill out.

The angel moved toward him, the sword still held high above him. Mark flinched as the huge hand slowly reached his face. He was dead. Life was over for Mark. The being, or whatever it was, would take one swipe and kill Mark instantly.

Bring it on. He'd decided that life without Katty and Bea wasn't worth living. Cut off his head. That was what was happening.

But, as the angel's hand reached Mark's face, it gently wiped away the tears. The sword was still upright, but the angel's hand was gentle and soft, wiping the wet away from his face. Both sides. Both eyes.

Mark blinked. The huge hand was so close. It touched his skin. He should be dead. He shuddered. His eyes locked with the angel's eyes. Something passed from the angel to Mark—a surge of power, but a knowing. A powerful landing of information, of knowing.

A knowing that God was on Mark's side. That whatever had happened to him at the prison, that whoever had actually attacked him through those escaping inmates, God was on his side and God did not lose.

Those eyes spoke wordless knowledge and volumes that Mark's God was greater. That his God had a plan, a plan to help Mark, a plan to prosper him and heal him.

Tears flowed freely now. The angel didn't move to wipe them away.

Mark blinked as ten more angels lined up behind the one in front of him. No. More like hundreds of angels all surrounding him, lining the walls, and outside the window.

"What is your name?" Mark finally found his voice and sputtered it out. "Who are—"

"Thus saith the Lord: You will recover with very little remaining pain or wounds. You will continue to serve as a deputy of the Lord Most High, Jesus the Christ. You will heal." The angel smiled—grinned, really. "Michael. My name is Michael." His smile became more gentle. "You will recover to father a child."

Mark blinked. "A child—"

"You will battle." Michael continued. "You will go to battle for the lost. You will redeem the lost."

Tears streamed down Mark's cheeks again. The pillow under

his head was wet. His face was wet. He didn't care. A child? The most powerful words ever spoken to him, and he didn't want to forget. Somehow, he knew. He knew this was real. He knew it was life changing. And he knew—

A surge of power slammed into Mark—almost as startling and as shocking as when the bullet had knocked him flat at the prison.

Breathe.

He'd never felt anything like what was flowing all throughout his body. He felt more alive now than he ever had before the prison break. A flash of a visual broke through the garbled mess of thoughts in his mind.

Katty. Bea.

He jerked upright. Sat upright. He had to get to them. He had to find them. He choked. He had to make them part of his life. Every part of his life. He would die trying to save them and get them back.

Alarms went off.

The huge angel, Michael, in front of him stepped back to give him room.

Mark braced himself on the table next to the bed, but it gave way and he almost fell out of bed.

A moment of truth could be the last brick in a wall built to keep others and life out. Or a moment of truth could be the spark that ignites a person to chase down their life destiny.

Michael reached out to steady Mark before he fell onto the floor.

His touch zinged Mark even further. A force or bolt of energy zapped him upright, and he pulled out an IV.

Alarms rang again, this time followed by the door bursting open with two nurses—actual nurses this time.

Mark yanked another needle out of his other arm and rolled out of bed onto the floor. So much for foot massages.

One nurse screamed. The other stopped short, seemingly blocked by the line of angels.

Mark didn't stop to figure that one out. All he knew was that every time Michael touched his skin, his head, something happened. A jolt of energy moved him forward. He rolled over onto his knees. Oh, dear God. That hurt. He felt around his chest, belly, his knees. As near as he could tell, there was a bandage over his ribs. The gunshot wound.

Deep breath. He grappled for anything to hold on to.

One nurse just stood there. She was probably overwhelmed by what Mark had been seeing—a roomful of angels. He glanced at her. Maybe not. She was in another world.

The one who had screamed came to and tried to help Mark up. "You can't! You can't get out of bed. You need rest to recover. The doctor has you on complete bedrest."

She stepped aside to make room for him to get back into bed, but that was the opening he needed to limp to the door.

He glanced around the room. He didn't have any clothes, just the hospital gown he had on. He spied his ball hat on a shelf above a closet and tried to reach for it.

Michael reached far above Mark and picked it up, handing it to Mark.

Mark froze for a minute, staring into Michael's eyes. Locked on each other. "Are you really—"

Micheal grinned and pushed him out the door. "Others are coming and you won't make it out with them in here." Immediately, he morphed into a doctor of sorts. Everything seemed appropriate except his long, flowing hair. "Gotta keep that."

Mark looked him over. "Looks good to me. Dr. Michael."

More personnel filled the doorway, blocking their escape, but Michael waved his hand at them with a flourish and Mark and Michael moved right through them. Another orderly waited in the hallway with a wheelchair. Michael sat Mark in it, saluted the orderly, and they were off down the hall.

"Wait." Mark pointed at the orderly. "Was that—"

"No time for that. We have to get you to your destination."

"My destination." Mark gripped the arms of the wheelchair. "What's my destination?"

THIRTY-EIGHT

Katty couldn't stop. She painted in Gamma's closet long past when the sheriff had dropped them off. Her back ached. Her legs were stiff. It had to be late.

She painted a whole wall—completely covered with painted babies and trees and flowers. She painted it all, alongside the other hand. Like, whatever the hand painted, Katty painted.

All in red. Only she saw what they painted on the walls—everything—the trees were trees in greens and yellows and browns. But the paint was red.

If Katty tried to understand this crazy, she'd be crazy.

Wait. Maybe she was. Only it wasn't the booze anymore. She was stone cold sober.

The paint set didn't run out of paint, either. It appeared to be as full as it was the minute they brought it home from the store.

The only difference was that every little paint well contained red. Every well filled with red paint. No green. No blue. No yellow or black.

Just red.

And every wall revealed a part of her past, the pain, the

cruelty, the trees or babies. A different scene on every wall. She couldn't not paint on the walls.

But every time she lifted the brush beside the other hand, she painted over the scene with red. Red paint.

It was like painting over her life … with the blood.

That sat her down next to a wall. With the blood.

She could still see the scene of Mom breaking her crayons and colored pencils through the red, through the blood.

Through the blood.

She almost forgot to breathe.

Through …

"Oh, Jesus."

Katty had no idea how long she sat there without moving. She could barely hear noises from the other rooms in the house. Bea must have been drawing or coloring because Katty heard her say the name of a color every once in a while. Noell must be washing dishes. Katty could hear water bubbling, dishes clanking … in a sink.

It became too much to take in. Was she really painting with limitless red paint, over pictures of her own past, hearing names of colors over the background of bubbling water?

Another wall appeared.

Katty held her breath. Hadn't she seen every painful and brutal scene of her life on every wall? Hadn't she seen enough pain and blood and—

This wall was different. The hand started painting white— even though the brush was filled with red? Her own brush, as she raised it to paint alongside, was filled with red.

This was her life in paint, through the red. But when the red paint in the brush touched the wall, right now, it turned white.

Katty filled her brush from the paint set with red. She intentionally watched the brush. As soon as she touched the wall, the paint in her brush became white.

This was a dream. It wasn't real. She must have fallen asleep on the floor in the closet. Sure. The stress. The pain of seeing …

Sob.

She must be dreaming. But the dream didn't stop. The paint on the wall turned green—turned into pretty green leaves flowing from a … basket. The white had taken shape into a dress? Like a person dressed in … white? An outline of maybe another person or something beside the white dress. Boots. Dark brown heavy boots. Familiar … boots.

Katty blinked at the memory of when she had puked on Mark's cop boots.

Mark's boots?

Those were Mark's boots. She had a very clear picture in her memory of her face down, puking on his boots.

But now, those boots were polished and shiny.

She followed the other hand with her paintbrush, on up from the boots to a body, to a face, to … green eyes.

Katty dropped her brush and fell back against something.

Someone.

She slowly turned around, knowing it could be Phil and his demons. Knowing it could be Mom and hers.

Green eyes.

Katty screamed! "Mark!" She patted his shoulder and his chest. "Are you real?"

Mark chuckled. "I am. I'm real. I'm not sure about …" He seemed to search the room and shook his head. "I …" He shook his head again and winced.

"Are you okay?" Katty checked the door. Bea was standing just outside the closet in the bedroom. Noell right behind her. 'How long have you …?" Back to Mark.

Mark cringed as he knelt down on one knee. He gasped, closed his eyes and visibly breathed, in and out a couple times.

"Mark. You're … still hurt. You … the hospital. How did you get here?" Those staring, dead green eyes morphed under the fully sparkling and alive green eyes open in front of her. "Am I dreaming?" Another breath. "You were … when they dragged me out of … the prison … you were—"

Mark reached into his pants pocket.

"You … your shirt. You're still wearing a hospital gown—"

He held out the most dazzling and beautiful ring Katty had ever seen.

"Will you marry me?"

THIRTY-NINE

A beautiful woman with brown hair tumbling around her shoulders stood at the end of … the bed? "Katty?"

A little curly head popped up and down. Bea?

Where was he? *Mark* must be dreaming now. He'd just been dreaming that he went to Noell's, found Katty painting in a … very strange room or closet and—

Katty smiled a sweet and shy smile. She glanced down at her left hand.

Mark gasped. "That wasn't a dream?"

Bea bounced up and down again.

"Bea. Settle. You need to be quiet. Mark is still healing." Katty moved closer, her eyes never leaving his. "You really don't remember this?" She held up her beautiful hand with that beautiful ring on it. She placed that hand on her other one, a confused look on her face. "Like in—"

Mark shook his head. "No. No."

She started to remove the ring.

"No!" Too loud. "Don't take it off. Please don't." *Breathe.* It hurt to shake his head. Behind Katty was a poster on the wall of a school calendar. A school calendar? Next to a bookcase. His bookcase—his childhood bookcase. There had to be books in there from … sigh. He started to raise up but gently laid flat again. "I'm-I'm in my old room."

"You sure are." Mom walked through the door, carrying a tray. "And as long as you're here, you better keep it clean." She paused, put the tray on the bedside table, and carefully hugged him.

"Mom." Mark glanced at Katty, then Mom, then Bea jumped up again. He patted the bed beside him. "Bea. Can you climb up here, next to me?"

Bea jumped, ready to launch, but Katty grabbed her and held her back. Katty obviously waited for Mom. They exchanged looks and Mom picked up Bea and gently sat her right next to Mark.

He blinked and swallowed. What just happened?

Bea snuggled in beside him as if that was the most natural thing in the world for her to do. She breathed out a deep sigh.

Mark chuckled because he had a deep sigh at the same time. Same time. Same deep breath. Bea and him.

Unbelievable.

Bea started to wiggle. She had her backpack on and struggled to sit up and take it off. She had one strap almost off her shoulder when Mom helped her with that one and Katty slipped the other one off. Together.

Again. Mark just watched the two women he now knew he loved work together to help little Bea, who he had loved from the very moment he met her.

She grinned as she sat upright, unzipped her backpack, and held up a chunk of wood paneling. Only she had it wrong side facing him. The back of that old paneling. Without seeing it, Mark knew.

A sweet, gentle smile was on Katty's face. She could see the other side.

Mom reached over to help Bea, but stopped when Katty moved to help Bea at the same time.

"Sorry. You should." Mom stepped away.

"It's okay, Phyllis." Katty shook her head. "It's just part of a painting." She helped Bea turn it around so Mark could see the babies and clouds that he knew were there.

He starred at the chunk of wood for a minute or so to settle his emotions. The baby and clouds seemed to take on a supernatural edge, like they were alive and moving on their own. Flying. Giggling. Beautiful. Then up to Katty. "The most beautiful painting there ever was … ever." Back to the painting. "Thank you for letting us save it before your trailer got destroyed."

Mom gasped. "Your trailer is destroyed?"

Katty nodded. "Yeah. Yes. It was terrible anyway and they're wanting the land to be used for … I don't know what. It's okay. We got what we needed … before." She visibly straightened, her shoulders back. "There were lots of things in that trailer we didn't need anymore. Lots of things from that time in our lives …" She glanced at Mark. "Things I don't need anymore."

"Yeah." Bea took a breath like she was going to preach or dive underwater. One or the other. "Those little bottles—"

Katty blew out a breath on Bea and tapped her on the mouth. "I was drinking a lot. And I'm not anymore." She hugged Bea. "I'm not perfect, but I don't need those little bottles anymore, right Bea?"

"You mean those little bottles behind the begtables?"

Little stinker! Mark corrected her. "You mean those vegetables?"

"I thought I had you fooled, Baby Bea." Katty laughed the most beautiful laugh—free and musical. "Instead, you had me fooled."

"Fooled." Bea shook her head. "What's that mean?"

Mom jumped into the conversation. "It means you are one

smart little girl, that's what it means." Mom clapped her hands and held them out to Bea. "Do you want to come into the kitchen and help me get some cookies?" She pointed at the tray. "I brought in some drinks, but didn't have room for those cookies. Want to help?"

"Cookies?" Bea stood up and let Mom help her down to the floor. "What kind of cookies? The ones with white frosting in the middle?"

They chattered as they left the bedroom. "No. These are homemade."

"Homemade?"

The voices trailed off, leaving the bedroom very quiet. Just Mark and Katty.

She stepped close to the bed and smiled. "Are you sure?" She fingered the sparkly ring on her left hand. "Your mom saw it. I know she did. She … it was hers, wasn't it? I can give it back—"

Mark held out his only unbroken arm. "She's the one who gave it to me. And if you don't want it, like in if you want your own that nobody else wore, I'll buy it for you. Just your own."

Katty jerked, her face startled. She shook her head. "No. No." She held her hand out and looked at the ring. "I love it. I love the fact that it was your mom's and … dad's." She gently leaned into his one-armed hug and softly kissed his mouth. She was so close. Touching her was all he'd ever wanted to do. Openly touch her, love her and now … he could.

He kissed her back.

"Look! They're kissing."

Mom shushed Bea. "We need to come back. Give them some time."

"No. No. Come in." Mark stretched his arm to them. "Don't leave."

Bea climbed up on the bed again. "Are you going to married Mommy?"

The question. Mark had wanted to ask that question for so

long, or it seemed like a long time. He knew he'd asked Katty in
… the closet, but here was Bea.

He cupped Bea's side of her face in his one hand. "Bea. Look
at me." Those beautiful brown eyes looked directly into his.
Those long black lashes. Her pure skin. "Is it okay if I marry
your mom?"

Bea became very quiet.

Oh, no. Had he misjudged her? Mistaken—

Bea sat up very straight, her head held high. "Mr. Mark
Depdy, Sir, you can marry Mommy only if you marry me, too."
Her little chin quivered, her mouth puckered. "Please." She
glanced at Katty, who was crying. Mom was crying.

Mark couldn't stop from crying. "Yes. Bea." He sniffed.
"Will you marry me, too?" He brushed the curly hair away from
her face. Oh, dear Lord Jesus. How could he be so blessed? This
little one.

Katty was to be his wife and Bea his daughter.

Mom had stepped away, presumably to give them some
space. Mark held out his other arm to her and waved her closer.

Back to Bea. "Will you? Will you marry me, Bea?"

Bea nodded in between sobs. "Yes. Mr. Depdy, Sir."

Mark pulled her down on his chest—pain or no pain—and
held her close. Very few times had he allowed himself to pick
her up, hug her, hold her. He'd always tried to restrain himself—
especially on the job.

But here.

Now.

He would never hold back again.

FORTY

Phil mumbled. "Stop hitting me." Somewhere in his brain rattled around pictures of little kids hitting him on the head. Little kids. Big kids. All colors of kids. All ages. "Stop! Stop hitting me. That hurts." Then right in front of them all was Bea. "Bea! Stop it. That hurts." They giggled. Laughed. They didn't care.

It did.

It hurt.

Then Dad joined the kids and boxed his ears in. "Listen to me, Phil. Ya gotta do what I say."

Phil knew what that meant. The clan was gonna meet tonight and Phil was to gather in the victims. Search the neighborhood for strays. Stray anything. Cats. Dogs. Snakes were the best. Even worms would do if he couldn't find anything else.

Bam! "Ow! Dad. I'll go. I'll find something."

Oh, what a headache. His ears throbbed. His whole head throbbed. He must have tied one on last night. Bad booze. Bad drugs. It'd happened before. Never this bad, though. Must have gotten into one hell of a fight … and lost.

"Coverage of the prison break." Some news show on … TV?

"Warden, can you tell us how this could have happened? Many visitors and staff could have died."

Phil swallowed. Damn Warden. "Yes, it was difficult to let it go to the level that it did, but we needed to flesh out as many of the leaders as possible." Yeah. Him. "We needed to draw the ringleaders out, to squash this evil for all time."

"That's impossible." Phil mumbled. "Never squash out the evil."

Someone snickered.

What?

Click. What? Where was he? Someone turned off the TV? Or whatever that was.

Even opening his eyes hurt. He tried to pull at whatever was wrapped around his head, only his arms wouldn't work. Only one eye opened. The other one seemed to be covered up.

He started to raise up.

"I need to move around. I gotta get to the bathroom." He started to move his foot to stand up, but he couldn't budge it. Something rattled. He tried to reach up and rip the covering off his head. He still couldn't move his hands.

A hand reached up and pulled off the covering. Phil screamed. "Ow. Ow! That hurt." The covering was all bloody and nasty.

With his eyes uncovered, he saw why he couldn't move his legs. They were shackled to the bed. "Why am I locked to the … bed?"

His eyes caught sight of a man at the foot of the … bed. "Why am I in bed? We were … we escaped." The man was holding a gun. "Didn't we?" He caught sight of another man beside a door. Another one on both sides of the bed. Two more by the window. All carried guns. Every one of them was dressed like a swat team. Armored.

He tried to raise his arm, but both hands were handcuffed to the rails of the bed. The handcuffs were like none he'd ever seen before. A little green light blinked and tiny buttons lit up. Like a high-tech combination lock on handcuffs? He held one up to the closest guard. "What's this?"

The door opened, and an enormous man stepped inside the room. Huge man. Long, black hair. Built. Muscular. The man removed his sunglasses, folded them into his chest pocket, and crossed his massive arms across his chest.

Just stared at Phil.

"What is all this? Why am I here?"

"You don't remember?"

Each guard turned to face Phil, guns trained on him.

"What … what're they doing? They can't do that." The room blurred. "What's happening? My eyes. I can't see right."

The guards aimed and fired.

Phil screamed. "Don't shoot. Don't kill me."

He couldn't stop screaming until he realized that what they were shooting was confetti. Streams and streams of colored paper and sparkles of glitter.

"What the? What are you doing?" Phil screamed and rambled. "This is crazy. You can't do this. Let me go. Unlock these—"

One by one, each guard removed his helmet.

Phil gasped. Their glaring yellow eyes pierced him. Matted hair hung down to the shoulders. Dirty skin looked like rotting, dried-up flesh.

They each resumed firing the guns, hitting every part of Phil's body. He looked down, but the confetti and glitter had morphed into tiny, black insects that immediately crawled all over his body. Stinging. Biting.

"Ow! Ow. No. Stop."

He was in some sort of terrible nightmare.

A bad dream.

This couldn't be real … could it?

"You've got to get ready! You're getting married in … " Noell checked her phone, "Two hours!"

Katty dropped the paintbrush and stared at the wall. She'd just finished painting her own wedding, cake and all. Never had she been so tuned into the spirit and right now she guessed, God. What? Who? The Holy Spirit? She didn't understand all that.

All she knew was someone else had been in Gamma's closet with her just now, painting the beautiful scene on the wall before her.

The hand had appeared holding a loaded paintbrush just as her own hand loaded paint from the paint set. Mark bought her a new, upgraded set of paints—a set intended for adult use instead of children. They had been in hard use for the last couple of weeks. As Katty held her hand to the wall, the hand painted alongside. Whenever Katty changed colors, the hand did too … somehow. The same color was always on that mysterious brush at the same time Katty changed her paint color.

"Mommy." Bea stepped carefully inside the closet with Noell. "So pretty." She sincerely didn't want to mess up her beautiful white wedding dress, but always wanted to rush inside the door to see what Katty had painted. Bea picked up the skirt to her dress and stepped closer.

"Careful Bea." Noell was in charge today. "We don't have time to get another dress for you." She slid down against the back wall as she allowed the painting to draw her in and mesmerize her. She reached for Bea and pulled her down onto her lap. Both were careful where the skirt of Bea's dress landed.

"See?" Bea pointed. "There's me." She rustled her new dress. "I can tell because it's the same dress as what I have on." Her head popped up to Katty. "Right, Mom?"

Katty found it hard to pull out of the realm she had been in when she painted that wall. When she painted any of them, for that matter. She glanced around the magical closet that had morphed into a room with many more walls than an actual room should have. All painted. Whenever she needed a new surface to paint, a new wall appeared. The hand appeared. There was always more than enough paint for what she or what she and the hand needed.

Quiet.

No one moved or spoke. Hardly breathed. Such a precious and holy hush.

Noell jumped and checked her phone. "We have to go get ready!"

"I'm ready." Bea patted her chest and the skirt to her dress.

"Yes. And let's get you out of here without getting paint all over your beautiful wedding dress. Okay?" Noell lifted her up and over the floor inside the closet, onto the floor inside Gamma's bedroom. "Good job. Now go on inside the room and I'll get up and try to pull your mom away to get the bride ready."

Bea jumped. "I forgot my basket." She rushed into the closet, swishing her dress.

Noell leaped, trying to prevent a terrible accident from happening this close to wedding time. She picked up Bea's basket and Bea all in one swoop and stood her up inside

Gamma's bedroom. "I think dish soap might take the paint out." She twirled Bea to inspect the dress. "She didn't get anything on it." She glanced up and Katty, then back to Bea. "I would have bet there was gonna be paint on it."

Katty still sat hypnotized by the painting. The bride and groom were at the center, surrounded by candles and angels and babies and clouds. Greenery created a backdrop. A beautiful Light rose from within the bride and groom, illuminating it all. Bea and a strange little boy held hands behind the bride and groom.

Huh.

Who was the little boy?

Noell reached down and pulled Katty upright. They stood, arms around each other's waists, caught in the mystery of the painting once again. "I don't know how you do it, Katty. You paint the exact likeness of you and Mark, especially. So amazing to paint free-hand so accurately." She pointed. "And Bea, too. And that little boy is so cute … but what … who is he?"

Bea rushed back into the closet. "Boy is gonna be at the wedding? Where?" She bounced, brushing her skirt against the wet paint. "Where is Boy?"

Noell grabbed her and checked her skirt. "Nothing. I don't understand it. She actually touched the wet paint with her dress and now there's nothing." She looked up at Katty. "How can that be? I saw her skim it against the wet paint." She cautiously touched the wall and held up her finger. "See? It's still wet." She stood Bea back into the bedroom, carefully keeping her finger away from Bea's dress. "Okay girls. We've got to get dressed." She looked at Bea and grinned. "Well, Mommy has to get dressed."

Bea giggled and pointed. "You have to get dressed, too, Noell."

One more glance at the wall. Deep sigh.

Unbelievable. It was Katty's wedding day.

Another sigh.

Noell pulled Katty up off the floor and hugged her. Katty was tired, sleepy, but all it took was Noell hugging her to wake her up and get her excited.

"It's your wedding day!" Noell screamed.

That. That was all it took for Katty to really embrace the day. To get excited.

"Come on Bea. Help me do my hair and make-up." Noell dragged Bea out of the room. They had set up what they were calling a Pamper Room in the dining room. They never used it for dining. So no harm done now in spreading out hair spray, curling irons, make-up and anything else thought of for beauty-making, all over the table and some on the floor.

Noell inspected Bea. "You need a little blush here. And a tiny bit of lipstick on your pretty lips." She smacked her lips together as she applied the lipstick.

"Not too much." Katty grinned from inside the bedroom, imagining those two smacking lips at each other. She stepped out of her shorts and T-shirt and breathed. She was nervous for sure. Excited for the day to really start. Still breathing in the power of painting the scene of her wedding. Stepping into the closet once again, she viewed the painting.

It was indeed beautiful. Beautiful twinkly lights had been sprinkled all over the scene. She gasped. She hadn't done that.

"Noell. Come here."

"What? Need help to zip up?" Noell glanced into the bedroom. "You're not are you? You have to get ready." Then she spied the painting. "When did you paint all of those pretty lights?"

"Lights?" Bea scampered into the bedroom and on into the closet. She blinked, looked up at Katty, then back to the painting. "Those lights. Those are angels, Mommy. Like when they 'peared in the car those times. 'Member?"

Katty blew out a breath. "I do remember, Bea." She leaned

over and picked her up. "You think they are angels, though? How'd you know that?" She shuddered. "I honestly didn't paint those." She shook her head. "Any of them. How did they get there?" She had experienced the hand painting alongside her own hand. Magical. Mysterious. Miraculous. Could this be the same? Goosebumps skittered across her bare skin.

"The angels were here, I think. And Boy told me that's what they are. He should know. He's an angel. He knows all about them … what their names are and … how they fly." So grown-up. So matter-of-fact. "He tells me stuff."

Katty checked Noell's face quickly. She wanted to laugh. She wanted to cherish the moment. She didn't want Bea to think that she didn't believe her. But, angels? "Well, I do remember all those pretty lights in the car with us. It always helped. It always felt more peaceful when we saw them."

The three of them paused.

"Katty. Get dressed! We haven't done your hair. Thank God you did your make-up." Noell took Bea from Katty, set her down, and watched Katty put on her wedding gown. She turned her around and zipped it up.

Bea helped—kind of.

"I have to go potty." Bea pulled on Noell's arms.

"Okay. Let's go." Into the bathroom they went.

They chattered and giggled. They were in the small bathroom off of Gamma's bedroom—so close. But the voices became a blur, buzzing, blending together.

Thoughts of yesterday afternoon with Mrs. T at the nursing home flitted through Katty's mind and layered over Bea's giggles and Noell's voice, as she checked herself in the mirror. She'd never had a beautiful dress like the one reflecting back to her. Clarence had made sure she found the right one and paid for it himself.

Goosebumps traveled up her arms, like someone was skimming up and down with their hands. Like it was real.

She felt so pretty, and she wasn't sure she'd ever felt that way. Time with Mrs. T yesterday had opened up a whole new and wonderful realm of being a woman. Mrs. T had told her things—things about being a woman in the physical, but also about the spiritual and emotional.

Katty knew that if Gamma was still here on this earth, she would have told her the same things as Mrs. T. Huh. Maybe Gamma had been with them.

Katty had no idea how all that worked … the spiritual stuff. But because of Mrs. T's prayers over her yesterday, Katty felt beautiful—not pretty—but beautiful in a way that she'd never known.

"Clarence is here!" Noell called out. "Time for this wedding to begin!"

One last check. Hair, done. Make-up done. Earrings from Clarence—diamonds. *Breathe*. Left hand beautiful ring from Mark—check. And Phyllis—check.

Breathe. Check.

Should have practiced. Should have worn this dress around the house—well, maybe just … so much emotion.

Can't cry. Can't cry.

Clarence was here. Clarence.

No crying.

As Katty stepped into the dining room, Clarence walked into the room from the front enclosed porch. He was dressed regally —almost like a king might—in a white tuxedo jacket over his usual Led Zeppelin T-shirt. Katty chuckled and then marveled. He was now over eighty years old, but carried himself like an athlete or … a king might. Bea was the first person his eyes seemed to land on. He stopped, his hands flew to cover his mouth, then he held his arms wide to embrace her.

Bea giggled shyly. She'd never done that before. Never been shy before.

Katty knew Bea felt pretty in her own wedding dress of

white. White because she was pure. A pretty cropped white sweater trimmed with pearls over the dress. Her hair was up in a knot that only Noell could have created.

Noell.

Noell stood to the side, enjoying Clarence and Bea and the sweetness of the moment. She was stunning herself in her bridesmaid dress of the lightest pink. Long flowing skirt and close-fitted bodice with short sleeves. Her long, blond hair swirled in chunks around her shoulders and waist, with tiny light pink ribbons woven throughout her hair. She blotted at her eyes and realized Katty was watching her.

A stream of divine love flowed between them—between Noell and Katty. They had started off badly, but only because they had both been hurting from past experiences. But over time —time that now connected them to each other—they had become deeply attached to each other. Cousins, yes. But more than that. Sisters. Family.

Making those ribbons with Noell and Bea had been a highlight of getting things ready for the wedding. They wove Bea's ribbons around a headband, so maybe it might stay on at least during the wedding. The dance afterward? Maybe not. Didn't matter.

Bea giggled again, and Katty realized that Clarence had set Bea down and had glimpsed Katty.

Tears streamed down his weathered tan cheeks. Those blue, blue eyes. He was weeping.

"No. No." Katty swallowed, her hand at her chest. "Don't make me cry."

He slowly walked toward Katty, his arms out wide, tears running freely. "I never used to let myself cry when I was in prison. I'd tell myself not to cry. Inmates would beat a guy up if he'd cry. So I got in the habit of holding it in." He stopped right in front of her. "Until I met you." He turned to point at Bea. "And you."

Noell picked Bea up and swayed with her in her arms. Like a momma rocking her baby.

Babies swirled around them.

Clarence embraced Katty. His aftershave would always be her favorite.

Maybe.

FORTY-TWO

"She remembered." Jasper smiled at Jerahmael. "They both remembered. I thought you might be crazy for adding those lights on the painting."

Jerahmael laughed. "If Katty wouldn't have remembered, Bea for sure would have." He patted Boy's head. "Or this guy would remind Bea. Right Boy?"

Boy seemed to be in another world—even different from the invisible world that angels and demons usually dwelt in. "Doesn't Mommy look pretty?"

They all gazed toward the entrance of the nursing home as Clarence drove up. He hopped out and ran around to help first Noell and Bea out of the car. He held out his arm to them. Only Bea couldn't reach it, so they clasped hands as he escorted them to the door.

Then he rushed back to the car and opened the back door for Katty. As she stood up and brushed the skirt of her gown, she glanced at Clarence, then at the nursing home building and the surrounding area. She even seemed to glance at the park.

A quiet hush fell over the angels positioned all around the grounds and inside the building. The moment Katty stood, they all sensed the fact that a queen in the kingdom had arrived and she partly sensed the change herself.

Angels had been summoned in from every league, every realm, each and every position. Each one lined up along the border of the nursing home property. Even Jasper was in awe at the sight of them. Each huge being was dressed differently, but in elegant clothes of every color. In robes that flowed in an unseen breeze. In never before seen armor that had protected in every battle known to the invisible world. Badges of honor, medals won, crowns earned and cast at the throne of The Ever Living One.

Jasper loved the pageantry so on display. "Mrs. T did a good job of praying in protection." But he knew it was minimal in comparison to what was presented daily in heaven.

Clarence said something to her, and she nodded and smiled.

Boy ran out before the angels could stop him. "Mommy! You are so beautiful."

Katty seemed to stop and listen. She shook her head and let Clarence walk her up to the entrance door.

Boy slumped.

"Oh-oh." Jasper leaned over to Boy. "She heard you in her heart."

"No, she didn't. You're just trying to make me feel better." Boy turned to look at Katty and wiped one eye. "I wish she knew. I wish …." He brightened. "At least Bea sees me."

They nodded with him.

Bea waved at them. Noell, confused, shook her head. Maybe someday.

The music started. People from the town, residents from the nursing home, and staff had all begun to gather. Even though it was at the nursing home, the decorations were just beautiful.

"It seems like a church." Jerahmael wondered.

"Better than a church." Jasper bowed low as Michael entered the space.

This warrior commander angel entered, grinning and laughing with the others. He winked as he walked past Jasper and Jerahmael. "You get to escort the queen. Joyous occasion." He leaned into Jasper. "Well done, my friend." He glanced behind him as Katty and Clarence entered the dining hall. "Never, never, never give up. The Ever-living One has the victory!"

Others near him heard his declaration and repeated it, louder. "God has the victory!"

Jasper laughed. "See what you started? It took generations to get them quieted when Joshua defeated Jericho!" He shook his head. "But then that's what you intended for today. Am I right, Commander?"

Michael only grinned as he stepped into position.

Jerahmael poked Jasper. "Isn't that Noell's Gamma, right there? Holding Boy's hand?" Many beings and humans overlapped several realms. A beautiful sight to see, for sure.

"I believe it is." He knew. Such a grand woman of God.

Boy waved. Ah, Boy.

The minister stepped forward, and a shout broke out from the armies of angels. For Mark, their hero took his position beside the minister. Angels and beings raised their weapons. A shout went up again. Many of the warriors were men of old who fought alongside King David, but who lived in many realms and generations.

Jasper nodded. "Those men of old." He knelt as they strutted past, their leather cloaks covered polished armor over robes of rich golds, blues, and purples. Several carried small shields, daggers sheathed to wide leather belts, and pouches hung across their shoulders. Always ready for battle. Many battles had been fought alongside those warriors.

Many did not understand their origin. Humans here at this joining of Katty and Mark did not understand the importance and significance of this union and the victory that had been won. For the victory that had been won for every son of God.

Flags flew atop rods. The breeze that moved them was the literal breath of God. The posts were raised high upon the stone cathedral and castle bearing colors of gold, but every color known to the Kingdom of God.

Jerahmael laughed and pointed. "Hey. Look at Bea's skirt. We should reveal that. Humans are seeing it as clean and pure white. But we see it as colorful … beautiful."

"You're gonna get her in trouble." Jasper folded his arms across his chest.

"Boy will stand up for her. He'll protect her."

They nodded in unison and a Light shone on the skirt, revealing a rich rainbow of colors in the human realm. No one noticed because people were lining up. They would, though, soon.

Recorded music filled the dining hall as Clarence stepped in the aisle alongside Mrs. T with her walker. Arm in arm.

"It hasn't been that long since those two married, has it?" Jasper grinned. "I mean in earth years."

Jasper nodded. "She is one amazing Pillar in the Kingdom."

Every being in the Kingdom bowed low as she walked past. Clarence grinned and wiped his face repeatedly, his head held high. He might not know her like the angels knew her, but he also realized that she was the second love of his life—the first being Annie. Two chances at love.

A shout went up from the spectators. "He's here!"

Jesus.

Every knee bent as He entered the dining hall. Even a couple of humans could tell something big was happening, even if they didn't bow.

"He's here!" Boy knelt and dragged Bea to her knees, as well.

"What? Who?" Bea checked around her. "Clarence?"

Jesus was all in white robes with an ordinary brown sash and pouch over his body. Simple. No weapons. A smiling face as all the attention turned to worship Him. He shook his head, still grinning, and pointed down the aisle toward where the wedding couple would stand.

Clarence returned to the back of the room after escorting his wife to her seat at the front. The music soared. He grinned as he looked to where Katty stood.

Mark stepped next to his mom and held out his arm to her. She was already in tears. Wiping her cheeks, she shook her head. "I knew I'd never make it to the end." She almost whispered. "This is just like I saw in my dream." She leaned over and kissed his cheek. "I love you, Son."

A group of angels followed the two up the aisle. They had their own escorts. They stopped at her seat. She embraced him and kissed him again. Wiped it off and sat down.

Mark hesitated, looked to the front at the minister, then turned and walked to the back where Katty's mom, Louise, stood in all her glory.

Angels had checked each person as they entered the dining hall and had restrained tiny demons back outside. None allowed in the holy place set aside for Mark and Katty's wedding.

Mark held out his arm to her as a gentleman should and she did her best to make him uncomfortable with the way she leaned close to him and the way she had dressed. He was doing his duty nevertheless, and seated her across the aisle from his own mother.

"Good job." Jasper whispered to Rael, Mark's guardian. "Well done." They hugged each other and pounded each other's backs. "Well done."

Jasper watched as Rael followed Mark to the front. He towered over poor short Mark—but then he towered over everyone here. He had been appointed to stand guard with and for Mark. A true warrior indeed.

No one could see but the angels, as tiny baby angels flew up and around Katty, draping a beautiful veil over her that completely covered her all around, clear to the floor. The babies giggled and rearranged the veil. The veil was semi-see through but sprinkled with tiny lights and color splotches all over it. Beautiful.

"I like it," chuckled Jasper to Jerahmael. "It suits her, don't you think?"

Jerahmael seemed mesmerized. He blinked and nodded. "The artist in her would want that, I'm sure." He smiled. "Perfect."

FORTY-THREE

Clarence stood still for a minute, staring at Katty. But she could tell. He'd looked at her many times over the year, in many different ways—from disgust to lovingkindness to whatever this was.

Katty knew.

This was the love of a father, a grandfather.

Tears wet both his cheeks. Someone slipped him a handkerchief. Who? Oh, dear Harold. But he was crying, too.

"Stop it, you two." Katty wanted to burst. This was true love from men who wanted nothing from her. They adored her.

And Bea.

Bea looked beautiful. Her little white dress ... huh? She might have already gotten it dirty, but Katty wasn't one to call her out for it. Katty liked getting dirty herself. Only ... this wasn't dirt. "Bea?"

But she started up the aisle, seemingly floated with ... it almost seemed like her arm was bent as it would be if she had an escort. She didn't, though. But—

"She's walking funny, isn't she?" Clarence stepped next to Katty. "Is she okay?"

Katty nodded. "I think so." Angels? Bea was always talking about angels. Could it be true? Little stinker made a big deal of throwing rose petals all the way down the aisle. She kept changing hands to hold the basket. Some petals flew into the air without her moving her arm. What?

Clarence chuckled as he stepped beside her. "She's really getting into that. Kinda seemed like she has help—like the petals jump into the air for joy, all by themselves."

Katty laughed. She guessed that was it. The petals jumped for joy, right out of the basket. A quick blink of a vision of when she had been in Gamma's closet painting this scene and it had been just as magical as Bea now tossing the petals and when she put her arm down to grab more out of her basket, some flew in the air by … themselves. Just as magical.

Clarence checked her face and wiped a tear off her cheek. "Katty, my daughter, my own. You look beautiful."

She felt every word. Every word he said, the way he looked at her. She peeked down the aisle at where Mark was standing. The way Mark looked at her now, the way he kissed her. Oh, stop, Katty. Her face was hot. No. Not now.

Noell stepped in front of them. "Where's Guy?"

"What?" Katty had all but forgotten about the best man. "Oh no! He must have gotten called to duty somewhere."

Clarence stepped next to Noell. "I can walk you down and come right back for Katty."

Just as they stepped out, Guy rushed in—full dress cop uniform—and took Noell's arm. "I guess this is where I'm supposed to be, right?" He seemed unusually nervous as he wiped perspiration off his forehead.

"Good job, buddy. Right on time." Clarence patted him on the back. "You did good."

They stepped in time down the aisle, beautiful. She, tiny and very blond. Him, huge and muscular and dark-skinned.

"Too bad he's married." Katty whispered as Stephanie, his

wife, slipped in the back with their two kids. She waved and shook her head.

"It's okay. Glad you made it." Katty turned back to Clarence. "I didn't even realize he was late or even if he was coming."

Clarence choked. "Bride's privilege." Noell and Guy had reached the front and stepped on either side of Mark and the minister, turned around and faced them.

The music soared again. Whoever was doing the music was doing a great. Seemed to know when to tone it down and make it louder.

"Your turn, Mommy." Bea, from up front, dropped her basket and clapped her hands. "You are so pretty."

The entire room erupted in laughter.

"Shall we?" Clarence kissed Katty and took a step.

"No. No." She backed away a step. "I can't. I … "

"I remember way back my first time. And again with Mrs. T." He shook his head, incredulous. "I got a second chance." Shook his head again. "I wanted to run. But just keep your eyes on Mark now."

Katty looked up front. Mark was fidgeting, too. But he was smiling. Waiting. Almost bowed slightly.

"Keep your eyes on him and you'll be fine."

She took a step.

Clarence took another step.

She stepped forward one more.

Soon, they both stepped together.

Those green eyes.

"Good job. He's a good man. And you are a good woman with little Bea and more to come."

"I hope—"

They stopped, facing the minister. "Dearly Beloved. We gather together in the Presence of Jesus Christ, our Lord and all of these blessed witnesses to join together—"

She didn't hear another word until, "Who gives this woman …?"

"I do." Clarence turned her toward him, kissed her through the veil, and embraced her. Oh, his hugs. They held on for a minute longer, pulled apart, and gazed into each other's eyes. Every moment that Clarence had been there for her flashed through her memory. Like someone in heaven had started her memory scroll of every time he had helped her, stopped her from doing stupid, held her and adopted her.

And now, she turned to Mark. So many more memories flashed through. Times when he'd been sent to arrest her. She'd been so drunk. Funny, not funny. He'd always been kind and respectful. He'd saved her art wall—fought her to do that. Those green eyes and dark lashes.

This had to be a dream.

And it was until Mark said, "I do."

The minister paused. Everyone stared at her. "Oh!" She blinked. "I do."

"You may kiss the bride!"

Applause broke out. Shouts of joy burst out. Bea jumped up and down, clapping her hands. "Good job, Mommy. Good job, Mr. Mark, Depdy, Sir."

Mark laughed, lifted her veil, grinned, and kissed her.

Again. And again.

The music started again for them to march out, but Mark stopped it. "Please. I'm sorry. Please. There's something I must do to complete this marriage."

People in the back shushed others, and the room quieted.

"Uh, I'm sorry, but there's something … er, someone I have to …" He blew out a breath and blinked. He leaned down to Bea, knelt on one knee beside her, and reached for her hand.

Bea had never had an embarrassed minute in her life. She had never acted shy like she was now. "What Mr.Depdy—"

"That."

"What?"

He reached inside his coat and pulled out a tiny box.

She watched him intently.

He opened it and showed it to her. "I married Mommy today, but will you marry me too? Will you let me be your Daddy?"

Her expression changed from confusion to wonder. "My Daddy?" She looked up at Katty, her eyes wide. Back to Mark. "My Daddy?" Her chin quivered. It finally must have sunk in. She whispered it, almost trying it out. "My Daddy." Back to Mark. "I don't have to call you Mr. Depdy Mark Scott, Sir, anymore? I just get to call you … Daddy?"

He nodded and wiped his face with his coat sleeve.

Bea giggled. "Okay."

Mark whooped, dropped the box, and scooped Bea up in his arms.

The whole dining hall broke out in applause and laughter. Oo's and ah's.

Somehow, the box got picked up and handed to Mark.

"Thanks Boy." Bea hugged Mark's neck and let out a wail.

Mark jumped and held her out so he could see her face. "What's the matter? What's wrong?"

"I'm so happy."

Katty couldn't take her eyes off Mark. Who was this man? He was the angel. She whispered, "Thank You Jesus."

Mark heard her. "Yes. Thank You, Jesus." He pulled Katty into his arms with Bea still hugging his neck.

Hands patted her back, Mark's and Bea's. People gathered and hugged and cried. Clarence. Phyllis. Mrs. T.

Mom stepped forward, but paused just shy of touching anyone. Something was weird. She looked the same, a trashy, revealing dress, too much skin, top and bottom. But something was different.

She stepped up to Katty, looked her up and down, smiled, and opened her mouth.

Mark put his arm around Katty's waist and pulled her close again. He leaned into her, almost in front of her, blocking Mom.

That didn't stop Mom from being her abusive self. "You're still a—"

Katty cleared her throat, kept Mark's arm around her waist, but stepped forward, facing her mom. "There is nothing you can say to me that will hurt me. This is my wedding day. And if you can't be happy for me, then … then be gone."

Mom jerked her head, her shoulders back, her chest out. "You can't do that. I'm your mom." Her chin jutted out, her eyes squinted.

Phyllis stepped in and greeted Mom. "Won't you join me at the cake table? It looks yummy."

Mom resisted until Sheriff Dennison helped guide her away.

Katty, Bea, and Mark were in their own little dream world. They still heard words, people laughing and visiting. Mark set Bea down and pulled the tiny box from his pocket again. He knelt before Bea and opened it. Inside was a fragile necklace with a golden cross hanging from it. He removed it and held it out to Bea. "Turn around and let me put it on, okay?"

Bea stared at it a long time, then up to Mark's face, nodding. As soon as he clasped it around her neck and she turned to face him, she turned into a young lady. She patted the necklace on her chest and stood straighter. "What if I break it … Daddy?" She almost curtsied, bowed her head. Who was this child?

He cupped her cheek in his hand. "You won't."

"Mrs. B, it's time for your meds. Let go back to your room." The nurse maneuvered her wheelchair around guests.

There was cake. Punch. Cookies.

The music changed from wedding music to dance music.

Clarence gently steered Mrs. T to dance. So sweet. No walker.

Guy swooped Stephanie into his arms. What a beautiful couple. Their kids followed behind.

Mark, Katty and Bea stood together. People greeted them.

Noell danced with her neighbor … Fletcher? Were they?

Katty shook her head. Everybody should be in love today.

Bea giggled every once in a while. Were the angels dancing? Was that why she laughed?

Mark tapped Katty's arm. "What's … or who … Bea seems to hold someone's hand." Mark checked Katty's face. "What's—"

"Get used to it."

Let the wedding feast begin.

FORTY-FOUR

The judge almost growled. "I hate it when I see familiar faces in my courtroom again and again." He shook his head and slammed the gavel down.

Bam!

Katty jumped at the sound. She'd never been in front of this judge and she was also immediately glad she hadn't been. Glad she wasn't Phil today. This guy might be just the one to dish out what Phil deserved. Why did these things, these court cases, take so long to happen? She would have crucified Phil the very day of the insurrection instead of six months later.

She peeked behind her as the people from the earlier case walked out. More people filed in from the back, lugging cameras and notebooks. No. The media? Clarence slipped in beside her, patting her hand, then her belly.

"So glad you're here." She grabbed his hand.

"Me too. Looks like a circus already." He stretched to scan the room. "Sorry I'm late. Mrs. T stopped me to … well, you know."

Katty smiled and nodded. To pray. Thankful. She needed it. Thankful for Noell. She had wanted to be here for support, too, but she decided she and Bea hadn't been to Mrs. Gelda's in a long time. Hot chocolate called to them. If Bea had figured out where her mom was right now, she might have followed just to pound on Phil again.

Mark stood behind the last row of seating. He stood erect, straight, and tall. He caught her eye and winked. Then back to business. His new uniform was pressed and emphasized his muscles. A person couldn't even tell he'd broken his arm or leg. He still limped. She blew out a breath and eyed her ring. Her face felt hot. She'd heard that pregnant women had hot flashes. The ring, their marriage, and the rising bump on her belly all felt like a dream.

Back to today. Mark was one of the deputies serving in the courtroom today, along with Sheriff Dennison and Guy and two new ones. Who was running the department with Chantelle? Katty realized, since she had spent more time with the woman, that Chantelle didn't need anyone to protect her. She was one tough woman. Katty's heart warmed. She loved Chantelle.

As she faced the front, she pulled her sweater closer around her shoulders. From hot flash to cold chills. Didn't they heat this place? No one else seemed cold.

Katty jumped when she felt a hand on her shoulder. Her other shoulder. Clarence had his arm around her and patted her. She breathed in deeply of his aftershave. He was warm.

"Glad Bea didn't have to come." Clarence whispered.

Must be time.

Sheriff Dennison gathered the papers that the judge passed to him. Thankful for the sheriff. The judge had demanded that Bea attend the proceedings, and the sheriff refused. That was a big deal—refusing the judge—considering the judge's demeanor today. Seemed like he would get his way in everything. But the Sheriff got his way.

"Bring in the prisoner, bound and gagged."

Bound and gagged?

Sheriff repeated what the judge just said, and a side door opened. Metal rattled and feet shuffled.

Immediately, a blast of cold air rushed into the courtroom. *Don't look. Don't look.* But she had to. They were halfway back, so she didn't have to crane her neck, but she kept her head down. As Phil and his deputy guards entered, Clarence pulled her closer. She hadn't realized it, but she had tensed.

"You're trembling." Clarence grasped her closest hand.

Phil shuffled into the room with shackles on his legs and feet and handcuffs, pulling his hands behind his back. A weirdly medieval mask covered his mouth, with leather straps locking behind his head.

Katty gasped. Others behind her gasped. He had no ears. She'd done that. She'd ripped one off and shot the other one. He growled as his eyes met hers for a split second. She leaned deeper into Clarence and glanced his direction. Yes, Phil's lack of ears, but could the other people see the mask?

The judge himself was wide-eyed, but quickly shut his surprise down.

Deputies pushed Phil right up to the judge's bench. His lawyer shoved his chair back and hustled to stand beside his client. "We have a trial. This man is innocent until proven guilty."

The judge stared at the lawyer until he backed down.

"Do you see a jury here?"

The lawyer glanced behind him. "Uh. No. But my client deserves a fair trial."

"From what I've read of his record, he doesn't deserve air. What he has dished out over these last what," he checked his files, "ten years or more? Fifteen years? What he's dealt his family, his child?" He glanced up at Katty.

Someone growled. The deputy yanked on Phil's arm.

She squirmed. She couldn't get any closer to Clarence than she already was. The judge wasn't going to call her up there, was he? She glanced over at Clarence and he shook his head without breaking eye contact with the judge. Deep breath.

He pounded the gavel down, making the whole courtroom full of people jump. "I declare this man, Phil Daynton, guilty of first-degree sexual assault, domestic violence assault, attempted kidnapping with intent to abuse and harm, prison breakout, and murder."

Something shifted. The courtroom blurred. Was that smoke? Had someone started a fire in the courthouse? She rubbed her eyes.

The judge was still there, but there was another judge right beside him, holding up a golden gavel, ready to pound it down at the same time. This judge had on white robes and a crown on his head. Was … was that God? They spoke the same words at the same time. "I strip this man of all parental rights." Someone added, "In the name of Jesus Christ."

Again, both judges glanced at Katty. "Katelyn Randolph Scott is absolved of any charges made against her." Someone added, "For all time."

Katty blinked.

"Phil Daynton will serve time in prison until hell freezes over."

Silence.

Who said that? The earthly judge stared at the one with a crown. Could they see each other? Was this really happening?

Two gavels slammed down.

Bam!

Two angels stood and yelled, "Court adjourned!"

The smoke dissipated and Guy was left standing alone beside the stenographers desk, looking like he'd just seen a ghost. Well, he might have just seen the angels.

Was all that her imagination? Strange things had been happening the last year or so. Gamma's closet was still part of her everyday life.

The guards turned Phil to push him out. His eyes met Katty's. They were wide, and he appeared to be in shock. What had *he* seen? He couldn't walk. He had no ears. He stumbled as they tried to steer him out the door. He seemed to be five men— all stumbling and tripping.

The other deputies, Mark included, rushed to escort Phil out.

And there they were.

Mark in full-dress cop uniform.

Phil in shackles.

Angels appeared in full angel dress. Wings stretched up and out.

Clarence leaned in as he and Katty stood up. "You seeing this? Am I crazy?"

Katty nodded. "Am I crazy?"

FORTY-FIVE

This was the real dream. A dream come true.

Katty breathed in as she shifted on the sofa. Surprisingly, her arms got tired. But she never tired of holding him.

Little Teddy was perfect. He had green eyes, as near as they could tell, since he was just days old. And his daddy's long dark eyelashes.

Perfect.

His little tuft of hair seemed golden. Perfect.

Tiny fingers. She opened the baby blanket. Tiny toes. Perfect.

A vision—memory maybe—of when she'd birthed Bea gut-punched her hard. By herself. In her car. She'd been drunk. Didn't have the presence of mind to find towels to wrap a baby in. Just rags she'd found in the trunk. She didn't remember inspecting Bea at all. It had been about her next fix, her next drink.

A tear slowly tracked down her cheek.

She moved her hand in such a way that her diamond sparkled. It was so beautiful. The sun caught it just right and beams of pure light burst out against the walls. So huge. There had been a time when she might have—no, would have—sold such a keepsake to buy booze or drugs. Back to Teddy. But at this moment in time, Katty realized that she would sell it for him —to feed and clothe him and Bea.

Oh, for such a time as this.

Bea walked into the room carrying Daryl & Dumpty books and sat down on the rocker. No surprise there. "Mommy, you're crying." She dropped the books, rushed to Katty's side, and kissed her cheek. She was still Bea: snarky, smarty pants, picky. But something had changed in her. Maybe having a daddy was it. Or having baby Teddy to play with, to take care of, to hold.

Maybe Katty had changed. She had, but—

Bea leaned over Teddy and breathed him in. "He always smells so good." She sniffed again and thought a minute. "He smells like Boy. Like angels."

Katty smiled. "Never, never, never stop talking about angels and all that stuff." She patted Bea's behind for emphasis. "Got it?"

Bea giggled. "Ok, Mommy." She leaned against Katty's shoulder and watched Teddy, touched his cheek. "He's so cute. So perfect." Back to Katty. "Was I that perfect when I was born?"

"Of course you were. You were beautiful." She lied. She didn't remember. *God help. Bea was perfect, wasn't she, God?*

A deep warmth filled her heart. Like every time she looked at Teddy. But now it was almost like God had answered that Bea had been perfect in every way. That He had been there when Bea was born.

Another tear.

"Knock, knock." The entrance door pushed open.

Bea hopped off the sofa and ran to the door. "Mr. ... Daddy!" She held up her arms to Mark.

He laughed as he put down the bags of groceries. "Mr. Daddy sounds okay. You can call me that." He rushed Bea and growled. "Just as long as it's Daddy, too!"

Bea squealed as Mark threw her in the air.

Katty checked Teddy. Not even a sound. He didn't move. It was like he had been here all his little life. Well, he had. Katty smiled.

"Help me put away the groceries, Bea. Okay?" Mark put her down and picked up a bag. "Can you carry that one for me? Show me how strong you are."

Bea picked it up, but peeked inside. "Daddy!" She screamed. "There's a jar of peanut butter in there." She lugged it along behind him. "Is that for me?"

He laughed out loud and gave Katty a look. "No other kid would be so excited about peanut butter, right?" He walked to Katty and leaned his head against hers, lingered there, and kissed her forehead. Then he kissed Teddy. "How's my little Teddy?" He choked up, then wiped his eyes. "I can't help it. He's real. He's ours."

"He is on both counts." She glanced down at Teddy, then up at Mark. "Bea said he smells like the angels."

Mark sat down beside Katty and looked at Bea. "Does he?"

Bea nodded. So solemn. "Just like Boy." She glanced at something on the sofa beside Katty. "Just like you." She cocked her head. "He says Teddy smells like heaven. That's what Boy said. He should know. He lives in heaven, I think."

Katty almost forgot to breathe. Who was this child called Bea?

Nobody said anything.

Bea got up and carried her bag into the kitchen. "Peanut butter ..."

Mark didn't say anything, got up, and sat back down. "She is gonna get along great with Mom."

Katty's turn to be silent. Maybe so. Maybe so. Bea now had a sweet—maybe pushy—grandma that Katty could count on to not mistreat Bea. Her own mom. Never. "She already does get along with your mom." Katty hesitated. "And that's just fine with me."

He kissed her, kissed Teddy, and went into the kitchen to help Bea. Their voices and laughter filtered into the living room, like butter on bread. Katty chuckled. Down to Teddy. "That's so funny. Like butter on bread." She thought a minute. "Like peanut butter and jelly, those two." She shook her head. Those joyous voices from the kitchen were like a warm blanket on a wounded and tired soul.

Phyllis. It must be hard to not be the only girl in Mark's life, like she had been. Now he had three girls. Katty knew Phyllis had been a big part in praying for her and Mark to be able to conceive a child. Katty had been so messed up internally.

Phyllis had prayed for them, with them.

Bea. Bea wanted a baby brother or sister so badly. She prayed every night for one. Her precious words to God ... so powerful from one so young. It had always been, "Jesus, please make a baby in Mommy's tummy. Please? I know You can do that. You made me inside Mommy's tummy."

But then, Mrs. T had taught Bea to pray. Whatever had been preventing Katty from getting pregnant—inside her—hadn't had a chance with Bea and Mrs. T praying. And Phyllis.

Thankful.

Something bounced behind her head.

Oh-oh. They didn't have cats, but Mark had commented just last night that he wondered if they had mice, because he had heard a sound in the bedroom. A mouse or bird outside?

Something bumped her arm from beside her ... from the side that Bea had looked at. The side when she had talked to ... Boy?

Breathe.

"B-boy?" Something bounced again. Beside her. Behind her head. On the other side. Behind Teddy.

What was going on? She could take ... Boy. Maybe. Even though she felt it was Bea's imagination, she still felt it was okay. He seemed okay, and Bea loved him.

"Mommy?"

Quiet.

"Mommy?"

Bea was still chattering in the kitchen. Mark answered her.

This wasn't—

"Mommy?"

God Almighty. Help. What was this? These were the voices from inside the trailer. When she was drunk. Not now.

Ever since they had moved in with Mark after their wedding, the voices had stopped. Katty had been sure that the voices were just a figment of her drunkenness.

But now.

Here. Here they were again. She wasn't drunk. She was sober. Had been for over a year? Two? Close to two?

Teddy stirred. Must be getting hungry. Again. She loved feeding him. Felt so close to him. Amazing she could make breast milk for him. Do something good for him.

Could that make up for her past? Could taking good care of Teddy, for birthing him, but feeding him. Giving of her own body for him. Could that make up for the abortions?

She'd had a dream last night. Hadn't told Mark. The only reason it wasn't a nightmare was because all the babies that had appeared in her paintings had been there. Laughing. Giggling. Loving her.

"Boy?" She stopped. "I don't know how to say this. I don't know how to do this. If this is even real. I can't even see you." She began again. "Can you forgive me for … a … aborting you?"

Something bounced against her, waking Teddy.

"Mommy! We love you, Mommy."

"W-we?" Katty sucked in a breath before she lost courage or before Mark and Bea came back in the room. "Boy?" She swallowed. "I'm sorry for … for aborting you." Tears streamed down her cheeks. "I want to love you." She looked down at little Teddy. "Just like I love him." *God help.* "I want to name you …

what was the old man's name? Nelly's husband." A thought dropped in. "No. Clarence. I name you Clarence." She wiped her cheek with her sleeve. "Is that okay?"

There was some kind of bouncing and commotion next to her that could not be explained except for a little boy—her little boy—bouncing for joy right next to her.

Katty could almost see him. He lunged at her, opened his arms wide, and hugged her.

No way.

Katty jumped and almost screamed, but caught herself in time. "And one more thing." Get it out while the chance is at hand. "I love you … Clarence. I love … you all."

There was such a ruckus around her. Bouncing. And … voices? Laughter? Giggles?

And of course Bea and Mark chose that moment to walk back into the room.

"Mommy!" *That* was Bea. "Mommy. The babies are here. They're bouncing." She dropped her sandwich, but didn't seem to care. Bea paused and appeared to listen. "She named you Clarence?" To Katty. "Mommy! Boy just said you named him Clarence!"

Katty barely nodded. Very freaked out. Very stirred.

"They're laughing." Bea stopped. "Boy said you named him Clarence!" She stopped, then screamed, clapping her hands. "Like *our* Clarence!"

Teddy's eyes popped open, but he didn't cry. His little chin puckered up, but he didn't cry. He just watched Bea bouncing up and down. And … maybe …

Mark looked like they were crazy, but Katty could tell he was trying not to laugh. Trying not to run out the front door—forever.

Were they crazy?

Bea was so excited—seeing all the babies and Boy there. "Mommy. My angel … and your angel. They're all here." She pointed. "One. Two. Three. Four. Wow. I can't. Well, I can count to one hundred. But. There's lots. A really big one behind Daddy. Lots of babies. Lots of angels. Mommy!" She stopped. "A new angel. Teddy's angel?"

"Bea."

Only Bea couldn't hear her. She was dancing, seemingly with someone. Swirling and circling. With someone. Laughing. Clapping.

Katty handed the baby to Mark and grabbed Bea's hands and spun her around. And again. They danced and laughed. Back and forth. Around and around.

"Katty." Mark was in his right mind. "You better sit down." He looked down at Teddy. "You just had a baby."

Katty laughed, her face to the ceiling. "I just had a baby. I just had a baby. I just gave birth to another beautiful baby!" Never had she laughed with such joy and freedom. She sat and pulled Bea onto her lap, held her tight.

Mark scooted closer beside them, his arm around Katty and Bea. He shook his head. "We are … I am—"

Bea crawled over into his lap right next to Teddy. "Look Mommy. The babies are all around us. Around you."

Katty kissed her, kissed Mark, kissed Teddy. "Thankful."

Thank you for reading my books! If you liked Resurrected, would you consider leaving a review anywhere you purchase books? It is a huge help to any author!

Follow me on BookBub here, Goodreads here, Amazon here.

Ask for the books at your Public Library. Even though you get to read them for free, I get a little kick-back, too.
It's not all about the money, but it helps when I pay an editor or book cover designer.

This is Katty's Story. There might be more to come—in another book.
They've become like family to me and I hope also to you.

There is a trilogy (or more!) for Clarence and Harold, too, and The Timmelsen & Dexter Agency—a detective agency they run from Hillcrest Nursing Home. Michael is in it. Katty and Bea. Noell appears, too.

Yeah, Phil is jumping up and down. "What about me?"
Ugly, evil man.
But what if …

Noell is drawn to that pool in Rescued, Book 2. What are her other gifts? She goes to strange places in her own trilogy! Science. Creation. The Brain. That kinda stuff!

If you want to keep up with my characters (literally!) go to: www.bonnielacy.com. Scroll down and you'll see "Join My Newsletter." There you can fill in your info and hit the subscribe button. There's always a giveaway. I won't blow up your inbox, for sure … just keep you up on releases, maybe a doodle, and excerpts from my daily journals. You'll be added to my email newsletter list, but you can unsubscribe anytime.

Keep in touch.

Be Blessed!

ACKNOWLEDGMENTS

I admit that writing this third book, Resurrected, in Katty's Story, (sixth book in The Great Escapee Series) is bittersweet for me. It's been a heavy trilogy to write because of the themes: prison, abuse, addictions, and abortion. Writing the angels and little Bea helped lighten the load, as imagining what the angels might be up to is one of my favorite things to do anyway. And how could a four-year-old girl not add sweetness, humor, … and trouble?

But also, knowing that writing Katty's inner life is probably over, saddens me. Characters usually find a way to worm their way into story, no matter what I might think or plan. So it might not be the end. It's just a resolution to her trilogy and her character arc.

Some of you might not like the fact that Katty's mom, Louisiana didn't change at the end of the book. I know. It hurts in real life when some people don't change. Or when we can't see that change as *we* would want it to happen. That's hard. It's my heart to see everyone be what Jesus died on the cross for them to be, but God created us all with a free will. Sometimes that free will chooses differently from what I'd love to have happen. I guess I'm not God, huh.

I wonder if He feels that way? I wonder if … well, I'm pretty sure that it hurts Him when we choose a different path from what He offered to us.

You've heard this before probably. He didn't want robots: "Yes Sir, no Sir, whatever You want, Sir."

I am, along with Katty, learning to find out who I am in

Jesus, and who I am not. I'm not that angry woman of years ago, and I am learning who I am without anger.

Am I perfect?

No.

But, He is. And He lives inside of me. And I trust Him. He does not lie (Titus 1:2). If He says the old me has died, so it has. There's a new me that I must discover—just like Katty in my story. (2 Cor. 5:17)

Disclaimer: All of the businesses and stores, the nursing home, that I write about are amazing—amazing places and amazing people. When I write from Clarence's, Katty's, or especially Phil's point of view, think about it. Clarence is an ex-con. Katty is an addict and post-abortive. And Phil is a murderer—evil!

If there was no conflict, no weirdness, no evil, there'd be no readers. I don't like boring books and I'm sure you don't either.

But reality? Non of us are perfect. Only Jesus in us is perfect.

But I believe God's Word. What does it mean when it says, "Entering into this fullness is not something you figure out or achieve. It's not a matter of being circumcised or keeping a long list of laws. No, you're already *in*—insiders—not through some secretive initiation rite but rather through what Christ has already gone through for you, destroying the power of sin." Colossians 2:11-12 Message Translation.

I know. I don't get it all, either. But I believe.

The magic in Gamma's closet. This is fiction, right? So I can make it all up. But I love that stuff. What if it *was* real? What if it *is* real? What if some of the scenes are real?

I love the wonder of God's Kingdom. And I love to try to create that wonder in my stories. Did I succeed? Only you, the reader, know if I succeeded.

I often ask God why I can't prophecy like others seem to. Or travel in time like some movies show. But maybe. Just maybe through my writing, as I "see" scenes in my spirit, maybe I am prophetic. Or at least able to share what I see through the Holy Spirit. If any scenes resonate with you or speak to you or if you are curious about any, please contact me. We can learn together. Contact me here: randbl@risebroadband.net or there is a contact page on my website: www.bonnielacy.com.

A huge thank you to Dearly Beloved. He works hard driving truck, is gone a lot, and provides so I can pursue my writing career.

Thank you to my kids, who are always asking how the book is going and encouraging me to keep at it. Keep on pushing. Never, never, never give up! They are my mentors, next to Jesus!

Thank you to my grandkids—all ten of them—for keeping me laughing, hugging, and thinking. Your questions, your kisses, and your texts are always wonderful and loved.

Thank you to Jane Dixon-Smith who always understands where I want to go with a cover. I never stress over them. A book cover designer has such an important gift to draw readers to pick up a book.

Thank you to Steve Rzasa, my editor. I am so grateful for him. I always get nervous when I send the manuscript to him, but when he sends it back, what I need to change is so clear.

Thank you, Jan. I don't know how you do it—read my manuscript three and four times, send it back to me, I revise and read it multiple times and send it back to you. Then you read it again—three or more times! Thank you, dear Sister. You are more than a blood sister. You are a friend, a confidant, my sister in Christ.

Thank you Prayer Warriors. I know, beyond any doubt, when you are praying. I might have, at that moment, bowed my head into my hands, totally freaked out by what I'd just written. But, you prayed. God heard. And my heart stilled, quieted. And I knew it was your prayers that helped me write on. Thank you.

Thank you to the police departments, the fire departments, the military. You keep us protected. You serve, you fight, you give your lives so we can live free. I pray that continues for The United States of America!

This, copied from the last book, Redeemed. Not being lazy. Worth repeating.

Thank you, Readers. There are many of you who stay in contact (always feel free to contact me via text or email!), asking when the next book will be out, emailing with what that book meant to you. I can write another day/month/year when you do that. It's not about flattery. It's about genuine heart-felt encouragement that keeps me at the keyboard.

I pray that my books point you to Jesus Christ, Yeshua, the Son of God, the Anointed One. There are so many words we could use (and I did!) but he is kind and compassionate, too. Back to the verse at the front of the book, Redeemed: *"It is because of the Lord's loving kindnesses that we are not consumed, Because His [tender] compassions never fail. They are new every morning; Great and beyond measure is Your faithfulness." Lamentations 3: 22, 23. Amplified Version.*

His kindness and faithfulness. He never fails. He never lies.

Ask Him. Believe in Him. Breathe Him in. Take another breath.

He is here.

Believe.

Want to read my own story of regret, anger, and addictions?
Buy Rage Rising: My Walk Through the Dark Tunnel of Rage
here on www.bonnielacy.com or wherever you purchase books.

"To be honest, I go back into that awful tunnel—not really
because I want to—but because it's home. I have to learn to take
a different path.
This is one woman's story of her walk through that dark tunnel
of anger."
Get Rage Rising: My Walk through the Dark Tunnel of Anger
here.
www.bonnielacy.com

Sign up here to receive my email newsletter! Keep up with new releases, Kickstarters, any new doodles and free short stories!

Thank you for reading this book and spending time with me in my imagination!
Please email me and tell me what you thought of Resurrected.
Did you like it … or not? How did you feel after you finished it?
Did you want to throw the book (at me?), or did you want to read more?
I invite you to always feel free to contact me with any comments or questions. Please stay in touch. Writing is a very solitary adventure and it encourages me to no end when you contact me!
Either at randbl@risebroadband.net or bonnie@bonnielacy.com.

RESOURCES

Addiction:
www.teenchallgengeusa.org

Abortion:
www.rachelsvineyard.org
https://grief-to-grace-lsi.squarespace.com/
https://savethestorks.com/
www.reassemblelife.com
They Lied to Us, They Lied To Us Too
Abby Johnson https://abbyj.com/
And Then There Were nonehttps://abortionworker.com/
Pro Love https://proloveministries.org/
Loveline https://loveline.com/
40 Days For Life https://www.40daysforlife.com/en/
Dr. Alveda C. King https://www.alvedaking.com/
Patti Giebink, MD https://unexpectedchoice.com
https://theyarenotforgotten.com/
Video on website is gripping
https://abortionsurvivors.org/
https://www.prolifespeakersbureau.com/josiah-presley
https://www.claireculwell.com/
https://abortionsurvivors.org/
https://abortionsurvivors.org/supporters/sohl/

Prison Ministries
https://www.godbehindbars.com/
https://www.behindthewireministries.org/

ALSO BY BONNIE LACY

Fiction:

Released

Rescued

Restored

Revealed

Redeemed

Resurrected

Nonfiction:

Rage Rising: My Walk Through the Dark Tunnel of Anger

Cash Envelopes: You've Never Had So Much Money

Cash Envelopes: You've Never Had So Much Money Companion Workbook

www.ingramcontent.com/pod-product-compliance
Lightning Source LLC
Chambersburg PA
CBHW061525210726
48287CB00006B/1837